Summer of '63

Brian Leyden.

BRIAN LEYDEN

Christmas 2016

ISBN: 1530961262
ISBN-13: 978-1530961269

"For Josephine, in appreciation of her courage, attitude, and positive outlook on life – an inspiration to all of us."

ONE

The summer holidays had started and I took my time walking home from school. Shortly before the house I heard a wheezy rattle, and felt a hot scratchy sensation in the bottom of my lungs. So, while I waited for my breathing to recover, I dawdled on the bridge and looked down into the river.

Insects hung over the bright water and a huge, metallic-green dragonfly circled and then landed on a stone in mid-river and rested there like a brooch. I enjoyed the soothing sound the river made, where it ran around the flat-topped stones in the shallows, and then its trout-brown waters slipped into the shade under the archways of the bridge. I loved, too, the way the old stone bridge neatly divided the village in half; the private houses on either side of the bridge mostly two-storey with solid blue-Bangor slate roofs. The biggest, where we lived, had the pub, the shop and post office, the telephone kiosk, petrol pump and the raised Pink paraffin tank with the brass tap for filling quart and gallon cans.

The phlegm in my chest loosened as the bout of wheezing passed, and I caught the sweet smell of blooming lilac from the shrubbery backing onto the river. From the sulphurous heaviness of the air I guessed at a thunderstorm brewing, and my attention wandered to the lightning rod fixed to the gable of the pebble-dashed church that stood on the edge of the village, then the hillside graveyard, and above that the new concrete tanks so people got their water on tap instead of using the village pump, with the spout like a lion's mouth and a curved iron handle like a tail.

There was an Iron Bridge too higher up the valley for the colliery workers who needed to make their way down off the mountain. Leafy whitethorn hedges divided the mountainside where the colliery workers lived into small farms. The majority had marshy bottom fields full of buttercups bordering the river, summer meadows higher up, and then steeply-sloped pasture fields before the heather covered mountain crests, that I would have the whole summer to explore. Downriver from the village, an abandoned railway crossing had notices bolted to the gates warning people to keep their cattle off the narrow-gauge track, even though the train didn't run anymore.

The coal train stopped a couple of years ago, but standing on the same side of the river as the post office and shop, you couldn't miss the iron-roofed workshops, bunkers, stacks of coal and colliery offices at the place everyone called 'the siding' from the days when the train was still running. Nearly every man living in the valley worked at the siding or in the coalmines. The mines were tunnelled straight into the sides of the mountains above the village and followed thin bands of coal sandwiched under the heather and the rock. Digging their tunnels deep into the mountainside the men of Arigna risked getting killed or badly hurt by rock-falls or heavy machinery, or choked by pockets of poison fumes after blasting. But it was only the owners who called these rough tunnels cut into the sides of the mountain coalmines. The workers called them pits, and called themselves pitmen.

In the evenings, the pitmen rode home from work on the back of the fleet of trucks that replaced the coal train. Some owned Honda motorbikes for getting to and from the pit, and the rest walked home on foot in their pit boots and Wellingtons with the tops turned down. The pitmen washed only when they got home, so it was hard to tell the men apart when all you could see was the whites of their eyes in faces caked with coal dust.

Even on the side of the road after work, the pitmen hunkered down to talk to one another like they were still under the low roof of the tunnels where they spent their days crouched down in the dungeon dark. I found it a strange and, at times, an unsettling place to be an outsider, with a father who had never set foot in one of these pits, and instead of a helmet and carbide burning lamp wore a tan shop-coat, fawn cardigan and a clean white shirt and necktie every day.

Daddy ran the shop while Mammy looked after the pub. With Mammy in charge of the pub, some people said behind Daddy's back it was clear who wore the trousers in our house. And at school I heard some of the other boys say that Daddy was 'so dry he'd fart dust'.

But my mother didn't drive, and every Tuesday and Saturday my father had to load up the big blue van that stood outside the shop and drive around the whole of the valley, and then up onto the mountain where his customers waited along the sides of the road for the travelling shop to bring them their messages.

The travelling shop went as far as the Iron Bridge and then, at Whistle Hill, on the very top of the mountain, turned around and came back down into the valley by the Top Road.

It was on account of the travelling shop that people got used to Daddy being the one who sold the women their detergent, and totted up what was owed in the book on pay days, while Mammy looked after the pub and made threats when the pitmen got rowdy, and called time when it got late, and told them 'you don't have to go home but you can't stay here'.

Most people got used to this being the way things were done, most people that is, except me.

The back door into our house was constantly bolted, unless Mammy had to put out washing or sort bottles in the yard. And I was not allowed to have a front door key. The heavy brown wooden door onto the village street had a steel bar permanently across it on the inside in any case. So the way into our house was always through the pub, with whoever was drinking there looking to see who was coming or going through the door into the house marked 'Private'. It made me feel noticed. Marked out.

Now, after I left the bridge and went into the pub, I had to wait a minute for my eyes to adjust to the gloom after the brightness outside. I looked hopefully in the direction of the shelf at the other end of the room. It was still empty – a sight bound to put Mammy in a bad mood. Even though they had promised her faithfully it would be here by Tuesday at the latest, the people from RTV Rentals still hadn't come with the new television.

President John F. Kennedy, the 35th President of the United States, was coming to Ireland on a special four-day visit, and hundreds of people were expected to turn up at Dublin airport when his plane landed at eight o'clock in the evening. Mammy had her heart set on having a television installed in the pub before the President arrived. But President Kennedy would be landing shortly, and there was still no trace of the new television set.

Even though President Kennedy wouldn't be coming next nor near our village, Mammy had an American flag flying outside, and a string of red, white and blue bunting hung between the shop and the pub. Inside, the pub was done up with Presidential inauguration pictures, souvenir plates, mugs and portraits of the President and his lovely, posh looking wife and First Lady, Jacqueline Kennedy.

Mammy had gone to a lot of trouble doing up what she called the American Lounge and ordering a television, but she was going to Dublin herself to see the President make his State visit, and Daddy was supposed to be bringing her to the train station in Boyle. Only our family Mark I Ford Cortina car still stood outside the shop, which meant Mammy was still here: a development that didn't suit me one bit, since I had plans for when she was away, and if Daddy didn't get a move on she'd miss the train.

The American Lounge was empty and silent, and I went on through into the house, where I found Mammy in the kitchen. She wore her best pearl necklace and a matching pink jacket and skirt above the knee, just like the outfit she saw on the film star Grace Kelly. But Mammy also had her apron on and she was making a load of ham sandwiches.

"You're home early," she said.

"We got a half-day."

"Isn't it well for some? Now wash your hands and have a sandwich."

I went to the sink, washed and dried my hands, put a couple of sandwiches out on a plate and sat eating them at the end of the table. They tasted lovely and fresh.

"What time is the train?"

"I'm not going."

"Why, what's wrong?"

"Francie Curran is missing, and everyone is out looking

5

for him. I can't go until he's found – it wouldn't be right."

"But you really want to go," I said.

Mammy rolled her eyes and said, "When did your father ever heed me, or what I want?"

TWO

Francie Curran had a brother living in America who sent parcels that came to the post office home to his family. He had more brothers who worked in the pits. His sisters, Angela and Mary, used to share the desk behind me in Mount Allen National School. They were twins, and wore matching ribbons in their hair and matching white Aran cardigans to Sunday mass, and on school days had identical shiny faces scrubbed pink with carbolic soap. They were smiley, well-behaved girls.

Francie was the youngest and he didn't look or act a bit like the others. He was stunted and tubby, with short arms and white hair, and narrow eyes like they have in Mongolia. He didn't do a tap in school. Miss Costigan, our History and Geography teacher, only got him to stay in his seat by letting him play with toy soldiers. One time, when I asked Daddy why Francie always dressed in a soldier's outfit that must have come in one of the parcels from America, he said Francie was 'harmless'.

Francie loved his American Marine outfit, and wore it the whole time. Even in the classroom, it was a job getting him to surrender his toy Colt .45 cap-gun. And wild horses wouldn't get the helmet off his head.

My mother's eyes went to the clock, then back to the sandwich making.

"Who are the sandwiches for?" I asked, tempted to have more.

"Your father has everyone asked back to the pub for refreshments after they find Francie. And muggins has to get everything ready."

"I'll help," I said, hoping she might change her mind about cancelling her Dublin trip. She'd bought a new outfit specially, and she had a guest-house booked on the North Circular Road.

"Get more margarine from the shop," she said. "And if your father mentions butter, tell him margarine is good enough."

The hallway connecting the kitchen to the shop was stuffed with cardboard boxes, wooden tea-chests, and sacks holding onions and flour. And the overflow from the shop made the whole place so dark and boxy you had to watch your footing or you were bound to trip over something. But I made it to the door into the shop, without causing any breakages, and stuck my head around the jamb.

Mrs Daly, the Postmistress, sat with her back turned sorting postal orders beside the telephone switchboard. Daddy was busy with a customer.

Nora Greene, an old woman with a house on the mountain, stood at the counter pointing to a milk jug on a shelf behind Daddy's back. He fetched it down for her and the two of them stood looking at the jug on the counter. It was a nice *'Carrig Ware'* jug with blue and white bands, but Nora was trying to act like she hadn't her mind made up to buy it.

"Can you take anything off it?" she asked, looking for a reduction.

Daddy said, "Only the dust."

Nora nodded and got out her big black purse with the brass clip.

Daddy collected up a handful of the purple tissue paper used to line the box of oranges that came from Seville and stuffed the soft paper into the jug before going to the roll of brown paper, tearing off a length to wrap up the jug, after which he criss-crossed a strand of brown twine around the lot and smartly snapped the twine between his fingers and neatly tied up the ends to make a jug-shaped brown paper parcel for Nora to take home.

Though she'd never spoken a cross word to me, and looked harmless in her black hat, long coat and heavy stockings the colour of cold tea, I didn't like Nora Greene. I faded into the shadows and waited for her to leave.

The shop was quiet with the front door closed, but not bolted yet, as Daddy worked to get the last customer served so he could close for the weekly half-day on Wednesdays. The hands on the clock in its wooden case on the mantelpiece at Daddy's back reached one and I heard it chime. At one o' clock every day the shop closed for dinner.

Daddy had started out working as a messenger-boy in a shop in Enniscorthy when he was my age. He'd ended up running the business, until the owner's youngest son came back from America with new ideas. He took over the shop. Daddy and Mammy had to leave. And that's why we moved here, to what my father called 'pastures new'.

Nora Greene left along with Mrs Daly, and I delayed while Daddy bolted the front door.

With the door shut, he lowered the black-out blinds and the daylight dimmed on the brass weights at the weighing scales, on the tins of picnic salmon and jars of blackcurrant and strawberry jam. There were glimmers of

9

light too from the glass lids on the tin boxes holding arrowroot and ginger nut biscuits, and my favourites, the thin Marietta biscuits that were best dipped and softened in a cup of tea, or buttered and stuck together and eaten like a sandwich.

The portable rack of meshed-steel shelves that stood beside the petrol pump outside had been taken into the shop and left in the middle of the floor. It was loaded with cans of Castrol engine oil for cars and motorbikes. But there were still loads of wooden drawers in the shop full of dynamos and reflectors, spare spokes, tyres and puncture repair outfits for bicycles.

Household goods were kept at the back of the shop nearest the door into the house, where I stood, and I could make out washboards and galvanized tubs and boxes of Rinso soap flakes for clothes, and bars of Sunlight soap for scrubbing collars and cuffs.

It wasn't a bad life I suppose being a shopkeeper, but you had to get used to the smells: the perfumed soaps and the rubbery smell of the new Wellington boots that hung on strings from the ceiling; the chests full of loose Indian tea, and golden Clarinda meal, and the powdery lumps of carbide the pitmen burned in their lamps. The whole lot combined gave the shop an exotic smell I hadn't got used to yet and often made me sneeze. And it happened now, as I stepped into the shop, the sneeze taking me by surprise and also alerting Daddy to my arrival.

"Bless you," he said.

"Mammy is looking for a packet of margarine."

"Not Kiltoghert Creamery Butter?" he asked.

I shook my head. He frowned but moved to fetch the margarine from the cold room.

"Did they find Francie Curran yet?" I asked.

"He'll turn up when he's good and hungry," Daddy

said.

"If they open a jar of Breifne Blossom jam, Francie is bound to come running," I said. "He's stone mad for strawberry jam."

"The poor little fellah," Daddy said, and I left him to finish closing the shop for the half-day.

Transferring the packet of margarine to my left hand on the way out of the shop, I double-checked to make certain Daddy wasn't looking, and then bent down quickly to lift two small bottles of Fanta orange from the crate.

In the kitchen I sneezed again handing over the packet of margarine.

"Are you getting one of your attacks?" Mammy asked straight away.

"It's the shop making me sneeze."

"Did you take your tablets?"

"Not yet."

"Well take them now," she said.

I had to open the cupboard beside the sink and take out the little brown bottle full of pale pink tablets, and another even smaller brown bottle full of teensy white tablets. I ran the tap and filled a glass of water and put on a show of swallowing. Then dropping my hand, I stuck the pink and the white tablets into my pocket to get rid of them later.

As I rinsed my glass and left it on the drainer, a bell rang to announce a customer had opened and closed the door into the American Lounge.

"I'll finish making the sandwiches," I volunteered.

Mammy put down the knife she'd been using to cut the sandwiches into dainty triangles and took off her apron.

After she left, I washed my plate and dried it with the tea towel and put the plate and the drinking glass away. I liked having the place tidy, though we had so much stuff from the shop and pub taking up space around the kitchen, and the rest of the house, it was hard to keep anywhere except my own room neat and dust free.

The sandwiches I made looked flatter and rougher somehow than the ones Mammy did earlier. But I got through the job, and by the time I had used up all of the bread and ham, I could hear music coming from upstairs: the Beatles singing, 'Love Me Do'.

I put clean tea-towels over the plates of sandwiches on the table to cover them, and went out into the hallway to collect the two bottles of Fanta orange left out of sight at the foot of the stairs.

Several of the rooms upstairs were reserved for paying guests: engineers mostly visiting the pits, or officials checking weights and measures. But we had no one staying with us at the minute. When I reached the landing, I stopped at the door into Bernice Hickey's room. It stood firmly closed but I could hear the record player inside start up again. I knocked gently but got no answer.

I had an idea what Bernice was up to. And rather than enter her bedroom without her permission, I went to the end of the landing and raised the sash on the last window. Then I climbed out the window onto the flat roof of the American Lounge extension built onto the pub below.

The public road ran straight in front of the pub, while the yard at the back was full of crates and bottles. The flat roof on the new extension offered the best suntrap where a person could sunbathe unseen. It was only lately, though, that Bernice had started to take a deckchair out onto the roof, keeping close to her bedroom window because the height made her nervous. The Beatles song started up again almost as soon as it finished, so she must have the record player in her room on repeat play.

I found her sitting back in a blue and white striped

canvas deckchair with a towel over it. She had the sun on her face and her eyes closed.

Bernice would be eighteen on her next birthday in November, and as far as I knew she was an orphan. When my parents left Enniscorthy to come to Arigna to run the pub and the shop and the guesthouse combined that belonged to the colliery owners, Bernice Hickey already lived on the premises. Her job included accommodation, so you could say she came with the business. While no one ever said to me straight out she was alone in the world, I'd noticed how she never had people belonging to her visit. She got no letters or cards. And she never went anywhere. She'd come straight from an Industrial School to take up a job in the village shop. I couldn't imagine what it must be like to have no father or mother watching you like a hawk.

In the past couple of months, Bernice had started to wear her skirts and her hair shorter than normal, plus she had my mother demented playing the same Beatles songs over and over since their long playing record, *Please Please Me* came out in March. Daddy – who only ever listened to Jim Reeves – warned Mammy to say nothing. Bernice was a bright and capable girl, he said, and she didn't have much around here to keep her entertained. Deep down, Bernice had to know she was really good looking. But she didn't socialise much and she didn't have a boyfriend.

Without letting her know I was there, I watched as she stirred in the deckchair and raised one of her slim pale legs to see if she was getting a colour. I felt that uncomfortable tingle in the bottom of my lungs start again, caused this time by the smell of tar underfoot rising from the hot felt roof.

Her short dark hair was held in place with a headband and, as Bernice leaned forward, my interest moved from her raised leg to the pale delicacy of her neck and the way her chin rested on her chest where the rise of her breasts started below the neckline of her sleeveless white top. When I let the air in my lungs escape I heard a low asthmatic rattle. I tried to tell myself I wasn't interested in Bernice in a sleazy, wheezy way. But seeing how her candy-striped shorts and tight-fitting top displayed her womanly figure to full advantage my curiosity boiled over like a small saucepan full of milk.

THREE

Bernice was thirsty and hot looking and it made me happy to be able to display the bottles of Fanta as I approached.

"I got you a mineral?" I called out.

"Did you pay for those?"

I halted and said, "I can put them back if you like."

"No, I'll settle up for them later. Have you an opener?"

I produced the pocket-knife Bernice had given to me as my Christmas present. It had one short and one long blade I'd honed devilishly sharp with a whetstone from the shop. Alongside the smaller blade was a hook for catching the edge of tin caps on bottles. I bent and flipped off the two mineral bottle caps without spilling a drop, handed her drink across to Bernice, and proudly put away the pocket-knife. We were both thirsty and the Fanta tasted tangy and sweet.

"Are you working this evening?" I asked.

"I was supposed to be doing the bar for your mother so she could go to Dublin. And Mrs Daly was coming back to look after the switchboard. But I don't know what's going to happen now. I suppose you heard Francie Curran is missing."

I nodded and looked off towards the mountainside hoping to spot the search party. I could see nothing out of the ordinary. But what had been a clear sky overhead was growing darker. And in the direction of Drumshanbo, the muddy orange-coloured sky above the town was full of low booms and rumbles.

"Francie won't stay outside long if the thunder comes," I said. "He hates loud noises."

"A magpie flew straight across in front of me this morning," Bernice said. "I'm afraid something terrible has happened to Francie."

"He's gone missing before and nothing happened."

Bernice fanned her face with her hand, drank some more Fanta and said, "What if he ran into that lion and got attacked."

I hated getting into an argument with Bernice, but I had the *World Book of Big Cats* on loan from the library, and when you matched the pictures in the book with the descriptions of the mystery wildcat seen roaming the mountain this winter, I was convinced the sightings were of a large cat from the leopard more than the lion family: a puma, or a lynx or maybe an escaped jaguar from South America, but more than likely a panther – a black panther.

"It's not a lion roaming the countryside," I said. "It's a wildcat. Probably a panther. And panthers only hunt at night."

"It's definitely an escaped lion," Bernice said. "Potter's Circus let one loose on account of the blizzards this winter when they had no shows and couldn't afford to feed it. That's what I heard anyway. And it's already killed several sheep and baby lambs on the mountain."

Determined to hold my tongue, I walked towards the edge of the roof hoping to catch a breeze. The close dead heat had me in a sweat. And there was not a breath of air to stir the American flag on its pole. The rumbles too were getting louder, and if I kept a tight eye on the clouds where they were darkest I reckoned I'd soon spot a flash of lightening.

"Come away from there," Bernice said, seeing me right out on the edge of the roof. "You're making me nervous."

"If you don't like heights," I said, "you have to push yourself and fight back the fear. That's what I do when I get wheezy. I run against the hill until the attack goes away."

"I'm happy how I am," Bernice said.

She finished her mineral while I went back to watching the storm brew. The whole sky was now as purple as the outfit the Phantom wore in the 'ghost who walks' jungle comic books. Out of the corner of my eye I glimpsed a bright bolt of lightning. After several seconds the boom came, like the sound of a twenty-gallon iron tar-barrel being rolled across the cobbled heavens. More low booms echoed from the mountain slopes behind us.

Ever since the Cuban missile crisis last October, when the world stood on the brink of an all-out nuclear war, I kept having dreams about Atom bombs exploding. A fantastically bright detonation behind the mountain overlooking the village was followed by a giant mushroom-shaped cloud swelling to fill the entire sky as I waited for the shockwave to hit. But I woke up every time an instant before the Atom bomb blast struck and reduced me to a scorch-mark on the outside wall of our pub, as though incinerated by an almighty bolt of lightning.

Quick as a wink, a fork of lightning streaked across the heavens directly overhead.

"Wow!" I said, "Did you see that?"

Bernice was already out of her deckchair and on her bare feet gathering up her belongings to get off the roof. I moved to collect the metal and canvas deckchair. I was nervous about how to fold it properly, but it was lighter and easier to manage than I imagined, and I was happy following Bernice as she hurried towards her bedroom window, where the lace curtains had started to flutter.

We made it into the room ahead of the rain, but as I turned around to fix back the curtains I saw a perfect fork of lightning strike downwards out of the storm-clouds. I lowered and fastened the bottom half of the sash window just as the sharp crack of thunder reached us.

Bernice said, "Come away from the window."

I moved deeper into her bedroom.

She had a poster up on the wall of the Beatles looking cheeky with their mop-top haircuts and smart suits. And under the poster, Bernice had the PYE record player with the top open and the Beatles single on the turntable set to play at 45rpm. Just as I thought, the arm on the record player was lifted across and it would be playing again now only a ball of fluff had built up under the needle and the stylus just slithered across the vinyl and got stuck at the end making only a clicking sound.

Bernice stopped the record and then draped her towel over the bedspread and sat on the edge of the bed.

"See that brown bottle on the dressing table," she said. "Can you pass it over to me?"

Outside the thunderstorm was close enough for the noise to vibrate the single pane of glass in the window where the putty had crumbled and fallen out of the frame.

I gave Bernice the brown bottle and she uncapped it and poured milky pink calamine lotion into her hand. Next she got me to hold the bottle for her while she rubbed the lotion on one forearm where the skin looked red. Then she used her other hand to take up the extra lotion and rub it into the opposite arm where it too looked tender. I stood close and poured more lotion into her hands, which she rubbed on her legs and asked, "How's my neck."

"Kinda red too," I said.

Bang went the thunder, and it began to pelt rain against the window, and down onto the flat roof making puddles straight away.

She opened the top button of her sleeveless blouse and pulled the collar open.

My face felt hotter than any part of her sunburnt skin.

"Can you put some lotion on the back of my neck," she said.

I tipped the bottle gently to pour a small amount of the chalky calamine lotion into my hand, and I laid my hand on her warm neck, and gently worked the lotion into her skin. She moved her head around, and I could sense the pleasure it gave her to have her neck and shoulders rubbed.

The room itself had grown hot and airless and I was afraid I was going to start wheezing again, but the calamine lotion smelled lovely, and the perfumed heat from Bernice's skin didn't affect my asthma one bit.

She opened up another button, and I massaged her lower neck.

"That feels good," she said.

Rain swirled outside the window as the full force of the storm struck. But it was so dim and snug and cosy in Bernice's room it felt like we were cut off from the rest of the world. I wondered how far I could take this when a really bright flash of lightning lit up the whole room a brilliant blue-white. Ready to count off the seconds in my head between the flash and the peal of thunder, I barely got past one before we heard an incredibly loud bang. Bernice flinched, and I increased the pressure of my hands on her shoulders to reassure her. A burst of hailstones beat against the window.

"It's all right," I said. "We're safe here."

She reached up, put her hand on mine, and began to draw me closer. I was ready to ease back onto the bed alongside her, when the next violent crack of thunder exploded with a monstrous bang, as if the sky overhead had just been split open by an almighty sledgehammer.

Bernice slid out of my grasp and got down on her knees, pulling me down alongside her so our elbows rested on the coverlet, and our knees were on the rug on the floor. The whole room lit up again, and another cannonade of thunder rattled the glass in the window.

"*Hail Mary, full of grace, the Lord is with thee,*" said Bernice. And I had to take up the prayer at "*Holy Mary, mother of God…*"

Bernice winced at the next lightning flash and shot of thunder, but kept up her prayers.

I felt like telling her it would be better to let go of my hand and make me stand safely back. If God intended to strike down anyone with the next bolt of lightning in this overheated, summer downpour darkened bedroom, it was bound to be me, the sneaky wheezing best friend holding her hand, who should be fried alive by heaven's highest voltage for the secret thoughts and longings going on inside my head that I could not mention, on pain of death.

FOUR

When she had her prayers said Bernice looked at the alarm clock on the dressing table.

"Janey Mac!" she said. "Is that the time?"

I left her alone to run a bath and get changed in comfort, feeling strange after being so close for what felt like an exceptionally long time in the privacy of her bedroom.

In my own room, I went to the window and looked out to see if the storm had cleared. The afternoon light was unnaturally dim and brownish, but the downpour had stopped as suddenly as it hit, and coils of steam rose from the wet road making the air hazy and damp. A lot of rain had fallen, and when I looked towards the river I could see racing torrents of brown and white water flooding through the eyes of the bridge after what must have been a cloudburst further up the valley.

If poor Francie Curran was still stuck outside he'd be very frightened and very wet.

I emptied the exercise books and used copy books, pencil case and ruler out of my school satchel. I wouldn't need the books again until September when I'd be studying for the Group Cert at the end of second year. In my first year I'd missed a load of days on account of my asthma, and was struggling to keep up. In second year I'd have to make a fresh start, but even now I felt wheezy again, on account of the strong smell of greenery after the rain. So I lay down on the bed for a short rest, and looked again at the library book on big cats.

I turned to the picture of the panther and studied it closely. With all of my heart I longed to catch sight of the mystery wildcat the pitmen had reported seeing on the mountain several times over the past year, convinced it would look exactly like the great cat in the book.

So far, the sightings of the wildcat were few and far between, and happened only at a distance as the pitmen were going to work early in the morning or on their way home at night. Yet ever since the snow melted in the springtime, I'd been scouring muddy gaps between the farm fields outside the village for big animal tracks. As the weather improved, and the level of the river dropped, I'd walked the riverbanks on both sides on the lookout for drinking places a panther might use, and checked the sandbars for paw-prints. And finally, on the side of the mountain, I found what I was looking for.

Just five minutes walk from the Bog Lane used to reach the turf-banks on the top of the mountain, I'd come across white feathers on the ground. The trail of feathers led to a hiding place dug into an embankment. Inside the hiding place, I'd found bits belonging to the leg and head off a rooster where the panther had stopped to eat. There were tracks too. The tracks weren't very clear, but they'd been made I reckoned by a large predatory cat.

Soon after that discovery, I found a deep, natural cavity behind the rock-face near the panther's lair. With a branch broken from a mountain ash tree I'd measured the depth of the hole between the rocks. It was good and deep. Next I threw stones into the hole to make certain it had a solid bottom. The stones hit a dry floor, making it a perfect pit to lure and capture a prowling big game cat.

Now, with the summer holidays started, I meant to get the trap up and working. Only I had a problem at home to get over first.

Panthers only hunted at night. And I wasn't allowed to go near the mountain after sundown. I wasn't really supposed to go anywhere after dark. Mammy said it was bad for my chest to be outdoors once the dew began to fall. She said any kind of night air was bad for my breathing. And even in the summertime I wasn't allowed out without a vest.

But with my mother supposedly going to Dublin, I planned to get hold of some good strong cart rope from the shop, which I could use to climb down into the hole in the daylight. Once I got down into the hole I meant to use the stones I'd tossed into it to block up any gaps or chinks through which a large cat might escape. I reckoned the few openings I'd seen were too tight for a panther to squeeze through, but I didn't mean to take any chances.

Finding that readymade pit on the mountain was a lot handier than having to dig a hole myself. And the final part of the plan was to use more lightweight mountain ash branches and clumps of heather and grass to cover up the opening. It would be too dangerous to leave the hole hidden overnight. Anyone could fall into it. And I couldn't count on the panther just walking over the booby-trapped hole in the ground either. I would need bait. Only I hadn't worked out yet how to execute that part of the trap.

I'd told no one about this plan, especially not Bernice, because it would be just too embarrassing to explain why I was so determined to catch the panther by myself.

On account of my weak chest I didn't play football, or any other sport. And it was doubly hard to join in as a newcomer to the village when my mother kept forcing tablets and tonics on me, and really didn't want me out of her sight. Even though I was fifteen now – having been held back a year after I changed schools – she still treated me like a child. Trapping the panther would be a perfect way to prove my courage, and show everyone I could look after myself. Yet that was only part of the reason I wanted to catch the wildcat. Ever since I arrived I'd found this part of the world unsettling. I'd felt shut out, anxious and unsafe. And it didn't surprise me to learn about a dangerous beast roaming the mountainside: a darkly mysterious threat to match my personal unease. By trapping the panther I could not only make a manly impression on Bernice, I could lay this constant feeling of unnameable dread to rest.

Without knowing it I fell asleep. When I woke I had gluey eyelids and a dry mouth. I put away the library book alongside my stack of *Commando* comics and went downstairs where I helped myself to a glass of water and saw from the clock in the kitchen it was coming on four in the evening.

I felt torn between the wish to avoid going near the public bar, or take a look in to find out if Francie Curran had been found. He would have got an awful drenching if he was still outdoors when the thunderstorm struck. And I hoped he'd been rescued, or made it back safely by himself, and didn't end up in the hospital with pneumonia. Possibly, my mother had gone to Dublin; although she'd hardly have left without saying goodbye and leaving a list of instructions for meals and bedtimes and what shirt to wear on Sunday.

After rinsing my glass and putting it away, I went down the hallway and braced myself to step into the American Lounge.

The minute I set foot inside the door Mammy said, "I'm blue in the face calling. Where were you?"

"Upstairs."

"How many times have I told you the safest place in a thunderstorm is under the stairs."

I didn't mention about being in Bernice's room.

Business was quiet after the thunderstorm. Mammy had just two customers, Eugene McPadden and his son Gerry.

Most of the pitmen worked from eight in the morning until four in the evening, but Eugene and Gerry, and a small gang of pitmen, did the back shift in Rover pit from four o'clock in the evening until midnight. Their job was to drive the pit deeper into the mountainside using the coal-cutting machine, and to leave enough coal ready to keep the rest of the pitmen busy the next day getting the coal to the surface.

Because the coal cutting machine was a two-man job, Eugene worked alongside his son, Gerry. Every evening Eugene came into the pub for a drink before work. And while Gerry was only a couple of years older than me, he was a fixture now on a high stool at his father's elbow, in rough working clothes, drinking a pint of Bass and smoking one of his father's Navy Cut Players.

Unless the machine got stuck or broke down, both men would return at the end of the back shift to coax a late drink from my mother. At the weekends, too, Eugene and Gerry often kept Mammy up until all hours waiting for the Sunday night poker game to finish in the pub and sometimes, if it got really late, in the kitchen. The other pitmen treated Eugene as their superior, though one time, when I was earwigging on the older pitmen, I overheard them say how some of the sheep that disappeared off the mountain over the winter might have been killed by a strange black cat, but more had been lost playing poker against Eugene and Gerry, who sold the sheep they won at cards to Ambrose Luck, the butcher.

Even when a week's wages, or a farm field, got won and lost, nobody had a bad word to say about Eugene especially, because it was Eugene who stood up for the pitmen whenever they had a dispute with the pit owners over pay and conditions. And if the pitmen didn't get what they wanted, he was the one who brought the men out on strike.

Mammy was fond of Eugene, who wore his hair combed just like President Kennedy and dressed up smartly on Sundays in a dark blue suit, a white shirt and knitted tie with a gold clip to match his signet ring. His wife was a heavy, plain-faced countrywoman who looked years older than him. Meet them out together and Eugene had little or nothing to say. But when he was with my mother he was all talk and swagger. If I didn't know better I'd say he was making eyes at my mother.

Now, even though the two men were on their way to work on the back shift and not out looking for Francie Curran, Mammy had treated Eugene and Gerry to a plate of the freshly made sandwiches.

"So, I was standing there in the bank minding my own business," Eugene said to my mother, "when I turned my head and saw them coming through the door waving guns around the place and shouting at everyone to get down on the floor."

"What did you do?" Mammy asked.

"I did exactly what I was told," said Eugene.

"I was waiting for me father outside," Gerry said. "The bank was about to close for dinner, and I had no idea it was the getaway van beside me the whole time with the engine running."

It took me a second or two to realise Eugene and Gerry were informing Mammy that armed raiders had robbed the Great Northern Bank in Drumshanbo. The two pitmen were eyewitnesses to the bank raid that must have happened while I was dillydallying on my way home from school. I hung back at the edge of the counter to listen and find out more.

"They grabbed the bank manager," said Eugene, "put a gun to the butt of his lug, and ordered him to open the strong room."

"Where the pitmen's wages are kept," Mammy said.

Eugene didn't have to answer. Even I knew it was the Great Northern Bank where the colliery owners got the money that was divided out into the brown paper pay-packets the pitmen queued up to collect from the colliery office every second Friday evening. The pitmen got a small amount of money for the first two weeks, and at the end of the month they got their full pay packet. The raiders had robbed the bank when the pitmen were due the bigger amount.

"They must have had inside information," Mammy said. "Because it's not every week the bank would have that kind of money."

"They cleaned the place out – lock, stock and barrel," said Eugene, "and then they took off for Dowra."

"Back across the border where they came from," said Mammy.

Gerry looked like he was thinking about something else as he interrupted his father's account and said, "Tell Monica what Red Paddy Reynolds said to Miss Costigan the teacher."

"When the raiders burst in the door," Eugene said, "Red Paddy was standing at the counter cashing a creamery cheque. The raiders had black balaclavas on and said they'd shoot him on the spot unless he got down on the floor. But Miss Costigan was there too, dressed in her finery on her way to Dublin Airport for President Kennedy's welcoming reception. And she refused to lower herself, or lie down alongside the rest of us. So they knocked off her hat and forced her onto the ground."

"The poor woman," Mammy said. "She must have been terrified."

Eugene said, "She asked Red Paddy, 'Are they going to kill us?' And he said, 'You can be certain sure of it, Mam'."

Eugene and Gerry burst out laughing. "You can be certain sure of it," Gerry mimicked Red Paddy's gruff voice. "Jeez! He'd be some comfort in a hostage situation."

Gerry and Eugene laughed even harder. But I was upset hearing what happened to Miss Costigan. She was kind to me in Geography class because she knew I had an interest, and often took the whole class on educational trips to see the turbine hall in the local power station, the sugar-beet factory in Tuam, and even the Spring Show at Ballsbridge in Dublin. Plus, she called JFK's Presidency 'the new Camelot'. So I was glad Mammy didn't join in the laughing. Instead she looked at the time and got busy filling empty pint glasses with stout.

Eugene and Gerry helped themselves to more sandwiches while Mammy filled pint after pint until a row of drinks lined the counter. Glancing through the clear top-half of the picture window with the word 'Bar' on the frosted lower half, I saw the first of the coal-lorries stop outside. A bunch of pitmen began to climb down from the back.

As the truck pulled up, Eugene collected his change off the counter and said, "We'll go before we stay."

Gerry finished his drink and followed his father.

The line of freshly poured pints stood ready on the counter, needing only to be topped off to be fit for dinking. Every evening as soon as the pitmen finished their shift they came into the pub thirsty for strong drink and Mammy knew not to keep them waiting.

"What about the pitmens' wages?" she called after Eugene. "The bank will hardly get to replace the money before Saturday?" Eugene barely paused in the doorway as he called back over his shoulder, "Brace yourself, Monica. No one is getting paid."

FIVE

The daylight slanting through the pub window turned blue with smoke as the pitmen lit up. Their cigarettes stood out white against their faces black as stoves, and while their hands were washed, their wrists and fingernails were dark with coal dust as they counted out the grimy notes and coins carried around in the pit all day to pay for the pints they collected off the counter now 'to wash down the dust'.

The pitmen had their helmets off, and the hair on their heads was plastered tight against their scalps from sweat and damp and the track of their pit helmets. Many still carried their extinguished and battered brass carbide burning lamps hooked to their belts, and even though they were free to circulate around the bar, they kept close together in the same teams in which they worked underground as shovellers and drawers and brushers.

Even at the weekends, when their wives and mothers and girlfriends were with them, the pitmen had their own seats and tables in the pub. Almost everyone in the valley was related by family or through marriage, and whenever someone from outside arrived the pitmen stuck to their own company.

I could feel an uncomfortable tickle in my lungs, and my eyes were starting to water. The cigarette smoke was really getting to me, but I held on hoping to find out more about the bank robbery. But nobody had anything worthwhile to add to Eugene and Gerry's firsthand account.

The theft of their wages by armed robbers didn't overly concern the pitmen. In fact, the raid on the Great Northern Bank put them in good humour, since nobody liked the manager who was so mean they said 'he wouldn't give you the steam off his piss'.

Hearing the jokes get rowdy, Mammy eyed me to say it was time to leave.

And I was ready to slip off of my own accord to escape the smoke, when Red Paddy Reynolds walked into the bar. Red Paddy had worked in the pits along with the other men in the pub, but he was retired now: a bachelor with land along the river who spent most of his time drinking. Instead of going straight to the bar counter, as usual, he waited at the door and took off his cap. Something I'd never seen him do before, not even at Mass where he stood out in the front porch along with what Mammy called the other *oinseachs*.

The top of Red Paddy's head was completely bald, but he had one long strand of carrot-coloured hair which hung down by his ear. He licked the tips of his fingers and used the dampness to plaster the strand back across the top of his head.

Seeing him try to make himself presentable the pitmen began to look at him.

One said, "What's up with you, Paddy?"

"I have bad news."

"What's that, Paddy?" my mother called out from behind the counter.

"Francie Curran is dead."

"Ah no!"

"Lord have mercy," several voices said at the one time.

Red Paddy twisted the cloth cap in his hands and said, "I'm after finding him below in the river field."

"God between us and all harm," my mother said.

"I'd say he went into the river at the Iron Bridge," said Red Paddy. "And the flood took the body down with it."

Mammy went to the optic and measured out a double whiskey. She added a dash of red lemonade and served Red Paddy as soon as he sat down on his usual high stool at the lower end of the bar where he had a track worn in the wallpaper from resting the back of his head against the corner wall. The noise in the pub died down, though not for long. The pitmen found it sad what happened to Francie, but it was an accident, nothing could be done about it, and they soon began to talk again as normal.

My first instinct was to go and see Francie for myself. Only I wouldn't be allowed near the body, probably. And on second thoughts, I could find out more by going back into the house and up the hallway to the post office.

Every phone call in or out of the valley passed through the switchboard in the post office. Phone services were from eight o'clock in the morning until ten o'clock at night. And though the post office and shop closed for business at five, the switchboard had to be manually operated until ten. Bernice did the switchboard at nights. She did Sundays too, from nine until half-past ten in the morning before mass, and again from seven until nine in the evening.

The switchboard looked like a school desk with an upright panel full of sockets and plugs and wires. It seemed complicated, although Bernice maintained it was simple to operate, and the hard part was passing the time. So I'd gotten into the habit of keeping her company in the evenings. Especially on long dull Sunday evenings when Bernice leafed through whatever women's magazines were on order and hadn't been collected yet, and I looked for new *Commando* comics, and we both sat reading out the best bits to each other.

Entering the shop now I looked past the magazine shelf towards the switchboard to where Bernice sat. The black roller-blind on the window beside the post office counter was down just over half way; enough to make it clear the post office was shut while letting in the early evening light. By angling my head I could see out into the street where a bunch of people had gathered around the green and yellow telephone kiosk.

Bernice had changed into a pale blue cotton blouse, a pair of blue jeans, and summer sandals. She smelled as sweet as if she'd just stepped out of the bath, but she was busy at work with the headset on putting through a call to the main exchange.

I moved up close beside her to overhear what was being said. Listening in on calls together was the other method we had for passing the time.

Sergeant Glacken in Drumshanbo came on the line. Bernice asked him to hold while she put him through to Doctor Ballintine, who stood in the telephone kiosk outside the shop.

With the connection made, the doctor cleared his throat and told the Sergeant he had a fatality to report. Having conducted what he called a 'cursory examination' of the body, Doctor Ballintine said he wished to report that a twelve year old schoolboy had accidentally drowned. The body had entered the water earlier in the day and appeared to have been swept downriver by recent flooding where it was deposited in marshy ground after the level in the swollen river dropped.

Gathered around the open door of the kiosk were Francie's father, and the neighbours who'd helped with the search. As the doctor informed the Sergeant what happened, Francie's father sorrowfully hung his head.

The river field where the body lay, Sergeant Glacken instructed, was to be kept out of bounds until he arrived. Doctor Ballintine said the family wanted to bring the child home. The Sergeant ruled out the request. No one should go near the body until the circumstances were thoroughly examined.

When the call finished, and Bernice removed the headphones, we watched Doctor Ballintine assist Francie Curran's father into his car and drive off, taking him home to what Bernice said would be a very sad house.

The rest of the search party broke up, some going into the pub and others going straight home.

"Poor Francie," said Bernice. "He hadn't a bad bone in his body."

"Doctor Ballintine didn't say how Francie fell into the river?"

"Going by what Francie's father said earlier," Bernice said "his mother kept Francie home from school knowing the holidays were starting. She let him play in the laneway setting up a checkpoint."

"He had a long plank he'd put across the road," I said. "And he'd shout, 'Halt – who goes there?' at anyone who came along."

Bernice said, "When he didn't come home for his bread and strawberry jam at eleven his mother got worried. She checked the lane and went as far as the Iron Bridge, and then she turned back to get help."

"He must have been caught in the thunderstorm," I said. "He could have been running from the thunder when he fell into the river."

Over the next hour Bernice had to put through several more calls one after the other. First, Miss Costigan got a call from her sister living in Galway to find out how she was doing after her ordeal in the bank, and if she wanted to come to Galway instead of Dublin to see the President on Saturday. Miss Costigan said she was too shaken to be going anywhere but she'd think about it.

Next, the undertaker, Long Tom Tymon, got a call from Sergeant Glacken asking him to bring his hearse to the river field in the morning to collect the body. Soon afterwards Doctor Ballintine came on the line using the telephone in his own house. He asked to be put through to the Superintendent in Boyle. I don't know who he finally got talking to, but he didn't get very far with his attempt to go over the head of Sergeant Glacken and have Francie's body brought home straight away.

It got quiet for a while. Then we heard a speeding car hit the brakes hard and slide to a stop on the loose gravel outside the shop. It could be a late customer desperate for petrol, or for cigarettes and matches, but this driver was in such a rush it crossed my mind it might be the bank robbers back to raid the post office.

I looked at Bernice and she looked at me.

Daddy had an iron bar he put across the shop door on the inside. It stayed there until the shop opened in the morning when he damped the wooden floor and swept out the dust. If the bank robbers wanted to rob the post office, and managed to break down the door, someone should have told them the safe was always locked at night and only Mrs Daly the Postmistress and the colliery owners had keys.

I moved to the window to peep around the edge of the blind. Lifting the hem slightly I saw a police car and then the driver, Sergeant Glacken, getting directions to the river

35

field from a couple of pitman leaving the pub.

The car took off hard and sped across the bridge. And I overheard one pitman say to the other: "He must think he'll get a promotion out of this."

His friend said, "Troth, he should have kept a tighter eye on the bank."

The switchboard came alive again, and Bernice had to put through a call to Doctor Ballintine. It was the Superintendent in Boyle. The phone in Doctor Ballintine's house rang at least nine times before the doctor answered, so he must have gone to bed early.

When he finally got talking to Doctor Ballintine, the Superintendent apologised for the late call, and for being unable to speak with the doctor in person when he rang earlier. He was calling now to inform Doctor Ballintine that an army crackshot was coming out from Boyle Barracks in the morning. Sergeant Glacken had strict orders to leave the body where it was until the crackshot arrived.

Doctor Ballintine got angry with the Superintended, saying it was 'thoroughly disgraceful' to leave the body of a dead child out in a field overnight.

The Superintendent kept his voice calm as he told the doctor there were stories circulating about an escaped lion. Fresh information, he said, furnished by a member of the public, placed the creature near where the drowned child may have ended up in the water. Animal tracks had been found at the spot.

"Utter nonsense," said Doctor Ballintine. With his voice steadily rising he told the Superintendent the wildcat story was a complete fabrication to explain sheep lost through poor farming practices after the bad winter. The authorities needn't waste time on a wild goose-chase bringing in this army 'hot shot'.

"Crackshot," the Superintendent said. And even

though he appreciated the decision would upset the family of the deceased child, the circumstances were unusual enough to warrant – that's what the Superintendent said – to warrant the calling in of a specialist army sharpshooter. The crackshot had served in the Congo and had first hand experience of tracking lions in the bush.

"It's not a lion," I whispered to Bernice.

"You said panthers only come out at night," she whispered back.

It was strange to hear the Superintendent, and the village Doctor, argue over the telephone whether the panther or the lion, or whatever kind of creature might be on the loose, was genuine or not. Never having seen the beast, there had been an element of doubt at the back of my mind, even after I found the dead poultry feathers, whether it was real or not. Now the authorities had linked the sighting of an unidentified large cat with the death of Francie Curran.

SIX

I waited on another while at the switchboard with Bernice until she finished her shift. Then, at ten o'clock, Mammy found me and ordered me up the stairs to bed.

A clammy haze hung over the tops of the trees and the roofs of the houses of the village, and from my bedroom window I caught sight of an occasional blue-white flash on the horizon like the thunder and lightning hadn't fully gone away, but the storm was too far off to matter. Climbing into bed I thought I might dream about Francie Curran, but as soon as my head hit the pillow I was out like a light.

In the morning, when I opened the curtains and lowered the top half of my bedroom window, a deep wide blue summer haze hung over the countryside. It was a lovely morning again after a muggy night. In the street below, Daddy set up the rack with the cans of Castrol motor oil beside the petrol pump. The breadman from Drumshanbo arrived with a tray full of batch loaves fresh from the bakery, and Daddy followed him inside to check the delivery against the docket.

I dressed quickly, hurried downstairs and helped myself to a good big bowl of cornflakes with milk and plenty of sugar for extra energy. An army marches on its stomach and I had a busy day ahead. When I had my plate rinsed and dried and put away, I sneaked into the master bedroom to find Daddy's binoculars which he kept hidden on top of the wardrobe where I wasn't supposed to find them.

In the scullery I undid the bolts on the back door and went out into the yard. Someone was bound to find the bolts off and fasten them again, but by that stage I would be safely away from the house. At the lower end of the back garden a hole in the hedge led to the ash-pit, and I had extended the path to make a trail along the river, although the quickest way to where I was headed this morning was around by the front of the pub, across the road and take a shortcut across the football field. I was determined to get a look at the battle-hardened sharpshooter back from the Congo with big game hunting experience, and while I had no idea when he'd show up, I figured if he was an experienced tracker he'd be an early riser.

To avoid drawing attention to my movements, I went around by the sideline instead of straight across the football field. I had only bad memories of the football field in any case, after the one time I got picked to play on the village team. They put me in goal and the match was a disaster because there was a deep hole full of muddy rainwater worn into the ground in front of the goalmouth. On the very first dive I made I got blinded with water, and soaked to the skin, and the ball ended up in the back of the net. We got pulverized that day. And when my mother saw the cut of me after the match she said I wasn't allowed to play again – not that the team ever wanted me back.

At the far end of the football pitch, the field dipped away into rough ground full of tall weeds and rubble from the original brick-wall of the ruined dam belonging to the iron foundry reservoir. Below the abandoned reservoir the damp bottomlands began. But just under the dry base of the iron works' wall I had scouted out a giant sycamore tree which was one of my favourite hiding places.

I'd nailed a couple of laths to the lower part of the trunk to make footholds, and I knew exactly which way was best for reaching the big lower branches that were as wide and smooth as a horse's back.

About half way up the tree I found a comfortable vantage point from where I had a good view of the fields bordering the river. I got the binoculars out of the case and raised them in both hands. Even when I got the focus clear I couldn't find the spot where Francie Curran lay. The summer grass was too long and the pasture field too full of weeds. And I knew Francie would be wearing his bottle-green coloured soldiers' outfit, making him harder to see.

I probably wouldn't even have found the right field only I noticed Red Paddy Reynolds standing guard near the gap. He had a double-barrel shot-gun rested in the crook of his arm. He must be afraid the panther would come looking for the body. But it would be an easy thing for a jungle cat to hide amongst the crop of thistles and blooming yellow ragwort covering the field.

Along with Red Paddy, a uniformed guard whose name I didn't know stood waiting for the army crackshot to arrive. In rural science we were told that ragwort was a noxious weed, and a land owner could be fined for having it on the farm. But the guard didn't look too bothered, and the two men passed the time talking and leaning on the top bar of the farm gate.

A strong sharp smell from the binoculars, and the hard carry-case hanging around my neck, reached my nostrils. That smell was the sort that could trigger a small wheeze at the bottom of my lungs, but if the rubbery chemical smell threatened my breathing I was ready to put up with it for the feeling of quiet power the binoculars gave to me being able to watch what was going on from a safe distance, unobserved.

I raked the field again with the binoculars and saw a dark green bump that must be Francie's body. Holding the binoculars as steady as I could manage, I finally made out Francie's legs and chest and the side of his face. For once, Francie had his army helmet off. It must have got lost in the river.

I kept the binoculars trained on his body, finding it hard to believe he was dead. Francie had always been so cheery and full of mischief, and now he lay completely lifeless in the long grass. Unless the men standing guard at the gap finally moved him, Francie would lie there until the clothes rotted off his back and the grey-crows picked his bones clean. I found that thought hard to take in. At any minute I wanted Francie to put his helmet back on his head, the way he did when he was a soldier pretending to be shot and he'd fling himself onto the ground for a few seconds only before getting to his feet again and telling everyone, 'I'm not dead'.

The morning warmed up, and bees began to drone amongst the sycamore leaves that had shiny splotches on them and tasted sweet if you licked the sticky spot with the tip of your tongue. The bees kept to the outside in the sunlight and didn't bother me where I watched from the shadows.

I don't know how long I waited up in the tree when a movement at the gap into the river field caught my eye. I raised the binoculars to see a green army Land Rover enter the gateway at speed. It drove fast across the pasture, mowing down the weeds in its path, and halted just short of where the body lay.

Even with the binoculars trained on the windscreen I couldn't get a clear view of the driver. I expected him to jump out and stride commandingly towards the body straightaway. But he stayed sitting in the Land Rover. Adjusting the focus I realised he had a big walkie-talkie up to his face.

At last, he put down the walkie-talkie and got out of the Land Rover. He was taller and slighter than the burly, square-jawed commando I'd been expecting. He wore khaki trousers and a short-sleeved khaki shirt with epaulettes and a black beret with a badge that caught the light, and his first action was to look straight in my direction. I held my breath and stayed stock still. The sun was in his face, but he had sunglasses on, and even at this distance in my concealed lookout post in deep shadow behind a screen of broad green sycamore leaves I was afraid he'd see me, and maybe even use his sniper's rifle to force me to show myself with my hands up.

Moving towards Francie's body the crackshot hunkered down and made a closer examination. It was hard to see exactly what he was doing, though I imagined he was looking for claw marks on the body. He stood up and raised his hand and waved to the men at the further end of the field. A big black hearse came through the gap and followed the tracks made by the army Land Rover. The hearse pulled up short of the soft ground where the body lay.

The uniformed guard and Red Paddy followed the hearse on foot. When they caught up with the hearse the undertaker, Long Tom, got out and started giving instructions. Long Tom was joined by Eugene and Gerry McPadden, who'd arrived as front seat passengers in the hearse. While the undertaker unfolded a large sheet, the uniformed guard, Red Paddy, Gerry, Eugene and the crackshot lifted Francie off the grass and put the body back down onto the sheet spread out on the ground. They wrapped the sheet carefully around Francie's body and lifted him again and put the body inside a plain pine coffin. I wondered if the undertaker kept one in stock, or had he spent the night making the special child-sized coffin. Either way, he screwed down the undersized coffin lid, and the men around him helped to load the corpse into the back of the hearse.

When they were done, the undertaker got into the hearse by himself. It moved off slowly, making a wide turn to avoid sinking in the soft ground before driving towards the gap, followed by the men who'd helped with the body. The crackshot kept a respectful distance behind the procession in the Land Rover.

A small crowd of people had gathered on the road to meet the hearse as it left the field. I spotted Francie Curran's father and the parish priest, Father Boland.

After a short stop on the side of the road for the priest to say a prayer, the hearse took off. The crackshot's Land Rover drove the other way; probably headed towards the Iron Bridge to look for tracks, and maybe even find the exact spot where Francie Curran got chased into the river by a large predatory cat willing to hunt in broad daylight.

I had a burning curiosity to go and look at the spot where the body had lain overnight in the long grass. But it didn't feel right. And it would be better to come back another time when everything quietened down.

I climbed down out of the tree and stretched my legs to ease the pins and needles. As soon as I got the proper feeling back into my legs I needed to get to work. Seeing Francie dead had made me realise I didn't want the crackshot to kill the panther.

You couldn't leave a black panther roaming the countryside free to do whatever it liked. But I didn't want it to end up like Francie Curran either, deprived of life forever. It was the panther's nature to hunt for food. And even if it had chased Francie into the river, it would be wrong to kill it. Somebody must have got tired looking after the panther and let it loose to fend for itself. So it was bound to be feeling lost and confused and hungry enough to hunt by day. It was only fair we do our best to catch it and return it safely to the mountain forest ranges where it belonged.

I hurried back to the house and returned the binoculars to the top of the wardrobe. When I came downstairs again Daddy was in the kitchen making tea.

His favourite lunch was a thick crusty slice of batch bread smothered in honey, washed down with a mug of milky tea. I left him to enjoy his bread and honey and tiptoed up the hallway, carrying my empty school satchel to steal the rope I needed for the panther trap. With luck, Mrs Daly the Postmistress would have gone home for dinner and I'd find the shop empty.

Unfortunately she was at the switchboard with a mug of Ovaltine and an arrowroot biscuit on the counter by her elbow. Stalling in the doorway I watched her for a minute or more. Her eyes were closed. Then I heard a soft snoring sound. She was fast asleep.

I'd read in a book on rough shooting in Scotland how hunters stalking in the Highlands could get within range of a stag without sending giveaway vibrations through the ground if they moved their weight slowly across the ball of the foot from their heels onto their toes. It would be risky but worth it if I could carry off my raid without waking up Mrs Daly. So I used the technique now, placing one foot stealthily in front of the other, as I entered the shop and moved past the snoozing Postmistress towards the spool of cart-rope.

Mrs Daly's breathing changed. I checked over my shoulder to see if she was still asleep. Her lips rattled but she didn't wake up.

The spools of rope were bolted to the edge of the counter in different weights, and I began to turn the middle spool of medium thick cart-rope until I had unwound what I judged to be enough. I was probably leaving myself short, but I got the feeling Mrs Daly was about to wake up. Wiping the palm of my hand on my jeans I got out the pocket-knife and was pleased by the way the sharp long blade sliced through the fibres. Everything seemed to be going well, when I heard the mechanism in the clock in the wooden case on the mantelpiece prepare to chime. Gathering up the cut length of rope, I bundled it into my satchel as the clock struck two and Mrs Daly began to stir.

After a swift dash into the hallway, I sidetracked to avoid Daddy and ducked into the good room to crouch behind the settee while he went past on his way to open up the shop.

With the coast clear, I took the stairs two at a time and made it into my bedroom, where it was a relief to shut the door behind me. In case I got quizzed about being spotted running out of the shop by Mrs Daly as she woke, I shoved the satchel with the rope under the bed until such time as I could smuggle it out of the house. With the rope securely in my possession, I steadied my nerves and got out my pencil case and a copybook with spare pages at the back. At the desk where I did my homework, I began to make a list of what I needed to bring to the mountain to set up the panther trap.

My pocket-knife topped the list; that and a flash lamp

for when I climbed down into the hole. Luckily, I had a flash lamp already that I used for going to the toilet at the end of the landing at night without turning on the lights. It could go into the satchel with the rope. Daddy's binoculars would also come in handy for keeping an eye on the trap from a safe distance when I had it finished. I'd need sandwiches, too, and a big bottle of Fanta in case I had a long wait. And then there was the question of what to use to lure the panther to the exact spot. To catch lions in Africa hunters used a kid goat tethered out in the open. Maybe I could borrow a lamb.

This was as far as I got when Mammy appeared at the bedroom door.

I closed the copybook.

"We're going to the Curran's house later," she said.

"To see Francie?"

"To pay our respects."

"Can I come?"

"As long as you don't get upset."

"I won't get upset," I said.

"Put on a clean shirt so. And give your hair a comb."

I closed the copybook with my big cat hunting wish-list and got ready to view my first dead body.

SEVEN

On the way to the Curran's house, Mammy sat in the front of the Cortina with her hands in her lap. Daddy drove, and I sat in the back looking between their shoulders at the road ahead.

We crossed the stone bridge and passed the last house in the village. Whitethorn hedges and thick white bands of pignut flowers grew along the verges of the road. The meadow fields behind the hedges were ready for cutting, and there was field after field of tall grass full of dog daisies and buttercup. Below the road I could see the sunlight sparkling on the river. On the far side of the river, deep gullies had been cut into the sides of the mountain by ancient streams. The sides of the gullies were thickly covered with hazelwood scrub and other shrubbery, and the surrounding slopes had great banks of prickly whin bushes stretching for miles.

It was easy to forget how much wild mountainside the panther had for roaming.

Daddy was a slow driver and he took great care when we came to the Iron Bridge. It was narrow with steel girder sides in the shape of Xs bolted and riveted together.

Looking through the spaces between the girders I could see the river flowing in the direction of the valley.

We crossed the narrow bridge at a crawl, and about half a mile further on we turned down an unpaved lane to Francie Curran's house. The lane was barely wide enough for the Cortina, so the people walking towards the house to pay their respects had to climb up onto the ditch to let us pass. Daddy smiled apologetically while Mammy looked straight ahead.

We drove into the Curran's yard where one or two more cars stood parked in front of the house, amongst them the crackshot's army Land Rover.

The County Council cottage looked like it hadn't been painted in years. Right in front of the front door odd sandals lay on the grass. There were no flowers anywhere, but a potato crop grew in ridges at the gable, along with a plot full of enormous heads of cow-cabbage. A sack of coal stood in the front porch, a pane of glass in the front door broken. We joined the line of people queuing to get inside; the women with their headscarves on, the men with their caps off, smoking cigarettes and speaking with their voices lowered.

After my efforts in the morning to catch sight of Francie Curran's body using the binoculars, I didn't know how I felt about seeing him close up. We shuffled forward slowly, and as we neared the front door I saw people who'd already been inside the house take their leave by the back door. They didn't look too shocked.

We made it into the front hallway and then the sitting room. There was no sign of the crackshot. But inside the sitting room door I saw a Holy Bible and a rosary beads left on a small table where the family had two beeswax candles burning. In an upper corner next the ceiling, the wallpaper had peeled away from the walls and there was a mouldy air of damp in the room. The older Currans sat in chairs, the twins amongst them. Everyone had to crush up against each other to fit into the crowded room, and I could hear a lot of sobbing and whispers.

Francie Curran's father sat in the chair closest to the coffin, and Daddy leaned over him and said, "Sorry for your trouble." He shook Mr Curran's hand.

Mr Curran mumbled something back and Daddy moved on.

Francie's mother was sobbing and one of the twin girls, Angela, put her arm around her mother's shoulder. My mother took Mrs Curran's hand and gave it a squeeze. I was next and wondered if I should squeeze Angela's hand. But I was too slow, and before I could do anything the pitman behind me jumped his turn and shoved me aside.

I was distracted anyway by the sight of the coffin and disappointed to see the lid closed. I'd been bracing myself to meet the expression of horror on Francie's face from having to run for his life and then falling into the river. Secretly I'd hoped I might learn something from the way Francie looked to help me avoid the same fate if I ever came face to face with the creature.

We squeezed out of the room past the people coming in. A woman dressed in brown caught up with us and said, "Go on through into the kitchen and get a cup of tea for yourselves."

I spotted the look Mammy gave Daddy. She wanted to go home. But these were Daddy's customers for the travelling shop, and he led us into the kitchen. Mammy agreed to have tea. It came in a blue and white willow-pattern cup with a chip gone out of the rim. And the glass of orange they gave me tasted watery. The biscuits too were Lincoln Creams, and soft.

A bunch of pitmen in their Sunday suits, their caps

stuffed into side-pockets, were drinking glasses of whiskey and bottles of stout and eating the sandwiches offered by a team of women going round with trays and teacups. When the woman carrying the teapot moved aside the pitmen were gathered around a stranger wearing an army uniform. The crackshot.

Clean shaven and handsome, in an officer material way, he had a high forehead, fair hair and alert blue-green eyes. His Tuf army boots were brightly polished, and he wore a short jacket over his khaki shirt. Seen up close he looked only a year or two older than Bernice.

Trying not to appear like I was ear-wigging on the conversation, I heard the crackshot say to one of the pitmen: "So, it was Gerry McPadden who claims to have seen this animal?"

The pitman said, "Gerry told me he was fishing from the Iron Bridge for a trout for the evening tea when he saw a giant cat. Like a wildcat only bigger."

"What colour?"

"Brownish like a lion, or maybe darker."

The crackshot said, "And then what happened?"

"He left the bridge and went down to the river bank where he says he found tracks."

"They'll have been washed away by the flood?" the crackshot said. "Did he see anything else?"

"You'll have to ask him."

A second pitman told the crackshot, "Francie's mother says he was playing soldiers near the Iron Bridge when he disappeared."

"You think this big cat might have been stalking him?"

"You tell me," said the pitman. "Isn't that what you're here for?"

I wondered if I should go over to the crackshot and tell him how Francie might have fired his cap-gun at the panther shouting, 'Halt – who goes there?' causing the beast to turn on him and chase him into the river.

All of a sudden the woman pouring the tea jumped at the sound of two loud gunshots, one fired straight after the other in the back yard. My eyes went to the crackshot, for the instant he heard the gunfire he'd reached under his tunic to where I glimpsed a concealed weapon. It looked like an army issue revolver. A split-second later, the crackshot was out the back door, and I was right behind him.

Red Paddy Reynolds stood in the middle of the back yard holding his shotgun. I was certain he must have spotted the panther and fired the shots to kill it or to drive it off. But there was no sign of the panther. And even the reek of cordite and gun-smoke rising in wisps from both barrels of the shotgun couldn't hide the smell of whiskey from Red Paddy's breath. While on the ground beside the outhouse I saw a freshly shot pigeon.

"I should have put lead in that buck sooner," said Red Paddy.

"Put away the gun like a good man," the crackshot said, closing up his tunic and acting like he hadn't been reaching for a weapon.

Red Paddy lowered the shotgun.

I crossed the yard to look at the fallen pigeon. When I picked it up off the ground, it was still warm, its neck floppy and a bead of blood gathered at the very tip of its beak. The shotgun pellets had torn away feathers from the pigeon's breast and, drunk or not, it was a fine shot. Then I noticed the pigeon had a number stamped on a metal ring around its leg.

"It's a homing pigeon that got lost," I said.

"There's no luck in a bird like that," said Red Paddy.

"Not now there isn't," said the crackshot and he

indicated I should put down the dead bird.

"Pishrogues," said the woman who spilt the tea.

Her hands trembled holding the teapot and she was disgusted with Red Paddy for upsetting everyone in the house. But the pitmen coming out of the corpse house were on Red Paddy's side. The pigeon had brought misfortune to the family's door and deserved to be shot.

I set the bird down gently on the grass and dusted off my hands.

People started to go back into the house, but I spotted Mammy and Daddy headed for the Cortina. Although it would have been useful to get talking to the crackshot, I was happy to leave. The whole atmosphere around the Curran household felt disconcerting, so risky in fact the army crackshot had parked the Land Rover where he wouldn't get boxed in, and brought a gun hidden under his tunic, like he'd been expecting trouble.

Shortly before the village, I looked over my shoulder and noticed the crackshot's army Land Rover right behind our car. I expected him to veer off for some reason, but he followed us over the bridge and pulled up behind us when we stopped at the pub.

We went into the American Lounge to go on through into the house. But while Daddy kept going to get back to the shop, I waited while Mammy had a word with Bernice behind the counter. The door into the pub opened and in walked the crackshot. He put down a canvas kit-bag and a carry-case for his rifle on the seat inside the door and approached the counter. He looked at Bernice behind the bar and then at Mammy and he said, "I'd like a room, please, if you have accommodation available."

"We have a vacancy, yes," Mammy said very politely.

"And how would you like to pay?"

"Cash in advance," he said.

He took a chunky black leather wallet from his hip pocket and counted off notes for my mother.

She swept the money up niftily from the counter and said, "I'll have a receipt done up for you."

"The morning is fine."

"And the name?"

"Welcome," he said. "Captain Frank Welcome."

"Welcome?" said Bernice like she didn't believe him. "What sort of a name is that?"

"We've had it in the family for years," he said.

"You're Welcome wherever you go," I said.

"Breakfast is at eight," Mammy said with a sharp look in my direction. "Give Captain Welcome a hand with his bags."

I made a bee-line for the rifle. I couldn't see the gun itself but there was a name on the strap of the carry-case: 'Mannlicher-Carcano'. Before I could pick up the gun Captain Welcome stepped in and said, "I'll look after that."

"Are you really a crackshot?" I asked, picking up the kit-bag instead.

"Time will tell."

"But you're here to shoot the panther, right?"

"You think it's a panther?"

"I do."

"Have you seen it?"

"No – but I found tracks."

"Panther tracks?"

"I don't know. A big cat anyhow."

"Why do you say that?"

"No claw marks," I said. "Cats can retract their claws, dogs can't. So it was definitely a big cat."

"Don't encourage him," Mammy said. "He's obsessed."

Frank Welcome looked at me and smiled in a way that let me know he was on my side more than my mother's.

"You'll have to show me," he said.

"Stop pestering the man," Mammy said.

She led the crackshot around by the bar, through the door into the main house marked 'Private', and up the stairs with the carry-case. I trailed after him with the kit-bag, which was a lot heavier than it looked.

As it banged against my leg climbing the stairs, I could feel at the very bottom of the kit-bag a dead weight like an iron skillet pot. It was also the right size to be the army issue revolver he'd carried earlier hidden under his tunic. I would need to see him unpack, of course, to confirm my hunch about the revolver, but at the doorway Mammy ordered me to put down the bag and make myself scarce while she showed Captain Welcome his room.

Even though we were rivals, in as much as I meant to capture the panther alive while his job was to shoot it, I could see the advantage in having Captain Welcome stay with us. It would make it easier to keep tabs of his movements, and to ask him about his plans. Unfortunately, I'd blurted out my information about finding tracks. He'd want to know where I'd seen them. He might even want me to show him the exact spot, in which case I had to avoid leading him to the nearby trap. I definitely didn't want him to know anything about that.

EIGHT

The following morning, as soon as I got up, I tread barefoot along the landing to the crackshot's bedroom door where I stopped and listened, but couldn't hear a sound from within. Then, before I could move, Bernice's bedroom door opened.

Seeing me rooted to the spot she said, "What are you doing, Leo?"

"Nothing."

"If you're looking for Frank Welcome, I heard him up and about earlier."

I felt stupid getting caught listening at the crackshot's door, but at least it was Bernice. She darted past in her nightdress on her way to the bathroom, and it made me feel better knowing the great thing about sharing the same landing was seeing Bernice first thing in the morning and last thing at night, often without much clothes. When I heard the bolt on the toilet door slide into place, I reached out and carefully tried turning the handle of the door into the crackshot's room. Locked. And he probably had the rifle and the handgun with him anyway if he was out tracking since first light.

Outside, when I looked up and down the road, there was no sign of the crackshot or the army Land Rover. On the bridge a bunch of girls sat on the wall talking and giggling and nudging each other. It was the absence of this silly mocking and messing that made Bernice so appealing to me. She was always herself, and didn't go in for any put-on girlie nonsense.

My first priority was to examine the spot where Francie's body had been found in the field on the other side of the river. To dodge the girls on the bridge, I crossed the road and made straight for the gate into the football field, headed for the big sycamore under the old iron works. Past the sycamore, the river made a wide loop where the water ran shallow, and it should be possible to cross without having to use the bridge.

The river had several dangerous deep turn-holes best avoided. But at other spots the water ran sluggish where wide sandbars and exposed rocks could be used as stepping stones. And with the disused iron-works reservoir wall at my back, I followed the river bank until I reached the crossing place I had in mind. I wore plastic sandals without socks, and the easiest thing was to leave the sandals on my feet and just roll up the legs of my jeans and wade the deeper parts.

The ground at the edge of the river was soft and full of green flaggers and horsetails and other marshland plants and wildflowers. Until I started to put my energies into stalking the panther, I used to catch tadpoles in jam jars to record their lifecycle, and collect wetland flower and grasses and press them between sheets of white drawing paper to preserve them. When the flowers dried out, I stuck them down with cow-gum and wrote their names in block letters with a HB 2 pencil after I found out what they were called in my book on wildflowers, grasses, rushes and sedges. If I took the trouble now I could probably find frog orchids and butterfly orchids. Instead, I waded into the water until it reached just short of my knees, then I paused to steady my balance and get used to the chill, and started to make my way across.

Mid-way across, the water was deeper and the footing trickier than I anticipated. I stopped to roll the legs of my trousers up higher. My legs and feet were numb, and I found it hard to keep my balance with the stones on the bottom moving under the soles of my sandals. It might be safer to turn back. But further down the opposite bank, a water-hen under the alders caught my eye, and when it darted away, I spotted a familiar object.

The green helmet had lodged in a tangle of exposed roots. Although I couldn't wade the whole way to the base of the alders, where the river ran too deep, I was able to reach out, and by stretching and balancing on one leg, hook the helmet with the tips of my fingers. It came away so easily I almost overbalanced and dropped it. But improving my grip, I pulled back quickly and backtracked to cross the river in a safer place holding my prize.

Gaining dry ground again on the other side of the river, my drenched sandals squelched as I walked, but I was in the river field now where Francie had finished up and I had his helmet. As soon as I got beyond the soft ground onto dry grass I sat down.

In possession of the very helmet Francie Curran never normally took off his head, I examined it for scratches or tooth-marks made by a big cat, but found only that the chinstrap and inside webbing were wet from being in the river. It told me nothing, and yet Francie would have had a fit if I'd attempted to lay a finger on it while he was alive. Amazed and proud to have retrieved it, several minutes passed before I noticed I was being watched.

Red Paddy stood under the far hedge beside Captain Frank Welcome's Land Rover at a spot where a large army tent had been erected in the shelter of the hedge. I got to my feet and, holding the helmet down by my side while making no attempt to hide it, I approached the two men.

A harsh static noise came from the walkie-talkie in Frank Welcome's hand as the volume rose before he switched it off. "I've been in touch with army headquarters," he said to Red Paddy. "I've made it clear that while the level of threat is low, there is enough substance in the reports of a dangerous wild animal on the loose to look into the matter further. I'll stay tonight with Mrs Rossiter and then set up camp, here."

Red Paddy said, "I'll keep the cattle out of this field."

Seeing me approach, the crackshot said, "What's that in your hand?"

"Francie Curran's helmet. I just found it in the water."

"What's your name again?"

"Leo. Leo Rossiter."

"Let's have a look at that, Leo."

When I held up the helmet for him to see, he took it out of my hand and said, "We ought to return it to the family."

"It's a crying shame what happened," said Red Paddy.

"Do you really think it was the panther chased him into the river?" I asked

"It's possible," Captain Welcome said. "And we have an eye-witness, Gerry McPadden who reported seeing a large animal in the vicinity. All the same, it's not enough to cause a public alarm."

"I've seen it," said Red Paddy. "A cat as big as a suck calf."

"Here in this field by the river?" the crackshot asked.

"No, on the side of the mountain."

"And Leo, you say you found tracks?"

Though reluctant to surrender the advantage the information gave me, I felt I had no choice but to come clean and say, yes.

"Let's take a look," Welcome said and started walking towards the Land Rover.

"Right now!" I said.

"I'll bring the rifle."

"Are you really going to shoot it?" I asked catching up.

"We'll have to find it first."

"You might as well be looking for a needle in a haystack," Red Paddy called after us.

Opening the door into the Land Rover Captain Welcome said, "And this needle has legs and won't be afraid to use them."

Giddy with excitement at the prospect of a spin in the army Land Rover, I opened the passenger door, which felt heavy and clunky, and sat into the front passenger seat, its worn upholstery hot from the summer morning sunshine. Along with the glove compartment, there were extra pockets made of green netting for holding maps, and Captain Welcome had a water canteen and a pair of army 'field-glasses' alongside the walkie-talkie that hung from a strap at his back. The Mannlicher-Carcano rifle, too, was out of its gun-bag and rested with its barrel pointing upwards between the driver and the passenger seats alongside the long handled gear-stick, which had a smooth round black top worn shiny from hard driving. The inside of the Land Rover as a whole had a distinct military vehicle feel that wasn't a bit like our family car, and it looked like Captain Welcome meant business, and had the full resources of the armed forces behind him.

We drove out of the field, not as fast as the first time I'd watched the Land Rover bouncing over the bumps and ridges in the rough pasture, but at an impressive speed that caused everything to rattle and slide and made me grab hold of the nearest handle to steady up.

"Do you know the mountain well?" he asked.

I said, "Pretty good."

"How about the old mines? The ones that aren't being used."

"There's Conlon's, and Flynn's and Noonan's," I said.

"Will we be passing any of those mines?"

"Conlon's old pit is at the end of the Bog Lane where we're headed."

"Do the old mines have disused out-buildings and sheds around them?"

"A few. But the only one with a proper shed is Rover pit."

I wasn't used to being taken so seriously, especially not by Mammy and Daddy, though maybe a little by Bernice. But Frank Welcome gave me the impression that as long as the quality of the information I supplied held up he would treat me as an equal.

We crossed the bridge and sped past the pub and shop where I saw Daddy outside filling a can of paraffin. He didn't see me.

Captain Welcome changed gears a lot, and I wouldn't have wanted to be going on a long journey in the rattling Land Rover, but it had plenty of power when we started to climb Chapel Hill.

"Turn right onto the Top Road, and the Bog Lane is coming up soon," I said. It would have taken me at least twenty minutes to climb this distance up out of the valley and we'd only been travelling for a couple of minutes. If the panther, as Frank pointed out, could cover a lot of ground between where it attacked and where it was hiding out, then so could we, and I could see the advantage in pooling information.

At the start of the Bog Lane he pumped the accelerator hard to begin the climb. Daddy never went over forty miles an hour in the Cortina, but Frank ploughed ahead up the Bog Lane as if we were still on the public road.

Pushing the Land Rover's capabilities to the maximum, we battered through deep ruts in the ground. The chunky tyres went into potholes and crunched over loose stones, sending them skittering away. We skidded too in spots, but quickly got traction again as we pushed hard up the steep rise until Frank eased off on the pedal where the ground levelled out and the lane grew grassy and narrow.

The going became smoother on the grass. We whizzed along, the summer breeze ruffling my hair. The sense of freedom was brilliant.

We met another steep rise in the lane at the place where the sloping mountain fields gave way to banks of thick summer bracken, black sallies and mountain ash trees, and the outcrops of rock and heather started above this final band of greenery.

Off to the right of the lane I could see the exact spot where I intended to trap the panther. I looked the other way and, thankfully, Frank Welcome was keen to keep going further on out the mountain, making for a dark outcrop in the distance: a spoil heap from the first of the worked-out coalmines he'd asked me to show him on this part of the mountain.

There had been fencing and stone walls on either side of the Bog Lane lower down, but now we had open mountain all around us. We drove through standing pools of peat-tinted water, thickened with gloopy green sphagnum moss and spirogyra. We arrived at Conlon's disused coal pit, abandoned years before. A deep cutting in a steep embankment led towards the dark eye of the pit entrance which was thickly covered in heather and wiry mountain grasses and clumps of rushes.

"The coalmine is a lot smaller than I expected," Captain Welcome said.

"They're all like that."

"Have you ever been into this one?"

"Only the first bit. The rest is too dangerous."

"Is it deep?"

"No, the roof is caved in. So you can only go in a short distance."

Captain Welcome turned off the lane and brought the Land Rover to a stop on top of the high point of the spoil heap, which extended out over the heather like a viewing platform. He reached for his field-glasses and got out. I followed.

There were several more rises to climb before we would reach the actual mountain top, but spread out below us was a panoramic view of summer heather with a breeze blowing from the south-west that sent silver waves rippling across the open moor.

"Smashing scenery," Welcome said. He put the field-glasses up to his eyes and did a three hundred and sixty degree sweep.

The Bog Lane we were using would end shortly, but I told him I had walked as far as the summit on my own, where I'd found a small lake called *Loughaun Bui* that disappeared in the dry weather. Captain Welcome said nothing and just kept reconnoitring the mountain. Grouse cackled, although we couldn't see them, and high above our heads the skylarks sang a song as piercingly lovely as the perfect blue sky. On the far mountain, however, curtains of rain fell.

After a methodical sweep of the terrain, his field-glasses tracked back and fastened on one spot. I looked in the same direction to find out what had caught his eye. A bunch of sheep appeared, running over the rise and headed our way. They looked like they were being chased. And my heartbeat quickened as a black shape pursued the escaping flock.

NINE

If Frank Welcome had the same thought as I did we were both disappointed. Behind the sheep a figure dressed in dark clothes waved a stick to keep the animals moving. As the person neared we saw it was a woman wearing a black hat and dark grey cardigan.

We stood by the Land Rover as the running sheep approached. Seeing us they slowed down but continued to climb up the side of the spoil heap to encircle us, and then they began to snatch up quick mouthfuls of anything under their feet they could eat. Behind the sheep came Nora Greene, the blackthorn stick she'd been waving in her hand now down before her to lean on it while she got her breath back. She was flushed, and short of breath, and her face tightened as she took in Welcome's army uniform.

"They were trespassing," she said.

"Whose sheep are they?" he asked

"Eugene McPadden's," she said. "But you'd have a hard time proving it."

"Why's that?"

"He counts them every day, but only from a distance with a pair of spy-glasses like yours," she said glancing at

Welcome's army issue binoculars.

"Where did you find them?"

"Tramping my flower bed – the third time this week."

"Have you spoken to the owner?"

"Arah, what good would that do? The sheepmen have me neighbour Johnny Wynn out of his mind. He has a house in Ballymote, and a farm of land here on the mountain, and every year he has lambs taken, fences cut, walls knocked and every bit of grass eaten. And now the doctor says he has a bad heart from running against the hill after other mens' sheep with only a useless hoor of a dog to help him."

"And what about the big cat they say is killing sheep on the mountain?"

The anger in her eyes became a merry twinkle and she said, "I hope it sweeps every last cursed sheep off the face of this mountain."

"Have you seen it?" Frank asked.

Nora looked towards the army Land Rover where she caught sight of the Carcano rifle.

"I have to be getting back to put a bit on the fire," she said. "But come down to the house for a drop of tea if you like."

It occurred to me that maybe she didn't want Frank Welcome to shoot the panther, or else she had no useful information, but wanted someone to listen to her complain about the sheepmen and the trouble they were causing her. Either way, Frank should just say no, instead of which he graciously accepted her offer.

"Hop in," he said to Nora, "we can give you a lift."

"No thanks," she said. "I'm in a hurry." And she took off walking.

We drove a short distance back the way we came, and I directed Frank Welcome to turn into a field where the faintest outline of a carter's-track was visible under the tightly grazed mountain pasture. Following the track, which had a few stunted hawthorns and clumps of whin bushes growing on either side, I pointed out the traces of the old potato ridges left behind in the ground after they were abandoned at the time of the Great Famine.

Nora Greene's house stood in a ring of sycamore trees within a dry-stone boundary wall. It was a pretty, three room cottage built like the garden walls from the surrounding field-stone. Even though there were few people around to admire the place, Nora had the walls whitewashed, the galvanized iron roof freshly painted, and the flower garden heavily coloured with tall pink and blue lupins and sweetly perfumed phlox.

On the rise at the back of the house Nora walked her shortcut home. Captain Welcome switched off the engine while we waited for Nora to come around by the back of the house to meet us at the front. When he opened the driver's door he spotted my reluctance to move.

"Aren't you coming in with me?"

"No."

"Why not?"

"I don't like her," I said.

Captain Welcome looked at me closely.

"She killed Martin Foley's mother," I said.

Captain Welcome closed the driver's door again and asked, "Who is Martin Foley?"

I wished I hadn't opened my mouth. But he kept looking at me, and I felt cornered and understood we were going nowhere until I explained.

It was Eugene and Gerry McPadden who confided the story to my mother. I wasn't supposed to be listening at the time, but didn't plan to tell Captain Welcome that part. So, I began by saying, "Martin Foley was the same age as me when his mother told him he was soon going to have a baby brother or a sister for company. Not long afterwards his mother went into her bedroom, because babies were born at home then and not in a hospital like they are now."

"I understand," said Welcome.

"The baby was a long time coming. His mother's bedroom filled up with old women looking to see what was going on and telling her what to do. But nobody would tell Martin what was happening. He just heard terrible noises coming out of the room. And then the women told Martin he had to leave the house to fetch a fresh bucket of water from the spring well.

"On his way back from the well, Martin heard his mother screaming. He dropped the bucket and ran into the house. Even though he started roaring for his mother, the old women wouldn't let him near her. Then Nora Greene took him away to spend the night in her house. He never saw his mother again."

Captain Welcome said, "That's terrible."

"Because he heard his mother screaming for her life, and he knew her bedroom was full of old women when she died, Martin was convinced the old women ganged up on his mother and killed her. He even threatened to kill Nora Greene," I said. "But he never got the chance, because she had him taken away and put in the mental hospital."

"Where is he now?" Welcome asked.

"They gave him electric shocks and tablets, and he was a long time gone before they finally let him out again," I said. "But nobody ever sees him. He's afraid to meet people, especially old women. If he's on the road and sees someone coming, he jumps over the ditch or breaks a hole in the hedge to get away as fast as he can."

Frank nodded and said, "Probably because he's still fearful of his neighbours."

"He sleeps outside," I said. "And he only ever visits his house when he's certain nobody is around."

I didn't add how I'd made it my business to catch sight of Martin Foley. And I'd succeeded once or twice, though only at a distance by hiding behind a ditch and watching out for him using Daddy's binoculars.

From what I'd seen of Martin Foley he wasn't old, but he wore a long black coat and he had a woolly grey beard and mad hair, and he was as near as I'd ever seen to a half-man, half-animal living in the wild.

"You understand, don't you," Captain Welcome said, "that Martin Foley's mother died in childbirth. Nora Greene and her friends didn't kill her. No matter what Martin Foley might believe, they were only trying to help."

"I suppose," I said.

"So come in and have a cup of tea. And don't be going around like Martin Foley making strange with the neighbours."

Until I shared the story just then, I never realised how much it troubled me, or how suspicious it made me of Nora Greene. I'd never accepted Martin Foley's notion that Nora and the other women killed his mother. Yet I had fallen into the habit of dodging and hiding from her whenever she set foot in the shop, or whenever I had to pass her house on the mountain, just in case there was a grain of truth in the story.

Nora stood watching us from her front door. She looked house-proud but uncertain, and I stopped stalling, grabbed the lever to open the door and go out to meet her.

"You have the place looking lovely," Captain Welcome said turning to admire the flower garden.

"The ground is sour but sure what can you do? Under bracken, gold; under rushes, silver; under heather, hunger," Nora recited.

Captain Welcome removed his army beret and had to duck his head stepping under the low wooden lintel of the front doorframe as we entered a flag-stone floored kitchen where a painted wooden dresser took up most of the opposite wall.

Neat rows of plates were lined up on the shelves of the dresser, and matching cups and mugs with blue and white stripes hung from hooks in a row. The end wall was taken up with a chimney breast and an open fireplace where a turf fire burned. Over the turf fire and its smooth white ashes, a black iron kettle hung from the swinging arm of a crane, with spare hangers for the cast-iron pots left by the hob.

A kitchen table stood in the middle of the room with an oilcloth covering and an unvarnished wooden form for sitting on. Nora made us sit down on either side of the fireplace in straw-bottomed *súgán* chairs with embroidered cushions.

She swung a steaming kettle out into the room, used a cloth to lift it by the handle and scald a big brown teapot, to which she added several generous spoons of loose tea from a caddie taken from the dresser. She had a rhubarb tart too under a glass dish, and we were soon served freshly baked tart with an extra sprinkle of sugar and tea coloured with strong cow's milk from her new blue and white jug.

I was a little wary of the tart, but the first cautious bite I took tasted sweet and juicy with rich buttery pastry.

"How is it?" Nora asked.

"It's good," I said.

I ate a larger mouthful and said, "It's very good."

Captain Welcome reached out and ruffled my hair. "There you are," he said.

I smiled happily.

The house and everything in it, including the tea,

smelled of turf-smoke, but in a good way. When Nora moved the turf basket aside, I caught sight of the movement of tiny silverfish darting hither and thither, and then we heard a chirruping sound.

Nora said, "It's the cricket on the hob singing. They only sing for people they like."

"What happens if they don't like you?" I asked.

"They eat holes in your socks," she said.

"I didn't expect to see a turf fire," Captain Welcome said. "I thought everybody around here burned coal."

"There's a few on the mountain still saving turf," said Nora.

"It's good turf?" Frank said, taking a hand-cut sod up in his hand. "I'm from Mayo where we like our turf as hard as a goat's knee."

Nora said, "It's off Eugene McPadden's turf bank."

"Oh," said Frank. "Does he compensate for his sheep trespassing with the fuel?"

"He gets his full due," Nora said. "I make certain of that."

She lowered her voice and looked out the little curtained window to double-check we were alone.

"There was an old woman lived here on the side of mountain called Katie Putt," Nora said, dropping her voice to a whisper. "She had no one to fend for her, and no money either, and she got into the habit of stealing turf off the mountain. She'd lift the turf while everyone was at mass on Sunday. That went on until Eugene's father, Vincey McPadden, got fed up of the old woman stealing the turf he had ready to sell. One Sunday morning, neither Vincey nor his oldest son Eugene appeared at mass. Everyone guessed where they were headed.

"Katie Putt was never seen again. Vincey and Eugene said the old woman got such a hop when they caught her stealing red-handed she turned around and went straight to Scotland to live with her sister. But a lot of people believed, though they could never prove it, the McPaddens threw her down an airshaft belonging to one of the old coal pits on the mountain. That's why no one ever saw or heard from her again."

Frank replaced the sod of turf in the basket and we drank our tea. For several minutes nobody spoke. Privately I felt stupid and ashamed. Nora Greene was no threat to me or to any youngster. She just wanted company to share a cup of tea and a chat, and to admire how nice she had her house looking.

And instead of being responsible for the death of Martin Foley's mother, she was the one living in fear. Eugene McPadden had her terrorised. His trespassing sheep besieged her garden daily, and she didn't dare complain because he sold her fuel for her fire, for which he got paid in full, because she believed he was responsible for the death of an elderly woman who'd dared to rob his family. I'd made a mistake avoiding Nora Greene, and it was Gerry and Eugene McPadden who'd made me wary of her. How far a rumour could be trusted depended on who spread it.

TEN

We stayed a short while longer at Nora Greene's open fireside, where I found myself at ease in a way I'd not felt in anyone's house since we moved into the area. But it turned out she had nothing useful to tell us about the panther. Twice at night she'd heard noises behind her house. She blamed the commotion on cats fighting, being too nervous to go outside and properly investigate.

Early one morning she'd seen what looked like a large dark animal on the side of the mountain prowling around the spoil heap where we'd been earlier. She could not say for certain what it was. It could have been the mystery cat or it could have been Eugene McPadden trying to keep out of sight while he counted his sheep from a safe distance with his spy-glasses. Then again it could have been her eyesight playing tricks.

We'd been on the mountain several hours, and with the evidence gathered from Nora inconclusive at best, I figured that as soon as we were done talking we'd go home. We said goodbye to Nora, who sprinkled us with holy water from a little font inside the door before we left. Then as we crossed her front yard, Frank asked me to show him the spot where I found the panther tracks. I had gotten used to his company, and could see how his transport and my local knowledge of the mountain doubled our chances of success, so leading him to the right place was not a problem.

We drove out the grassy carter's-track, turned up the Bog Lane, and when we reached the rim-rock again I said, "Stop."

Frank parked the Land Rover at the side of the lane out of the way, just in case a tractor or an ass and cart had to get past. Then he took up the Mannlicher-Carcano rifle. He also checked the breast pocket of his combat shirt where he kept a spare clip with extra rounds of ammunition. Seeing him take these precautions made me wonder if I'd been foolish scouting the mountain on my own without a weapon to defend myself if I stumbled across the panther or it stumbled on me. I'd even crawled into the panther's hiding place unarmed.

"Mind where you're walking," I said as we penetrated the rough ground on foot. "The slime on the rocks makes them slippery."

"Thanks for the warning," Frank whispered. "But let's stay as quiet as we can."

My cheeks turned red knowing I'd slipped up. We were in open countryside with no trace of the panther, but that didn't mean to say it wasn't in the vicinity, or holed-up and sleeping exactly where we were headed. So I concentrated on the expert deer-stalking method I'd picked up from the book on rough shooting.

Neither of us spoke a word until we reached the place I had in mind, and then I gestured for Frank to draw level with me and pointed to a man-made section of dry-stone wall with a small square entrance built into the clay embankment.

Frank indicated he understood. Bringing the Carcano around in front of him to be able to fire from the hip, he advanced cautiously. After a couple of paces he stopped and sniffed the air. Then he advanced on the opening.

I hadn't been back to this spot since I'd found the remains of the dead chicken. It was just too nerve wracking to go through that tight opening in the embankment believing it could be the panther's secret lair. Even Frank, his rifle at the ready, took the precaution of crouching down, picking up a stone and pitching it into the dark opening.

As the stone was swallowed up by the darkness beyond the threshold he cocked his head to listen. He tossed in a second stone, and when nothing happened he moved forward. When he got as far as the opening he reached into his pocket, got out a shiny metal pocket sized torch and put his arm into the opening first and bowed his head to peer inside. Satisfied with the situation he crouched down and crawled the whole way inside and disappeared.

I waited for what felt like a full minute but was probably only a few seconds. Seeing and hearing nothing out of the ordinary I began to move forward. Approaching the silent opening I said quietly, "Frank, are you all right?"

"All clear," he said.

I got down on my hands and knees and crawled under the lintel stone.

The entrance was tight, but past the narrow opening there was room enough inside for several people. Frank raised the torch and the space around us was revealed as manmade: a beehive-shaped chamber with enough room to stand up if we wanted though it was easier to stay crouched down. A pale square of daylight came in from above through an opening that once served as a vent or chimney at the top of the dry-stone roof.

"What is this place?" Frank asked.

"It's a sweathouse," I said.

I told him how our teacher, Miss Costigan, had taken us on a field trip to show us another sweathouse like this one. She said people in days gone by would build a big turf fire inside the sweathouse and close up the doorway. The fire could burn for a whole day, and when there were only ashes and cinders left inside they'd sweep out the flagstone floor. The old people believed that taking a sweat was a great cure for rheumatism. And with the inside heated up after the fire you crawled inside, took off your clothes, and stuffed them in the doorway to keep in the heat. Next you put a big cabbage leaf on your head to keep it cool. After an hour or so sweating in the dark you came out again and washed in the nearest cold stream and got dressed, went home, and after a hot drink, got straight into bed.

That was years ago, I said, and since that time most of the sweathouses had been forgotten about and were hidden in the undergrowth.

It was only when I found poultry feathers on the ground the trail led me to discover this sweathouse nobody seemed to remember anymore. The flagstones were gone from the floor. But there was a dip in the clay where a large animal had slept, and in the centre of the hollow I'd found the scattering of white feathers, a bit of a wing, and a scaly yellow shank with talons.

"What do you think?" I asked.

"It's a good hiding place," Frank said. "But I'm inclined to believe these feathers are the work of a fox."

He looked closely at the tracks I'd found earlier, but they weren't nearly as clear as I remembered them, or else they had gotten scuffed underfoot.

"I really don't think these are panther tracks," he said. "Though a big cat will mark its territory and there's an unusually strong animal scent in here."

I was disappointed we couldn't find definite proof of the panther's presence, but I didn't fancy being cornered in such a tight space waiting for the beast to come in through the door at our backs, and I was relieved when Frank said, "It's kind of claustrophobic in here."

He knelt down, poked the Carcano rifle through the entrance and crawled out after it with me close behind.

The dry-stone sweathouse sat in a hollow encircled by a sheltering ditch. We climbed to the top of the ditch where we could see the mountain fields slanting away below us. Beyond where the fields dipped the whole of the valley spread out in a fabulous panorama.

It was possible to see exactly how the narrow start of the valley opened wider as it dropped and how gullies taking water from the heights became a single river that wound in loops through the fertile lowlands, finishing in the lake at the foot of which stood the town of Drumshanbo.

Families were moving down off the mountain and at this height, apart from Nora Greene's cottage, the older homesteads were either abandoned or falling down. Most of the original cottages were roofless now and used as sheep-pens. There were one or two slate-roofed houses, but these were mainly lived in by bachelor hill farmers and elderly coal miners. People with younger families were doing their best to build nearer to the main roads.

Nestled on the side of Chapel Hill, the reservoir provided water round the clock, and it was only people like Nora Greene who walked twice daily to the spring well for water.

The 'siding' stood right in the middle of the valley. Coal Lorries came and went from the big yard bringing fuel to the electricity generating station built on the lakeshore. The coal burning power station had one lone tall smoking chimney and wasn't very big, though I had been greatly impressed by the size of the turbine hall when Miss Costigan took us there for a geography lesson.

Pylons brought the power to a substation, and creosote soaked poles carried the electricity lines along the sides of the roads, criss-crossing the whole of the valley, and climbing up the mountainside to bring power to the coal pits. New rows of telephone poles were starting to go up too. Cars were taking over from bicycles on the roads, and delivery vans were taking over from pony and carts, and you could see more grey Ferguson 20 tractors at work in the meadows than horse drawn machines.

As we sat taking in the view, I heard a strange beating sound in the air. Minutes later a helicopter appeared. From our vantage point on the mountain the markings on the helicopter's fuselage stood out clearly, as did the pilot and his passenger in the glass cockpit wearing jump-suits and aviation helmets.

Sometimes after a big gale a helicopter circled the area looking for fallen power lines, but this was a plain grey coloured helicopter with Air Force insignia. While we watched, it made several wide circles of the mountain, over-flying us at least twice and then leaving the mountain to cross the valley, heading in the direction of Dowra.

"Are they searching for the panther?" I asked.

"Probably the armed robbers," Frank said.

"Are you keeping an eye out for them as well?" I asked. "Is that why you wanted to know about old sheds on the mountain?"

"I'd like to see them caught," Frank said keeping his eyes on the departing helicopter. "Would you?"

"I'd sooner catch the panther."

"Well, let's get out of sight then."

As we got to our feet he said, "The kind of big game cat we're after could be watching us this minute, waiting for us to go away. So we'll act like we're leaving, and then circle back unseen and wait."

It sounded like a good plan.

Together we climbed the embankment and made our way onto the edge of the ridge where we walked in single file along the skyline to make our departure conspicuous before ducking behind a large freestanding boulder. We used other boulders for cover as we doubled back and slipped into a clump of bracken.

The tall green bracken grew thickly out of the soft ground, giving us perfect cover, and we crawled commando-style between the stems disturbing the undergrowth as little as possible. A rank smell from the bracken and bluebell pollen reached my nostrils, but the excitement of trying to outwit our prey kept my mind off these smells that could trigger my asthma. Advancing through the undergrowth we found a spot where we could slide down the perimeter ditch and return to the sweathouse.

I thought it unlikely the panther would have made its way back into the sweathouse so soon after we left, but I let Frank take the lead as he advanced at a crawl towards the opening and went inside without meeting our quarry.

Keeping low to the ground, I followed him into the dark beehive-shaped chamber. Now, all we had to do was stay quiet and wait. How long this vigil would go on for I had no idea.

Enough time passed for me to be able to see perfectly in the small amount of light coming through the chimney opening in the top. The very grain of the stone was clear, and so were the drips of water and the cobwebs in the chinks.

I passed the time moving my limbs every so often to stop them from going numb. The rest of the time I studied how each layer of dry-stone had been laid neatly one on top of the next without any two vertical joints in line. Whoever built this stone chamber knew what they were doing.

Frank kept the Carcano in front of him with the stock rested on the ground and the barrel pointed into the air. Even with the gun resting in this position I felt the tension of being in a constant state of alertness, listening for the slightest sound or movement outside. If we did hear something he would have to bring the rifle around instantly to its source and my job was not to get in his way.

As more time passed the world outside seemed to drift further and further away. Inside our silent, monk-like cell the grey light on the stone was so unchanging it could be any hour of the day or evening. We were completely outside the normal passing of time.

At some point my eyes closed and I drifted off into a light sleep.

A noise outside woke me. Opening my eyes I found Frank on the alert.

I had a crick in my neck but I held my breath and listened. A soft clinking noise started, as if a small run of stones had been dislodged and they were spilling down the ditch next to the sweathouse. The light coming through the doorway flickered as something passed by outside.

Frank raised the Carcano, eased a live round into the chamber and tightened the stock into his shoulder ready for the recoil when he fired.

At such close quarters the telescopic sight was no use, and I watched him press his face close to the Carcano to aim along the barrel using the metal sight on the end.

A dull thud came from directly above.

My brain was an instant ahead of my eyes in recognising the whiskers and enraged eyes that thrust through the opening above our heads.

"Don't shoot," I shouted.

As the rifle moved in a swift arc to fire at the opening, Frank swung the barrel past the target at my warning and he tilted back into me to avoid the reflex to fire.

The face above us vanished as quickly as it appeared and we heard footsteps running away.

"Who's that?"

"Martin Foley," I said.

It was his big grey beard I recognised, along with his mad hair that seen close up was a crude cap made from sheep's wool, with tufts of his own hair growing out through it.

He must have spotted us scouting out the sweathouse, seen us leaving and then curious to know what we'd been doing he'd decided it was safe to investigate. But his wild eyes had grown even wider when he found two people waiting inside the sweathouse; one of them with a rifle pointed in his face.

We probably gave him an even bigger fright than he gave us, even though Frank let out a long breath of dismay and relief as he popped the bullet out of the chamber, glad he hadn't accidentally shot a harmless local.

I studied the hollow in the clay floor and said, "He must sleep in here."

Frank said, "And now we know where the smell comes from."

ELEVEN

The sun was going down behind the rim of the mountain by the time we got back to the Land Rover. We drove into the valley, which was already in shadow. A rain shower had swept down the valley earlier, missing us in the sweathouse, but the tail end of the shower was still falling lightly on Chapel Hill where the road was wet and the runoff flowed on either side of the ridge of gravel in the middle with v-shaped ripples in the streams caused by stray pebbles. I'd been gone the whole day and I was hoping Frank would put in a good word for me and explain to my mother how I was showing him around the area.

After we drove past the church, I spotted Bernice up ahead. An open umbrella hid her head and shoulders but I recognised her short red coat and skirt. For some reason she was running as fast as her legs could carry her. I'd never seen her run so fast in my life.

In the Land Rover it didn't take long to catch up with her. But she didn't hear us coming up behind her and kept running. I got the impression she was in such a panic she didn't even notice Frank swing the Land Rover out wide to overtake her until we pulled up short and jumped out to intercept her blind flight.

Bernice collided with Frank and wrapped her arms around him.

"What's wrong – what's happened?" he asked.

"It's the lion," she said. "It's after me."

"There's no lion," Frank said.

I double checked and found the road in both directions empty, and the fields on either side showed no traces of a large animal path in the wet grass. Yet Bernice had worked herself into such a state she didn't believe us, and Frank had to keep reassuring her saying, "Nothing's going to happen. We're here. You're safe now."

It took Bernice another minute to get her fear under control. Finally she looked over her shoulder to confirm what Frank said. The road was empty.

"Tell us what happened?" Frank said.

"I heard it," Bernice said.

"Where?"

"Right behind me."

"Are you sure?"

"I went looking for you, Leo," she said.

"I was with Frank."

"I thought you might be up in that big sycamore tree where you're always hiding."

It surprised me to learn how well informed she was about my movements.

"When I couldn't find you I decided to go to the chapel to light a candle for Francie Curran. I was on my way home when I heard footsteps following me. I stopped and listened and the footsteps stopped too. I started walking again and I heard them again, coming up behind me. I knew then it was after me."

"Had you the umbrella up?" Frank asked.

"I had."

"Did you have it up the whole time?"

Bernice nodded.

"Walk on another bit for us," Frank said, "same as before with the umbrella wherever you had it."

Bernice settled the handle of the umbrella on her shoulder and slowly advanced towards the Land Rover. After a few steps she shouted, "There! There it is. Can you hear it?"

I looked around quickly, concerned Frank had left the rifle in the Land Rover. But there was nothing to see or hear – only the last of the raindrops dripping from the roadside trees.

Frank said, "Give us a look at that umbrella."

He took the umbrella, twirled it around, walked a few steps with the umbrella on his shoulder, and then he upended the umbrella, the top of which was dotted with droplets of rain.

"There, see," he said. "It's the little strap used to tie it up. Every time you walk it taps against the fabric and it sounds like someone is following you. That's why the sound stopped when you stopped, and started again when you started walking."

Bernice took the umbrella from him, flicked the offending short strap against the stretched fabric to confirm what he said, and then she closed up the umbrella using the same treacherous little tie that had given her such a fright.

"I'm glad you sorted that out," she said, "Or I wouldn't set foot outside the door again."

"Fear can get a grip on anyone," Frank said. "The trick is not to give into it."

My thought exactly, though I didn't say it.

We were so close to home I could easily have walked

the rest of the way home with Bernice, proud to be her bodyguard. But we rode in the Land Rover, where I sat in the middle with Frank and Bernice talking across me.

"You must think I'm stupid," she said.

"Never," Frank said.

"At the best of times I hate going outside alone," she said. "I'm always afraid I'll make a fool of myself in public. I'm fine when I have jobs that keep me busy. But if I have time on my hands, and I'm by myself, I get panicky. I get this feeling I'm going to cry. Or that I'll break down in front of everyone, and they'll think I'm a madwoman. And then I'll get sent back to the Industrial School. It's daft, I know. But I can't help it."

I'd never heard Bernice open up to anyone like this before, not even to me. And when Frank reached out and squeezed her hand, I couldn't believe the happy expression such a simple gesture brought to her face. Straightaway, I wished I'd done it first.

Mammy was ready to give out stink to me when I walked into the American Lounge, only she spotted Captain Welcome and Bernice along with me and politely told us that Brendan – she used my father's first name – had gone to see the colliery owners to discuss what to do about credit for the pitmen, who wouldn't get paid for another fortnight. We'd have to look after ourselves if we wanted supper.

We went through into the kitchen, where Bernice invited Frank to join us. He sat down at the table while Bernice got a bowl from the cupboard and cracked a bunch of eggs into it and whisked the mixture. While she lit the gas and heated the pan on the cooker, she got Frank to butter slices of loaf bread.

"I'd say you're not a great chef?" she said looking at the results.

"I have a black belt in cookery," he said. "One chop and you're dead."

Bernice smiled and dipped the buttered bread in the egg mixture and arranged three slices on the pan to fry. The smell of the hot butter and the egg mixture frying made me realise I was famished. I got plates and cutlery out of the cupboard. Then I had to move a stack of newspapers from the table before I could set three places.

"Is it true you fought in the Congo?" Bernice asked Frank.

"I'm just back," he said, giving me a hand to shift the newspapers and the magazines.

"The whole country came to a standstill when our lads got killed out there?" Bernice said. "It was in all the papers."

"The Niemba ambush?" I said.

Frank nodded and Bernice asked, "Did you know any of the men that got killed?"

"We weren't in the same regiment or anything," he said, "but yes, I knew them."

Bernice brought a big white dinner plate loaded with the first round of French toast to the table and told us to help ourselves.

"The long and the short of it is that we had no idea what we were letting ourselves in for," Frank said. "We took off from Baldonnell in American Globemaster planes because our own planes were so old they had thatched roofs."

I laughed, even though I probably shouldn't have.

"We landed next to the equator wearing heavy bulls wool uniforms that buttoned up to the neck, and hobnail boots and jam-jar leggings," he said between mouthfuls of

Bernice's home cooking. "You had men passing out with the heat. And the minute we landed we were marched off to Sunday mass. In the chapel we found the local men, women and even the children armed to the teeth. And there we were with rosary beads and scapulars and not a rifle between us. We saw trouble brewing but we thought, 'Ah sure we're Irish! Everybody loves us. All we have to do is say '*Jambo* – we come in peace.' But even though the native Baluba tribes' people were on our side, anyone with a white face was a Belgian to them. And they hated the Belgians."

"Is it true," I asked, "the Baluba's used bows and arrows?"

"It is," said Frank. "I even brought one home with me. It's with my stuff in the back of the Land Rover."

He tossed me his bunch of keys and told me to run out and get it. "It's in a wooden box inside the back door," he said. "The lock is worn, so jiggle the key around a bit, otherwise the door won't open."

Rubbing my hands to get the traces of melted butter and fried egg off them I went outside while Frank made the tea and Bernice got the next round of French toast ready.

A couple of minutes later, I came back into the kitchen carrying the lightweight wooden box with the word 'Ordinance' stamped on it. I put Frank's keys down beside the box. While searching for the arrow I'd taken a quick look for the pistol, but it must be in his room.

He raised the lid to reveal a blue velvet cloth wrapped around something long and thin inside the box. "When the Niemba ambush happened," he said, "the Balubas tried to warn our lads they were a war party. They wore leopard skin hats, and nailed one of their ceremonial hats to a tree. But nobody on our side understood what that meant. The patrol that went out that day had no interpreter with them either. The radios were useless. And they were far too lightly armed. A few antique Lee Enfield rifles that fired one round at a time, and could blind the eyes in your head with blow-back. Our lads looked like a soft target, and they were."

I wished he'd hurry up and show us the arrow, but he was so involved in telling us about the Congo he seemed to forget where he was.

"Of course the Balubas had some old blunderbusses as well as their bows and arrows, so it's hard to say who fired the first shot. Shots got fired – that's all anyone knows. It could have been them, or it could have been a warning shot from our side, or just an accidental round that got fired out of panic. And we only found out later," he said, "that firing warning shots into the air proved in their minds what the witchdoctors told them, that our bullets couldn't harm them. And then of course they had first fire. The UN had given strict orders not to respond to provocation unless we were in clear danger of being disarmed."

Frank beckoned me closer, loosened the last tie on the velvet wrapping, and took out a tribal arrow with a hardwood shaft bigger and stronger than I expected. "This is what they were armed with," he said. "And when arrows like this one start to fly you think it's some sort of a joke – like being the Lone Ranger with the Comanche coming after you."

He handed the arrow across for me to take a closer look. The feather at one end was big and amazingly soft, and the notch cut for the bow-string looked hand-made, though the sharply tipped arrowhead was surprisingly vicious.

"But if a man got hit by just one of these arrows he'd turn white as sheet in seconds. They're poison tipped, you see, with jungle plants and mamba snake venom."

I pulled my finger back fast from the arrow head. But Frank said it was scrubbed clean and safe. If there had been poison on it, and it got into my bloodstream, I'd be dead within three minutes.

"I've seen men shoot themselves rather than let the poison kill them," he said. "And soldiers who only got grazed with an arrow ended up with their arms and legs swelling up like balloons. It's amazing how Private Kenny lived to tell what happened. By the time we picked him up he was delirious and near dead with the poisoned arrows still hanging out of him. But he was made out of tough stuff, and the first thing he did when he stumbled out of the jungle after the ambush and met our patrol was to salute and give his name."

"Were you there for the ambush itself?" Bernice asked, carefully taking hold of the arrow I passed along for her to view.

"No, but I was with the patrol that came out to recover the vehicles afterwards," he said. "And that was a sad outing, I can tell you. Nobody could believe we'd lost nine men. But then we saw the spent red cartridge cases all over the road, and the vehicles themselves daubed with marks and signs done in blood – our lads or their own blood, I don't know which."

"Did you go into the jungle after whoever did it?" I asked.

"We had an idea who was involved, but in the end we just had to put up with our losses," he said. "There was some talk amongst the ranks about getting our revenge, but what we lacked in experience as an army we made up for in discipline. We didn't go in for reprisals like the Belgians. And to this day there's been no retaliation on our side for what happened."

He lost the thread of his thought, out of fatigue

perhaps, for he yawned soon afterwards, shoved his chair back from table, and returning the arrow to the box, said he had a report to write.

I was tired, too, and went to bed without a fuss expecting to sleep soundly after a busy day. But I woke up in the middle of the night feeling sweaty and breathless. My head throbbed and my chest felt tight, and I was so woozy and disorientated I wondered if Frank had been wrong, and a tiny amount of the mamba snake poison left on the arrowhead had gotten into my bloodstream.

TWELVE

My breathing sounded like I had an angry seagull trapped inside my lungs. I felt smothered by a strong chemical smell on top of the pollen smell from my clothes left on the bedroom chair. I'd picked up the pollen crawling through the bracken and the bluebells on the mountain when we were stalking the panther, but I couldn't place the choking tarry smell. It took me several minutes to realise the smell came from under my bed.

I found the flash-lamp, shone the beam under the bed to locate my satchel, fished it out and opened it up to confirm the stolen cart-rope was the source of the fumes. After getting out of bed, I stuffed the bag into the back of the wardrobe and closed the door tight. But the chemical and coarse fibre smell stayed in the air. I tried coughing to loosen the phlegm gathering in my lungs. Once I started coughing I couldn't stop. No matter what I did I couldn't get air. My stomach felt hard and tight like I'd swallowed a football.

I stumbled towards the window, shoved down the top half and, coughing violently, leaned out to find if I could breathe any better away from the fumes. My temples were throbbing and I was coughing so hard I thought I might throw up. Powerless to move I held on tight to the window frame in case I fainted and fell out.

My mother would be raging with me because I had ignored the two tablets I was meant to take every day. I took the pink one some days, especially if I felt chesty. But a lot of the time I either got rid of it, or broke it in two and only took one half and dumped the other half in the bushes.

If I could avoid it, I didn't take the white tablet at all. It was tiny but it tasted incredibly bitter and left a shocking bad taste in my mouth. Worse, if I took the white tablet in the morning it made me feel dopey for the rest of the day. So a lot of the time I only pretended to take it.

No matter what I did now I couldn't get my breath back. About the only thing I could do was lever myself further out the window. It was dangerous to hang out the window, since I could pass out during this coughing fit and topple out the whole way and end up on the road below. But whenever I got a really bad attack like this, and felt I was going to smother to death because I couldn't get an ounce of air into my lungs, I tried to calm my panic by imagining I was in a submarine trapped on the bottom of the sea as the air supply ran out.

Like the trapped submarine crew, I had to stay very calm and not panic and waste the remaining oxygen supply. Powerless to do anything else I had to have the will-power to wait patiently for my body itself to come to my rescue by believing the moment was coming when the air pumps would start working again and I could breathe life-giving fresh air into my lungs.

Until that relief came, the pressure on my lungs and heart was terrible. It felt like that wildcat I wanted to capture was trapped inside my own chest, yowling to get out and tearing apart my lung tissues and heart muscles with its lethally sharp claws.

Rather than dwell on the idea of my lungs in rags, and my heart about to burst, I stared off into the summer half-light, still coughing my lungs out, but imagining the black panther prowling free out there somewhere in the night, light of foot and purring, purring, purring in one long continuous uninterrupted breath.

I do not know how long this nearly unconscious state went on for, when I felt my mother's hands taking firm hold of me by the waist.

"Careful, Leo," she said. Her voice was gentle, to avoid further upset.

She eased me away from the open window safely into the room where I stayed on my feet, wheezing and gasping, but no longer coughing so violently. She brought her hand around and began to open up the first few buttons on my pyjama top.

"I have the Vicks ointment," she said.

She began to smooth the cold medicinal jelly into my bare chest with the tips of her warm fingers. The smell of the Vicks hit my nostrils straight away. Though I hated the sight of the stuff, and didn't want to end up with the over-powering stink on me I'd known throughout my childhood, the Vicks did help to release the tight airless pain in my chest, and the hard clenched muscles of my upper stomach.

She got me back into bed and made me take one of the tiny white tablets with a swallow of water from the cup on the dresser. The pink and the white tablets combined always made me thirsty, but I wasn't allowed much water at night because I'd wet the bed when we first moved here. It had been years since my last accident, but there was no way I wanted that mortifying business to start again. So even though the bitterness from the white tablet was already coating my tongue, I only took one further tiny sip and lay back exhausted.

My mother put a pillow under my ribs and got me to lie on my side, as demonstrated in the booklet on emphysema Doctor Ballintine who looked after the pitmen gave to her, which was full of pictures of breathless old men in striped pyjamas with pillows under their ribs.

Though I never mentioned it to my mother, this scary booklet was the latest reason why I fought back so hard against my condition. The effort I put into running against the hills, and dodging medication, was a direct result of my determination not to finish up like another one of those hollow-eyed, tubercular old timers.

I began to feel drowsy and as drained as if I had just run a full marathon.

"What brought this on?" my mother asked.

"I don't know," I said, though of course I had a pretty good idea.

Certain smells triggered my asthma, and when we moved here first my mother had thrown out the coconut-hair mattress on my bed and got a new one with springs. She had also trained me into being a stickler for keeping my room dust free. So I didn't dare mention the creosote-treated cart-rope hidden in the wardrobe. And thankfully the smell from the cart-rope was covered now by the pong off the Vicks ointment. My mother placed the palm of her cool hand on my forehead for a moment and then moved away from my bedside. I murmured thanks and almost immediately drifted off to sleep, the asthma attack over, my breathing back to normal.

Rubbing my eyes, I found my lashes crusty after a deep dead sleep. In a panic I touched the mattress underneath me, but it was bone dry. I looked at the alarm clock on the dresser and found it was after half-past ten. Frank Welcome had probably been up for hours. My sides and the lower parts of my rib-cage felt sore after the awful coughing fit during the night, but apart from that I felt fine. And I wasn't wheezing either. Just tired. Crossing to the bedroom window I opened the curtains and saw the green army Land Rover standing in the street below. The prospect that Frank Welcome had slept in late made me feel better.

In front of the shop, Red Paddy Reynolds stood by his Honda motorbike getting his usual order, a shilling's worth of petrol. He was talking to Eugene McPadden, and Gerry was there, too, sitting on the shop windowsill. They stopped chatting when RTV Rentals arrived. A new-looking red van pulled up in front of the pub, and a man wearing a tan shop-coat got out and went around to the back and opened the double doors wide. A second, younger, helper in a Fair-Isle sweater got out from the passenger side. The two men began to manhandle a bulky television set from the back of the van.

"Hey!" I heard Eugene McPadden shout. He jumped back from where he was standing beside the motorbike.

Red Paddy was so busy watching the RTV van arrive he'd overfilled the tank on his motorbike and petrol had splashed and spilled over. To stop his Honda from getting soaked in petrol he swung the hose away from the brimming tank, but the petrol kept coming, and a big splash from the nozzle landed where Eugene stood. Eugene reached out, grabbed the hose off Red Paddy and returned it to the pump. But more petrol splashed from the overfilled tank where Red Paddy couldn't get the cap back on straight.

The next thing Mattie Scanlon stepped out of the shop

smoking a cigarette.

Mattie was an old-age pensioner who wore on his chest the ribbons and medals he'd won serving in the trenches in the First World War. His veteran's medals might lead you to think he was a hero. But the pitmen said when Mattie was a young man he enlisted in the British Army only because his girlfriend dumped him.

He'd been going out with the same girl for years, until she got fed up waiting for him to propose, and she started seeing another young man from nearer home. Mattie joined the army when he found out she'd left him. But Mattie had only landed in France when he met the other man. He told Mattie he hadn't married the girl after all. As a matter of fact, he was never that interested in her. Mattie flew into a rage and they got into a fight. And that's how the two men spent the war, fighting with each other and not the enemy whenever they met in the trenches.

Both men survived, though Mattie had a shell explode beside him shortly before Armistice that damaged his hearing. And the girl on whose account he'd enlisted in the first place had gone off and married someone else. So Mattie ended up a bachelor with a chest full of medals for making it back from the Flanders' campaign alive but deaf as a post.

He was a chain-smoker and every day he went to the shop for cigarettes and matches, wearing a soft felt hat pulled down to meet the turned up collar of his overcoat with the medals, his face mostly hidden by goggley National Health glasses and the hearing aids, puffing away the whole time.

Gerry got to his feet and roared at Mattie: "Put out the cigarette."

Mattie didn't hear a thing. Unaware of Gerry calling out to him, he lit his next cigarette from the last one, and tossed away the butt.

For a moment the cigarette butt smouldered beside the dark stain of the spilt petrol on the ground. Nothing happened. It looked like the cigarette had gone out. But soon there was a flash as the fumes ignited and flames sprang up and began to travel at speed towards the standing pool of spilt petrol.

Eugene jumped out of the way of the flames.

Gerry made a lunge to rescue the motorbike. But Red Paddy got in the way and the bike fell over. Petrol poured out of the tank around the badly fitted cap. Eugene intervened to pull his son Gerry and Red Paddy away from the danger as the flames blazed around the Honda. As the fire spread, I saw Daddy coming out of the shop followed by Bernice. They stood in the doorway to see what was happening, not thinking how the petrol in the motorbike tank could blow up at any second and engulf them and the travelling shop parked nearby in one giant fireball.

Gerry spotted a galvanized iron bucket full of water used for topping up car radiators. He ran and grabbed hold of the bucket and tossed the contents onto the burning motorbike. The water only made things worse. The standing pool of petrol stayed lit on top while the water started to carry the burning fuel around by the base of the petrol pump towards the main holding tank.

Up on a platform beside the buried petrol storage tank there was the big iron tank to hold the paraffin. The paraffin wasn't nearly as combustible as the petrol, but if the petrol tank blew up it would more than likely detonate the paraffin, and there would be a massive explosion – enough to demolish the post office and shop and probably flatten our house.

Frank Welcome came running towards the fire. He had two of my mother's good blankets off the guest bed held up in front of him as a shield. With one blanket opened out wide he tossed it onto the moving stream of burning fuel, halting its advance towards the main tank.

Next, he jumped on top of the blanket and stomped out any escaping fluid still on fire. He swiftly followed this up by tossing the second blanket over the burning motorbike. For a moment the fire disappeared. But very quickly the blanket began to go brown at the centre as it charred from the heat of the flames threatening to burst through from underneath.

"Use the water on the blankets, quick," Frank shouted.

Eugene grabbed hold of a tin can full of water and tossed it on top of the smouldering heavy Foxford wool blanket.

"More blankets," Frank called, and my father ran back into the shop.

A passing coal lorry stopped, and seeing how the blankets kept the flames at bay, Eugene and Gerry got the lorry driver to drag from the back of the cab a canvas tarpaulin used in the winter to shelter pitmen getting a lift to and from work. Led by Eugene and Gerry, the driver ran with them carrying the tarpaulin, and threw it on top of the blankets covering the fallen Honda.

With the fire still trying to escape, Frank organised Bernice to stay by the water barrel, and he had Gerry pass the empty bucket back to Mrs Daly the Postmistress to pass it to Bernice to dunk and fill from the barrel while he took the full bucket and, though he risked being blown sky high or choked by the cloud of fumes and smoke, he climbed on top of the motorbike and aimed splashes of water at any spot threatening to reignite.

The chain gang provided a steady supply of water to douse the heavyweight tarpaulin, and there was no need for the blankets my father landed with from the shop. He stood in the doorway unheroically hugging the blankets; though the danger remained – the petrol left in the tank of the fallen motorbike might explode. At least the flow of burning petrol had been stopped around the pump, and its advance towards the holding tank cut off.

Frank kept on dousing the tarpaulin with more water to bring the temperature down. At the same time, Eugene and Gerry kicked up what dust and gravel they could find underfoot to cover the dark patches where the spilt petrol had soaked into the ground. I had a bird's eye view of the whole event. I wanted to join the action now and I grabbed my clothes, pulled on my jeans, and with my feet in my unbuckled sandals, half-ran and half-hobbled downstairs.

When I reached the street I heard Daddy say he wanted to call out the fire brigade to be on the safe side.

Eugene said that with sleepy Joe Dunphy driving it would be at least an hour before the fire brigade arrived. Instead Eugene set about organising the men who had arrived from the siding to help as word spread about the fire to shovel builders' sand from the back of a second lorry over everything.

It was clear from the way every one of the pitmen did what Eugene asked they respected him and were happy to do whatever he wanted.

When it looked like the fire had been safely put out, Eugene and Gerry and the other pitmen cautiously lifted away the tarpaulin and the fire-damaged blankets, exposing the charred and gutted frame of Red Paddy Reynolds's Honda 50. The seat was destroyed, the upholstery and stuffing burnt out and the front tyre melted where the plastic bag Red Paddy used for leg-shields had caught fire. All of the electrical wiring was melted by the heat.

"There must be some hoodoo on me," said Red Paddy. "First poor little Francie Curran finishes up in my field stone dead, and now me bike is after going up in flames."

"Come in and we'll get you a drink," said Eugene, leaving the men from the siding to tidy up the mess.

I looked around for Frank Welcome and saw him inside in the shop, where Bernice and Mrs Daly had him sitting on a wooden stool.

They had his boots and socks off, and the bottoms of his trousers rolled up, to allow Bernice to smooth zinc ointment on his shins and ankles where the flames had singed and burned his lower legs. By the look of things he would be getting careful attention from the two women for a while. And I had an opportunity I might not get again.

On my way downstairs to see the fire, I'd spotted Frank Welcome's bedroom door open. If I acted straight away I could take a quick snoop in his room and hopefully get a look at the pistol.

THIRTEEN

The door stood partly open, and a quick look into the bedroom told me Frank Welcome must have heard the commotion below in the street, dropped whatever he was doing, and grabbed the blankets up off the bed to tackle the fire. The signs were he'd been studying the map which had fallen onto the floor and lay on the carpet face up, along with some scattered pens, loose sheets of paper, a wooden ruler and tri-square.

I examined the map and found it was a detailed one of the area, and he had been using the pens, the ruler and the tri-square to draw boxes on the map, dividing the terrain into squares. Seeing the methodical way he was going about breaking the locality into search areas was impressive. If I wanted to catch the panther ahead of him I needed to be just as well organised.

It would be pushing my luck to stay much longer, but my eyes fell on the rifle case resting against the wardrobe. I felt tempted to take a peek, but I didn't think it wise to go near it. Besides, I was more interested in getting a look at his handgun.

I could see no sign of the kitbag. It must be stowed

away in the wardrobe. I tiptoed back as far as the bedroom door and listened. All quiet. Hurrying to the wardrobe, I opened it up and found a tailored dark suit on a wooden clothes hanger, a polo-neck sweater and pointy-toed boots, plus the empty kitbag. Beside the kitbag rested a leather satchel, like a pannier an army dispatch rider might carry on a motorbike.

The top flap of the pannier was open, and I spotted a belt and the revolver snug inside the leather holster. There was a ring in the base of the pistol handle and a braided cord that tied the butt of the pistol to the belt. If I laid hands on it I could easily get the holster and the cord tangled up, and Frank Welcome would know for certain someone had been going through his stuff. So I just looked the revolver over. Even partly hidden inside the holster the hand-gun seemed to throb with deadly force, and I suspected it would feel ice cold to the touch.

A large brown envelope had been tucked into the bag beside the holster. I listened closely for the sound of footsteps on the landing. When I heard nothing, I judged it worth the risk to have a peek inside the envelope. I had an idea it contained his official orders, which would be useful to know if he was supposed to shoot dead or corner and capture the big cat alive.

I lifted the flap and slipped out the document. Two photographs were paper-clipped to some sheets of flimsy paper. I didn't know the man in the first photograph, but it was clear the letter underneath was a report about him. The two men in the second photograph I recognised straight away – Eugene and Gerry McPadden.

The full dossier was several pages long, and all of the typewritten pages looked like they were copies made using carbon paper, almost as smudged as the copies made using the sheets of carbon paper tucked into the ledger in

Daddy's shop.

Although my hands shook, and my instincts told me to put the whole lot back where I found it, I couldn't help moving the photos so I could read what the heading on the page underneath said.

REPORT – BREAKAWAY OF IRA PHYSICAL FORCE MOVEMENT

1. Cathal Goulding. Housepainter. Activist. Jailed for failed attempt to seize weapons from army barracks in Felsted, Essex. Two failed attempts to set him free. Released in 1959. Became IRA Chief of Staff in 1962 after resignation of Ruairi O Brádaigh.

2. Since the ending of the IRA Border Campaign Goulding has advocated a Marxist programme to infiltrate unions and representative bodies in fishing, agriculture and social housing.

3. There is internal division between the advocates of Goulding's Leftist economic agitation and those determined to re-start the physical force campaign.

4. Recent intelligence suggests an armed raid on a provincial bank in the border

region has been approved by breakaway
physical force supporters to finance a
renewed campaign of violence.

5. No target has been identified but a
   raid is imminent.

6. County Leitrim shares seventeen miles
   of border with Fermanagh, and while the
   number of people in Leitrim actively
   involved in Republican activities is
   small there is significant behind the
   scenes support for the Republican
   cause.

7. While co-operative towards the Gardaí
   in all other respects, the local people
   will not, under any circumstances,
   divulge information which may be
   prejudicial to the activities of
   illegal organisations.

The second sheet of paper was stuck to the top one.

Before I could peel it free to read what it said about
'Local Involvement' and Eugene and Gerry McPadden,
I heard someone mount the stairs. I got the sheets back in
the envelope and the envelope dropped into the pannier in
the wardrobe. Aware of footsteps on the landing, and
guessing Frank Welcome was about to walk straight in on
me, I hunkered down in front of the map on the floor

"Hello," he said as he entered his room.

"I was looking for the old sweathouse on the map," I said smoothing out the map on the floor with my hand, desperate for him to believe me.

Maybe he was convinced, or maybe he was too smart to go straight to the wardrobe to check on his revolver and the document bag with the confidential dossier to see if I knew exactly what he was doing amongst us. Either way, there was no question in my mind he was secretly working for the Special Branch or Army Intelligence.

More than likely, he was turning over in his mind how to keep me from leaving his room and blowing the cover story he was here to shoot the panther. At any second he could employ his special training to overpower me, or knock me out, or maybe snap my neck and make it look like an accident.

With his eyes fixed on me I felt a creeping paralysis invade my arms and legs, robbing me of the power to save my life. The best I could manage was to stop the fear from showing in my face.

In the next instant we were both distracted by the clatter of a ladder against the edge of the flat roof, which was just below the level of the window. The RTV man dressed in the Fair-Isle jumper arrived onto the roof. Then Gerry McPadden appeared at the top of the ladder holding the television aerial by its centre bar between the prongs. He stayed on the ladder but reached up full stretch to pass the aerial to the young helper from the television shop.

The helper put the aerial down flat on the roof and Gerry vanished and then reappeared, passing up a short steel pole. With these essentials to hand Gerry joined the helper, and the two men began to fix the pole for the aerial to the chimney using steel wires and brackets. A long fat wire also came from a junction box fixed to the aerial and this wire dropped away over the edge of the roof.

I got to my feet to make certain Gerry and the other man noticed me along with Frank Welcome in his room. As I'd hoped, Gerry spotted me, waved, and then he took up the aerial again and held it against the pole, shouting down from the roof.

"How's that?"

I heard Eugene on the road below shout up at Gerry, "The picture is still very snowy."

The man in the Fair-Isle jumper slowly swivelled the aerial.

"That's better," Eugene shouted back.

I stepped around Frank Welcome. He made no attempt to stop me.

"I suppose we should go down and take a look at how they're getting on," he said.

Relieved to be getting out of the room alive, I led the way smartly downstairs into the public bar. Although I felt light-headed after such a lucky escape, I wasn't out of the woods yet. Frank Welcome had official orders to spy on Eugene and Gerry, and when I met them next I had to give absolutely nothing away. Any false reaction on my part could spoil everything.

We found Eugene in the American Lounge along with the man in the brown shop coat who had the television rested on the counter. To hide what I was really thinking, I turned my attention to the big PYE black and white set with the label on the side saying 'Made in Leixlip'. It had beige coloured tweedy fabric on the top half, and the bottom half was plain and dark with two big dials and several knobs. The wire from the aerial on the roof came in the window and stretched across the room, ending in a socket that went into the back of the television. A second wire for electricity came from the round-pin plug in the skirting. I glanced at Eugene, who stood looking at the screen where the picture kept rolling upwards out of sight with black bars in between. The man in the shop coat stood behind the television adjusting what he told Eugene was the vertical hold button.

"It's not the set," he explained, "the reception is poor."

"You'll get a worse reception from Monica Rossiter," Eugene said, "if she lands back from the hairdresser's and you're still fiddling with that picture."

He laughed at his own joke, and I wondered why it never occurred to me before how often he used smart remarks to hide the close watch he kept on everyone and every thing.

My father didn't often serve customers in the bar, but he came around from behind the counter carrying a tray with a picture of a trout on the bottom loaded with pints of porter and short glasses filled with whiskey. Mattie Scanlon had taken a seat at a low table under the window along with the team of pitmen who'd shovelled sand onto the spot where the fire had broken out at the petrol pump. When he had the drinks distributed, Daddy looked around the room and asked, "Did everyone get a drink?"

Red Paddy Reynolds lifted his pint and nodded where he sat on his usual high stool at the further end of the bar. The other pitmen raised and drank their pints with far-eyed expressions. They did not seem the slightest bit worried about getting back to work, and carefully replacing their glasses on the wood again after a long swallow they looked towards the television for something worth seeing to appear.

Breaking her usual habit, Bernice came out from behind the bar counter and stood in the middle of the floor alongside Frank Welcome to look at the television. One thing for certain, I would have to tell Bernice the truth about the crackshot and how, to the best of my knowledge, he was here to spy on Eugene and Gerry as much as he was here to kill the wildcat. But I couldn't open my mouth until I was absolutely certain of my facts. I had jumped to conclusions before about Nora Greene and been proved wrong. The safest course of action, for the present at least, would be to watch and wait to see what he would do next.

FOURTEEN

On the television the black and white picture stopped rolling and settled into a spotty view of flag waving crowds of people.

"Can you see him?" Bernice asked.

Staring at the screen, Red Paddy Reynolds had his mouth open: 'a great mouth for cooling soup,' my mother said one time.

Daddy looked at the television and then he looked through the open pub door at a customer headed for the shop. The television didn't truly interest him, and he just wanted to get back behind his own counter now that he had urged a free drink on everyone who helped put out the fire at the pump.

Turning to Frank Welcome Daddy said, "Will you have a drink, Captain Welcome?"

"I'll have a cup of tea if you're making one."

"I'll get it," Bernice volunteered as the picture on the screen shrunk away to a white spot and vanished when the man in the shop coat turned off the set in order to move it from the bar counter onto the waiting shelf now that he had the vertical and horizontal hold buttons properly adjusted.

While waiting for Bernice to bring the tea, Frank fetched his belongings from the guest room and got ready to leave. Meanwhile, Eugene and the man in the shop coat set about tacking metal fasteners to the skirting board to tidy up the aerial wire. With this job done the television was finally settled on the shelf with an American flag on one side and an Irish tricolour on the other.

Bernice was just serving Frank a cup of tea from the pot when my mother arrived back from the hairdresser. She had missed the excitement of the fire, but nobody mentioned it as we waited for her reaction at seeing the television finally take pride of place in the 'American Lounge'.

All conversation stopped in anticipation as the man in the brown coat pressed the power button. It was day four of the Presidential visit and President Kennedy was expected in Galway. In the afternoon he would be departing from Shannon airport so this was nearly our last chance to see him before he took off.

"The valves take a minute to warm up," the helper in the Fair-Isle sweater said.

At first, all I could see were people waving flags and a banner saying 'Welcome Mr President!' A troop of Irish dancers stood in front of the crowd, and above them there was a platform full of dignitaries. Then the President of America could be seen sitting higher up under a glass panelled roof.

Mattie Scanlon jumped up onto his feet. Clutching his hat to his chest full of medals he said at the top of his voice, "President John Fitzgerald Kennedy, large as life."

"That's Eyre Square in Galway," Captain Welcome said to my mother.

"God he's so handsome," my mother said softly and

touched her hair as if the President himself might be looking out from the television screen to admire her new hair-do.

Eugene crossed the room to stand beside my mother and Frank Welcome and, nodding towards the carry-case asked, "Can I have a look at the rifle?"

I felt a stab of alarm that Frank Welcome would allow a man he knew to be involved with the IRA near his firearm. But he didn't seem the least bit worried as he unzipped the broad end of the case and slipped the rifle out by the stock. He took the precaution, however, to test the safety catch and then he slid the bolt and double-checked the chamber and the magazine in front of the trigger guard to be absolutely certain there were no live rounds of ammunition before handing the weapon over to Eugene.

Eugene weighed and balanced the Carcano rifle in his hands.

"I can't believe how light it is," he said.

"Five and half pounds," Frank said. "Italian made, 6.5 millimetres."

"It's a long way from the old Lee Enfields," Eugene said, "But clunky compared to a Carbine."

Frank said, "The Carcano bullet wriggles less in the barrel and travels straighter."

While the two men admired the rifle itself, I had my eye on the leather pannier holding the army revolver and the secret documents Frank Welcome had brought down from his room. If Eugene knew Captain Welcome was holding a secret file on him and his son Gerry he would be more on his guard. And I admired the crackshot's cool leaving this information under Eugene's nose.

A neat protective case I hadn't seen before sat on the low table near the empty carry-case. Unable to resist, I opened up the lid and saw the telescopic sight for the rifle resting in the velvet lined impression of its own shape.

I picked up the sight and tried looking through it. The American Lounge was too dark, and all I could see was dim murky fuzz. I held the telescopic sight up to the television. The light became black and white and all of a sudden I could see clearly. As the pictures on the screen changed I found President Kennedy on his feet making a speech.

"If the day was clear enough, and if you went down to the bay and you looked west, and your sight was good enough, you would see Boston," the President said as I held him in the telescopic sight.

I centred the cross-hairs on the President's face. It gave me a weird sensation not letting the President's head drop out of the line of fire. If I had a rifle in my hands aiming from a vantage point on Eyre Square at this very moment and I fired, the bullet would go directly into the forehead of the President of the United States. I could hardly miss. Amazed by the dark power of the telescopic sight, I said out loud to the room, "It would be awful easy to shoot him."

"Mother of God," Mammy screeched when she realised what I was doing. "Put that thing down before you end up in a reformatory."

"He meant no harm," Frank said, loosening the telescopic sight from my grip and replacing it in its velvet-lined case.

My mother was on the point of saying a whole lot more, but she saw Gerry nudge Eugene with his elbow and both men looked towards the pub door. Sergeant Glacken stood framed in the pub doorway looking very officious in his blue uniform and peaked cap with a notebook in his hand.

Eugene handed the rifle back to Frank Welcome. And I waited for the worst. The Sergeant must surely have seen me pointing the telescopic sight at President Kennedy. At the very least I was in for a severe telling off. He might even decide to take me away in handcuffs until the President was safely out of the country.

"He didn't mean anything by it, Sergeant," Mammy said wrapping a protective arm around me.

"It's Eugene I'm here to have a word with," the Sergeant said, although he still hadn't taken his eyes off me.

"What can I do for you, Sergeant?" Eugene asked.

The Sergeant finally took his eyes off me and approached the table beside the window. "I'm gathering statements," he said, "from witnesses to the armed robbery in town on Wednesday."

"Did you hear anything more, since?" Gerry asked.

"I'll want a word with you as well," the Sergeant said ignoring the question.

"Sure I was off shopping for me mother, Sergeant," Gerry lied. "I saw nothing."

"All right so," Sergeant Glacken said. "But I'm told, Eugene, you were actually in the bank building."

"Who told you that?" said Eugene.

Eugene had been happy to give my mother a detailed account of the bank robbery, but even I could see he meant to hold back from the Sergeant.

With Gerry and Eugene acting cagey Mammy said, "Take the weight off your feet, Sergeant, and I'll bring you a drink."

"Thank you Mrs Rossiter. I'll have a small one."

Eugene and Gerry made a space for the Sergeant at the table. Frank Welcome replaced the rifle in its case.

I saw Sergeant Glacken eyeing the firearm and the telescopic sight. But with Frank Welcome dressed in his army uniform and Captain's insignia, the Sergeant chose to pay him no heed. He had enough on his plate trying to get

Eugene to co-operate with his enquires. Or, maybe he knew Captain Welcome was working undercover.

Lifting his peaked cap off his head the Sergeant wiped his brow with his forearm. He put the cap down in the middle of the table and got out a short pencil to write in his notebook.

Mammy served him a glass of whiskey and set down a little jug of water beside it taken from the tin tray Daddy had used earlier. She had whiskeys on the tray too for Eugene and Gerry.

Sergeant Glacken added water to his glass of whiskey, tasted it and licked the top of his pencil.

"Now, Eugene," he said. "I'm wondering if the raiders had recognisable accents."

Eugene looked puzzled and asked the Sergeant, "What do you mean?"

"Did they say anything to you?"

"No."

"But they told you to get down on the floor."

"They told everyone to get down on the floor."

The Sergeant looked at Eugene for a full minute.

"Were they carrying guns?"

Eugene said, "I couldn't tell."

"They must have been carrying guns?" the Sergeant said. His pencil still hadn't touched paper.

"You could be carrying a gun right now, Sergeant," Eugene said, "but I couldn't tell."

The Sergeant did his best to keep his patience.

"After they ordered you down on the floor," he asked, "did you notice anything?"

Eugene corrected the Sergeant and said, "After they ordered everyone down on the floor."

The Sergeant tried again. "After they ordered everyone down on the floor, did you notice anything? Anything at all?"

Eugene paused to consider and then he said, "Yes I did, Sergeant."

The Sergeant waited, his pencil suspended over his blank pad.

"When I was down on the floor," Eugene said in a way calculated to make the Sergeant pay the closest possible attention, "I noticed how dirty it was under the counter. You'd think for such an important bank they'd give the floor a better cleaning."

The Sergeant closed the notebook, got to his feet, finished his whiskey while standing and replaced the cap on his head.

"Good day to you, Sergeant," Mammy said, but he left without a word.

FIFTEEN

The village had fallen silent apart from the church bell calling people to the funeral mass. The shop, the post-office and the pub had closed their doors. Everyone in the valley seemed to be on their way to Francie Curran's funeral. But we weren't going. Daddy refused to leave the shop unattended on account of the fire. There wasn't the slightest chance the fire at the petrol pump could restart, but he wouldn't budge. And I realised that while he had been calm during and after the fire, the whole incident had upset and shocked him greatly.

Mammy didn't want me at the funeral either because she said I looked pale and worn-out after my asthma attack last night. Although it soon transpired that staying behind with me was an excuse not to have to go to the funeral. With the outside door bolted and the blinds down fully on the street-facing windows of the American Lounge, she put on the television and settled comfortably into seat with her feet up on a low stool to watch the final hours of the Kennedy visit. When she spotted me hanging about the bar counter she sent me up the hallway to fetch a box of Black Magic chocolates.

I went through the house to the shop and found Daddy wearing his good cardigan with the suede patches on the elbows over a starched white shirt and knitted tie. He was dressed to show his respect and, possibly, to give the impression he had been to the funeral.

The shop was empty and silent, apart from the sound of the clock on the mantelpiece. On top of the clock rested a pile of notes kept together with a wooden clothes peg. Long-term accounts were recorded in the ledger with the carbon paper in it. But Daddy had just made up a fresh batch of smaller credit notes by folding and cutting up the sheets of plain newsprint that came between the layers of boxed cartons of one hundred cigarettes. Until the cash to pay the pitmen had been replaced after the robbery, extra short-term credit notes would be needed. 'As long as they remember to settle up when they get paid,' my mother had warned Daddy when he got back from his talk with the colliery owners yesterday evening. He hadn't answered, but from the way he sifted through the credit notes now, he had money worries on his mind.

"Mammy is looking for chocolates," I said.

"Chocolates?"

I nodded.

He went to the display case to get a bag of Emerald sweets.

"She wants the good sort," I said.

To get hold of the box of chocolates, Daddy had to fetch the short ladder used to reach the high shelf where the luxury goods were kept. He took down a box of Black Magic and, using the yellow cloth kept under the counter for the purpose, gave the cellophane a wipe to clear the dust.

"I should have brought her to the train," he said.

"She told me she's mad you never mentioned her new

hair do."

To be fair to Daddy, she had her hair done before the cancelled trip to Dublin and came back from the hairdresser's this morning looking the exact same. But if he was a smart man he would have said something nice, because his lack of attention was one of the things she found so irritating about him.

Mammy herself of course was slow to offer praise, although she liked it when others noticed her wearing a new outfit, or new shoes – things Eugene McPadden never missed a chance to praise and win a polite flutter as she fobbed off the compliment.

Daddy handed me the box of chocolates.

Having no customers in the shop he could easily walk down the hallway with the chocolates and present them to Mammy himself, rather than entrust the job to me. But that was not his style. Likewise, the meticulously fair way he measured and cut penny wafers off the block of ice-cream in the shop meant I never felt hard done by him giving me less, but neither had he ever made me feel special with a little extra.

When I returned to the American Lounge, the television showed President Kennedy's helicopter leaving Salthill for Limerick. Mammy was so wrapped up looking at the coverage she reached out automatically and took the box of chocolates out of my hand hardly noticing me, and making no attempt to ask after my father. I waited around for a couple of minutes, hoping to get my hands on a chocolate or two. And it would be brilliant to set aside a couple for Bernice to share after she got back from the funeral. On second thoughts, though, having my mother stuck in front of the television busy eating chocolates gave me a chance to escape the house without her noticing.

In the empty village street, few traces of the blaze at the

petrol pump were visible, other than the gritty patch of builder's sand that covered the road, and the scorched remains of Red Paddy Reynolds's Honda rested against a wall with bits of blackened debris on the ground around it, his redundant crash-helmet hung on the handlebar.

If it hadn't been for Captain Frank Welcome's quick thinking and bravery on the spot, we could have been on the move again looking for another shop, with Daddy having to explain how the last place he worked got blown up.

Captain Welcome's swift intervention had saved the day, and he was clearly a man who could keep his head in a tight corner. His actions seemed to confirm he was a trained Army Intelligence officer. Even so, I could not rule out the possibility he got official reports to read all the time and then passed them along, so he might not strictly be on the trail of Eugene and Gerry. The Carcano rifle with the telescopic sight was exactly the kind of weapon a genuine army marksman would use. And when we had gone hunting for the panther yesterday, he acted like a man who knew what he was doing. On the other hand, hunting the wildcat gave him a perfect reason to systematically search the terrain, and gather information from locals who might not otherwise want anything to do with him.

As my mother mentioned when she first heard about the robbery, the raiders appeared to know the bank would be holding the pitmen's bigger monthly wages, and were acting on inside information. Information Eugene and Gerry could easily have supplied. So being in the bank on the very day when the raid took place might not have been a coincidence. They could have been there to see that everything went off as planned. They might even have been needed to help the robbers if anything went wrong.

Regardless of the crackshot's true purpose, I had plans

of my own to put in motion. First, I needed to know what Daddy meant to do about the travelling shop. He wouldn't want me going to the mountain with Francie Curran's burial on everyone's minds, and the possibility of a dangerous wildcat on the loose. If I did choose to go, I might have to dodge the travelling shop along the route.

Normally on a Saturday a daughter of Mrs Daly in the post office took over for Daddy in the shop while he took the van out on the road with Bernice. But today was different. Daddy had the fire at the petrol pump, and was reluctant to move. And second, most of his clients on the mountain were at Francie Curran's funeral.

Along with the usual orders for tea and flour and sugar and tins of treacle, the travelling shop also carried bottles of whiskey and heavy wooden crates full of bottled stout for the elderly pitmen who rarely set foot in the village. Regardless of the funeral, they would be out waiting at the start of mountain lanes leading into their stone cottages behind pine-tree shelter belts wondering what happened if Daddy didn't turn up with their orders for a half-dozen of stout in a brown paper bag. On top of which, they would have the empty bottles rinsed and ready to be given back, and were so dependable Daddy didn't even need to get a deposit, so they didn't get a refund the way my schoolmates earned money returning empties. He wouldn't want to let these older clients on the mountain down, even if he had no other customers.

So, as soon as Bernice arrived back ahead of the crowd still gathered in the graveyard I asked, "Are you doing the travelling shop?"

"I thought I'd be flat out here getting tea and sandwiches ready for everyone after the funeral," she said. "But Francie's brother is home from America, and he's taking everyone into Boyle for a meal. So I suppose it's the travelling shop for me today."

Daddy opened the shop door and began to load the van. Things like replacement broom and spade handles and zinc gallons for milking, and white enamelled buckets for carrying water from the well could be left in the van from week to week, but fresher foods like ham and sweetcakes had to be loaded just before the van set out.

He had the first box of goods loaded when he discovered a wheel on the travelling shop had gone down. The tyre on the inside back wheel was as flat as a pancake. Bernice examined the wheel along with him and said, "It's just like a thing that might happen."

Daddy got a large spanner from a tool-box in the van and used it to loosen the wing-nut holding the spare wheel in place. His hands got covered in dirt and he had grease on the cuffs of his good shirt. He wrestled the spare wheel out of storage, and then realised it was so long since the wheel had been used, it too was flat and the rubber cracked and useless because of age.

"We could take turns using the foot pump," he said, "but the tyre could go down again, and with no spare we'd be stuck on the mountain."

Word reached Mammy in the pub that the travelling shop was broken down. She came out to see what was happening, and found Daddy squeezed in by the side of the van nearest to the shop wall as he awkwardly fitted the jack to get working on the puncture.

She stood beside me and Bernice and we watched Daddy turn the lever and jack up the van until the punctured wheel left the ground. I passed Daddy the wheel-brace he'd asked me to hold. He fitted it to the first nut and gave it a turn. The whole wheel spun around.

"Oh, hell," he said. "I should have loosened the nuts first, before I jacked up the wheel."

"Typical," Mammy said under her breath and went back into the pub.

Daddy applied himself again to the job. With the wheel back on the ground he used surprising strength to get each of the rusted bolts loosened and then he set about jacking up the van once more. Before long he had the nuts out of their sockets and the wheel with the flat tyre off.

Sergeant Glacken drove past in the squad car on his way back from the funeral. He eyed the van but didn't stop. Then Frank Welcome arrived and pulled up beside us in the army Land Rover.

"Having trouble?" he said.

Daddy showed him the wheel.

"I'm going into town if you want me to take it and have the puncture fixed."

"Bring it to McGlynn's garage," Daddy said, "And tell them I'll be in next week for a new set of tyres."

Frank helped my father put blocks under the van to safely take the weight off the jack and then he loaded the wheel off the van into the back of the Land Rover.

"What do you want me to do?" Bernice asked.

"There's nothing you can do," Daddy said. "I'll load the Cortina and deliver what I can."

"Do you want me to come with you?" she asked.

"There won't be room."

"You can come with me if you like," Frank said.

Bernice looked uncertainly between Frank and my father.

"Go on," Daddy said. "Before Monica finds something for you to do."

"Can I come too?" I asked.

Daddy said, "Leave them in peace."

"Come on with us if you want," said Bernice. "I'm sure Frank won't mind?"

"The more the merrier," he said, and it flashed through my mind he might have plans for me.

Daddy reached into his trousers pocket and pulled out a fistful of coins. It was mostly pennies and half-pennies and tanners amongst the lint, but he also found a half-crown and gave it to me.

"I don't want you scrounging money off Bernice," he said.

I took the heavy silver coin and trousered it quickly. I had the price of several full-colour American comic books that could only be bought in town.

Bernice ran into the house to get her purse. Then Daddy went back into the shop, leaving me alone with Frank Welcome for the first time since he'd caught me sneaking a look in his room. I expected him to take the opportunity to question me further. And a part of me ached, in fact, for an opportunity to tell him I'd found the secret dossier, and let him know he could trust me. I was good at keeping secrets, even from Bernice.

He circled around the van to look at the burnt-out wreckage of Red Paddy's Honda, picked up the helmet and then returned it to the spot where it hung. If he had things he wanted to say to me he must have decided there were too many people around, with the steady arrival of mourners from the funeral now headed for the shop. Then Bernice came back wearing her summer cardigan and make-up.

"You look different," I said as we sat into the Land Rover with Frank driving, Bernice in the front passenger seat, and me between them like a third wheel.

The Land Rover crossed the bridge, where the younger crowd from the funeral had gathered. I was delighted they saw me riding high in the army Land Rover alongside Bernice. And my spirits continued to rise at the sight of the passing countryside beyond the village, the sunlit hayfields and whitewashed houses with doors and windows painted a familiar green. Sheds and barn doors and farm-gates, and even the caps of piers, were all painted in the same shade of green as we neared the home of *an Tóstal* – a festival for the tourists with parades and sports and a clean-up to show the country at its best. It used to be nationwide, but had died out nearly everywhere except Drumshanbo. And my father still did a great trade supplying *Tóstal* green paint to the surrounding homes and villages. Then, on the outskirts of the town, we drove under the leafy boughs of the beech trees of a walled estate. The branches spanned the road completely to make a long greenery-shaded tunnel after which we came out on the other side into a fresher light and the excitement of a day in town.

SIXTEEN

Drumshanbo smelled like strawberries. They were the main fruit harvest arriving at the Breifne Blossom jam factory, and the scent from the boiling vats filled the streets. In the autumn it would be apples, and over the winter months they imported canned oranges from Seville to boil into marmalade. After the coalmines, the jam factory was one of the biggest employers around; although the girls in school would tease each other that if they weren't careful they'd end up with a job in the jam factory shaving gooseberries.

We passed the Medical Hall, the drapery, the bakery and the Roxy Cinema where they were showing 'Tarzan the Magnificent'. Our first stop was McGlynn's garage where the yard stood full of TVO tractors, mowers and buck-rakes getting small repairs done with the summer hay saving in full swing.

Frank dropped off the tyre and said he'd collect it later. Then we went to the market yard and parked beside a stall selling from barrels full of herring. Another stall had pots and pans and butter churns. Clothes sellers had their cants set up too, some offering good Peter England shirts in boxes, and others had rails full of donkey-jackets and yellow and black oil skins.

One cant in the centre of the market had a big crowd gathered around it. When we made our way through the spectators we found Barney Maughan with a pair of pink flannel woman's drawers held up over his head. Stretching the underwear between his two hands he demonstrated the strength in the elastic.

"Passion killers," Bernice said to Frank. And she took a fit of giggling, which was a mistake because Barney Maughan spotted her.

"Come here to me, Mam," he said. "I want you for a minute."

Bernice tried to back away, but Barney had her now, and waving the knickers in front of her face he said, "Feel the quality, Mam.

"They're tailor made
And tailor stitched.
Cut with a hay-knife
And sewed with a pitchfork.
When you get stout,
You can let them out,
And when you get thin
You can pull them in.
You can wear them to high mass
Low mass or no mass at all
They're waterproof and bullet proof
They fit like an auld cup and saucer
And wear like an old woman's tongue
Peg them on your head
And give me a bob…"

He got a round of applause from the crowd for the recitation while Bernice freed herself from the old-fashioned pair of knickers dropped on top of her head.

Barney moved on to clinch a sale from a woman who held up a man's night shirt asking for the price.

"I'm mortified," Bernice said, but she was having fun. And it made me happy too, having her away from the house and enjoying herself.

A bomber-jacket on a wire hanger at the back of Barney's stall caught my eye.

"Do you like it?" Bernice asked.

"How much is it?" I asked.

"That's genuine leather," Barney said.

"Doesn't feel like it to me," Bernice said pinching the jacket between her fingers and thumb and moving on. I liked the manly cut of the jacket and would have bought it on the spot if I had the money, but Bernice said, "We'll take a look in Larry's."

We left the market yard and walked up the town past the Great Northern Bank. It was closed on Saturdays. And looking at its heavy bolted doors and sturdy red-brick front like a fortress commanding the town, you'd never guess the place had been robbed. But I noticed Sergeant Glacken at the street corner.

On our way to Larry's, Bernice asked if we could stop at the church. I thought Frank might not agree but he let Bernice lead the way.

In Arigna the chapel had cream-coloured walls and mostly clear glass in the windows, but the church in Drumshanbo was old and dark. The inside echoed and the stained-glass windows were fantastic colours, the stone pillars fancily carved. At a side altar, a rack full of candles burned before a statue of the Blessed Virgin Mary.

Bernice, wearing a headscarf taken from her cardigan pocket, made her way up along the women's side passing the Stations of the Cross to stand before the side altar. She put coins in the collection box and picked out a candle and lit it off a burning candle that would soon go out. She snuffed out the stub and passed it to me to dispose of it. I thought the candle-end might come in useful and stuffed it into the pocket of my jeans.

"What's the candle for?" Frank asked.

"A private intention," Bernice said.

He moved closer to Bernice and rested his hand lightly on her shoulder.

"Belief is a beautiful thing," he said. "But I have to confess, in my line of work, it's doubt that gets you an education."

I had a burning curiosity to ask Frank about his exact line of work. In this holy place he could hardly tell a lie. But an old woman with a sweeping brush rattled a kneeling board to get at the dust, and as a signal to stop our prattling.

We went out into the daylight again and turned left after leaving by the church gate.

"You'll enjoy meeting Larry," Bernice told Frank. I got the impression she was showing off how well she knew the town for his benefit.

Soon we arrived at a plain looking house with the front door facing onto the road wide open. It could be mistaken for an ordinary townhouse, but the windows were piled high with worn shoes. And the room directly inside the front door had a broad wooden counter loaded with more shoes; new shoes, second-hand shoes, shoes tied in twos waiting for repair, and tagged pairs of shoes waiting to be collected.

Teetering piles of duffel coats and jumpers were also stacked on every side, with close-packed sports jackets and suits suspended on cords criss-crossing the ceiling. Behind the counter, in the cluttered sales and mending area, an old boy seated on a kitchen chair was having his hair cut. Sheets of newspaper rested on the floor to catch the fallen locks. But when Larry Wren spotted Bernice, he immediately abandoned the hair cutting and left the steel clippers dangling above the old boy's ear.

"Well, if it isn't Bernice Hickey," Larry said, and he took hold of a pair of wooded crutches and hobbled to meet her. He had a club-foot and a hunched back as a result of polio when he was a young man, but he was otherwise a handsome, bright-eyed bachelor.

"Come back here," the old boy called after Larry with the clippers still stuck in his hair.

"It's good enough," Larry said.

"You haven't finished."

"Tomorrow, tomorrow," Larry said.

He released the clippers and waved the old boy out from behind the counter towards the door. After he left, Bernice said, "We're looking for a leather jacket."

We weren't really going to buy a jacket; I hadn't the money. But Larry obligingly moved a heap of sheepskin coats aside to expose a jumble of leather jackets to rummage.

"Have you me shoes ready?" a voice called from the open doorway.

"Try that pile," Larry pointed with his crutch to the pile of shoes due for repair.

"Ah Larry!" the young woman said, "I'm going dancing tomorrow night."

She began to search through the heap of mismatched shoes and said, "I see one here. But where's the other?"

"I'm closing. Come back after the dinner."

"You haven't laid a finger on them," she said lucky to have located the matching shoe.

"I'm weak with the hunger."

"If I do the cooking," the woman bargained, "will you do the shoes for me?"

"Throw a chop on the pan," Larry said happily. "And open a tin of peas. And there's Ambrosia creamed rice pudding somewhere."

The young woman looked at us and rolled her eyes before she went obligingly into the kitchen to get Larry's dinner.

Larry grabbed his crutches and tucked the padded ends under his armpits to go behind the counter again to the bench where he made repairs. A smell of lamb cutlets cooking drifted out from the kitchen as Larry expertly cut a new sole and tapped in tiny brads and then got to work on the heel.

"Try this," Bernice said and I put my arms out behind my back and reversed into the jacket she'd picked out.

The leather was soft and light and felt really comfortable.

Frank in the meantime had found a stack of woollen hats. Searching through the pile he stopped and withdrew a black balaclava. He waved the balaclava for Larry to see and asked, "Do you sell many of these?"

"The pitmen wear them on the mountain," Larry said, "To keep their ears warm."

"Anybody have cold ears lately?" Frank asked.

Larry went back to his shoe repairs, keeping his head down.

"How much is the leather jacket?" Bernice asked.

"It doesn't matter," I said. "I can't afford it."

"Name your price," Frank said to Larry.

"That's a new leather jacket," Larry said.

Frank put down a twenty pound note.

Hearing the rustle of paper money, Larry stopped concentrating on the shoe repairs and turned around. He looked at the money on the counter. Then he looked at Frank and he slowly shook his head. Frank laid down a ten pound note and a five pound note on top of the twenty.

Larry said nothing but kept looking at the money. Bernice had no idea what was going on. And if I hadn't found the dossier in his room, I would never have guessed Frank wanted to use the money for the jacket as a way to pay for information. But either Larry hadn't sold any balaclavas lately, or he was afraid to open his mouth.

"Are you fixing my shoes, Larry, or should I put this tin of peas back in the press?" the woman called from the kitchen.

Larry looked at Frank and then lowered his eyes and picked up the five pound note. "Good health wearing the jacket," he said to me. "And if you're not happy bring it back tomorrow."

Perhaps Frank didn't want me to have the jacket, but he'd paid for it now. And when Bernice said it looked really smart on me her flattery welded it to my back.

We left Larry to get on with his shoe repairs and eat his dinner, and the mood got lighter when we went to B J Early's, where Bernice bought a replacement stylus for her record player. From there she led us straight to Donnelly's on the High Street. It was a cross between a newsagent's, a souvenir shop and an ice cream parlour; what the Americans would call a Drug Store. To celebrate President Kennedy's visit, Donnelly's front window had an American flag and an Irish tri-colour on crossed sticks above a large formal portrait of President Kennedy in a gold frame rested on an easel. Underneath, were Kennedy mugs and scrolls and souvenir pens for sale. Bernice and I were in agreement, we told Frank, that Donnelly's was the best thing about the town.

Inside, we made straight for the chrome stools lined

along the shiny-topped counter. At home I'd sometimes make floats to share with Bernice by filling regular drinking glasses with lemonade and then adding a wedge of ice-cream to make the concoction frothy. In Donnelly's they made real knickerbocker glories with proper scoops of ice-cream with pink and green dashes of raspberry and lime cordial, dressed with triangle cut wafers and a cherry on top, plus long-handled spoons to eat the ice-cream from tall, conical glasses.

We lined up at the counter and ordered, me seated alongside Bernice and Frank at my shoulder.

Frank held a silver cigarette case out to Bernice.

"Smoke?" he said

She shook her head.

While the woman in charge got the order read, I swivelled my stool around and slid off to go the toilet. Passing the rack I spotted a new intake of full-colour American DC and Marvel comic books. I was tempted to have a look, but at the same time I wanted to live up to the manly feeling I got wearing the new leather jacket so I walked past the display.

Sliding the bolt behind me on the toilet cubicle door I removed the jacket, unbuttoned my shirt and took off the vest. Getting rid of the vest was a relief and I bunched it up and stuffed it into my jacket pocket. Then I went and stood in front of the hand basin and looked at my reflection in the mirror.

My face was too long and I pulled down the skin under my eyes until I could look into their red rims. I pinched the sides of my mouth until my lips puckered. It was clear I would never have the clean-cut open features of Frank Welcome or his confidence and flinty authority. But wearing the leather jacket with my shirt opened down an extra button at the neck, definitely improved my appearance. And I made my way back to the counter feeling cooler.

It jolted me though, to find Bernice had moved up a place at the counter onto my stool to sit next to Frank. My heart sank to see them enjoying their knickerbocker glories and looking so perfectly happy in each other's company.

"Oh!" said Bernice when she saw me. "Didn't you get any comics?"

"No," I said, and took the seat to one side. I dug the long spoon into the ice-cream in the frosted glass, and doing my best to swallow the feeling they'd subtly written me off said, "These are on me."

SEVENTEEN

After we left Donnelly's, and picked up the wheel repaired at McGlynn's garage, Frank asked Bernice, "Is there a back road out of here?"

"I suppose we could go around by Ballintrae," she said. "But it takes a lot longer and I'm not sure of the way."

"We're in no hurry, are we?" he said.

We took the Dowra road out of town, and after a mile or so branched off onto a minor road going in the direction of the lake and Ballintrae. Soon the road got so narrow the sides of the Land Rover brushed up against the fairy fingers lining the ditches while gangling briars scraped against the paintwork. Frank wrenched the wheel to swerve around potholes. Then just when it looked like we'd taken the wrong road we came to the bridge at Ballintrae. At first sight it seemed fit only to take pedestrians. It had light iron guard-rails only and planks not solid concrete underfoot. Below the planks a rush of bright water teemed over the top of two massive wooden sluice gates, the tumbling water falling a frighteningly long way down to the lower level.

In front of us, a man struggled to lead a donkey and cart across the timber bridge with the thundering flow of water spilling over the lock gates. He wanted to get his load safely to the other side, but the donkey pulling the cart was having none of it. As we looked on the carter took off his overcoat and put it over the donkey's head. Unable to see the water through the gaps between the boards under his hooves the donkey was less afraid and stopped baulking. Slowly the man led the donkey out onto the bridge. When he reached the other side, the carter removed the coat covering the donkey's eyes and ears and man and beast looked cheery after their safe passage.

"Can I borrow that man's coat," said Bernice.

"You'll be fine," said Frank, starting to take the Land Rover across.

It was a tight squeeze and it seemed to me we were too heavy for the planks that rumbled under the Land Rover's rolling wheels. At any second I expected to hear a board crack and give way, and too late I realised Bernice and I should have gotten out and walked across. Bernice pressed her face into my chest, and I wrapped my arms around her so she wouldn't have to see what was happening. While Frank kept us on a straight course, edging ahead slowly, I couldn't tell which made my heart race fastest: the threat of the bridge collapsing or having Bernice so firmly in my arms.

"Is it safe to look yet?" she asked when the rumble of the planks under the wheels of the Land Rover, and the booming noise of the falling water, lessened. I wanted her to stay exactly where she was, but I had to tell her we'd made it across. She drew her face back from my chest and smiled up at me. The old closeness between us was back.

Picking up speed again we found ourselves on a rarely used back road. At the next Y-shaped fork Bernice said, "I think we can turn left here for Arigna but I'm not sure."

"Where does the other fork go?" Frank asked.

Bernice said, "I have no idea."

"We'll risk it for a biscuit," said Frank and veered right.

We started to climb away from the lake and the hedgerows began to thin out and give way to bare ditches and dark-bottomed drains. It looked as if we had reached a dead end, but we continued along a rough track that brought us thorough a belt of pine trees and out at a junction just below the Iron Bridge.

"How far are we from the main working coalmine?" Frank asked.

The Iron Bridge gave me my bearings and I said, "Drive on towards Whistle Hill, it's not far."

We passed Noonan's worked out mine and its stacks of abandoned iron rails and the broken remains of the timber-built hutches like miniature coal train wagons the pitmen once used to transport coal to the surface. Further on up the road we came to Rover pit. This was the biggest pit in Arigna, and a load of cars, motorbikes and bicycles used by the pitmen to get to work stood parked out in the open. There were pathways, too, striking out across the open mountain used as shortcuts by the pitmen who walked to work and home again in the evenings. After a bunch of smaller outbuildings, a single great shed with a vaulted iron roof stood on top of a row of block-built coal bunkers. Frank drove around by the shed and bunkers to where a truck waited to be loaded with coal. Another truck, partly loaded, stood ready to carry the pitmen home at the end of their shift.

As we circled the shed it became clear how it was the final destination for the hutches that carried the coal out of the pit. The open end of the shed allowed the loaded hutches to be hauled inside, through hanging rubber flaps, using a braided steel rope that stood a short height off the ground. A second steel rope and set of rails took the empties back underground. At the far end of the shed the loaded hutches were tipped up and emptied into the coal bunkers. From there the coal went into steel chutes high enough above the road for the coal to be funnelled into the backs of the standing trucks that transported the coal to the valley where it was graded and sold.

Only a handful of men worked above ground, unclipping the hutches from the steel rope, tipping them into the bunkers and gathering up the small medallions, the pitmen called palms, that they clipped onto their hutches underground to make clear which team of pitmen down below had loaded them with coal.

There could be delays between the loads, and right now the steel ropes were at a standstill. As we sat in the Land Rover looking on, a group of pitmen began to gather around Eugene McPadden. Every so often the oldest of the pitmen at Eugene's side looked warily towards the dark eye of the pit.

Frank said jokingly, "Eh up! – there's 'trouble at mill'."

Gerry McPadden stood alongside his father amongst the upset looking pitmen. The older pitman walked away, put a hand to his forehead, and then thought better of his decision to abandon the others, and came back to have further words with Eugene.

"Eugene is the union rep," Bernice said. "And the man with the hand on his head is the Firesman, Peter Tim. He's in charge of the day shift."

Frank got out of the Land Rover and Bernice climbed out after him. I would have preferred to stay where we were. In full operation a working pit was an extremely dangerous place for unwanted visitors. You had steel ropes blindly dragging lines of hutches in and out of the pit using the powerful haulage engine. And you had to contend with wads of slate and lumps of stones being thrown onto a massive spoil heap, and more coal falling from the bunkers, and the comings and goings of the trucks. It wasn't a place for sightseers.

Gerry was the first to spot our arrival. He was clean-faced yet because he hadn't started his shift, and he welcomed us with a big smile, which I reckoned was intended more for Bernice than for me or Frank. As we arrived alongside Gerry, the Firesman, Peter Tim said to Eugene, "We're running out of cover."

A second pitman said, "The roof is getting crumbly."

Another pitman said, "And you and Gerry undercut the seam last night so we're getting water behind us."

"I'm putting in another pump," said Peter Tim.

"The water is teeming in," the first pitman said.

"Wait so, and I'll take a look," said Eugene.

"Is there a problem?" Frank asked.

"We have a rising seam of coal causing all kinds of problems," Eugene said. "Can I help you?"

Frank said, "I was interested in seeing what you do here."

"I can take you down with me now if you like," Eugene offered.

Before Frank even had a chance to answer, Gerry said, "We'll get you a helmet and a lamp."

I didn't like the smile that passed between Gerry and Eugene. It had the feel of their planning a prank underground on the newcomer – something the Arigna pitmen were known for. A photographer from a Sunday newspaper got great pictures earlier in the year after being taken underground, but the reporter along with him wasn't able to speak for hours after being frightened out of his mind when the pitmen left him alone underground without telling him they'd be back.

"What about it, Leo?" Gerry asked. "Do you want to

know why you shouldn't leave school too soon like me?"

"Stay here," Bernice said. "I don't want you getting into trouble."

I dreaded the thought of being taken underground, but I didn't want to be seen chickening out either, or acting cowardly in front of Bernice.

"Give me a helmet," I said.

"Right, so," said Eugene. "Gerry can mind Bernice 'till we get back."

If I'd known Gerry was staying behind I'd have said no. But it was too late to back out now.

Eugene led me and Frank into the big shed, the whole front end of which was taken up with the massive haulage engine. Its great iron pulley-wheels were at a standstill, and would turn again to spool the steel rope only when Eugene got the trouble sorted underground. Old jackets, overalls and a line of pit helmets hung from a row of wooden pegs on a rack. Eugene found us lamps and helmets and adjusted the inside webbing to make the helmets fit. My first concern was keeping the new leather jacket safe, and I took it off and hung it on a peg though I knew I wouldn't be warm enough underground.

"You'll freeze to death," Eugene said, and found a smaller sized oilskin coat for me to wear. The insides of the sleeves and the back of the neck of the oilskin coat felt perishing and damp but I was glad to put it on even though I had to roll up the cuffs because the sleeves were too long.

In single file Frank and I followed Eugene out of the shed and down the short incline to the mouth of the pit. Bernice stood with her arms folded looking on while Gerry said, "If we're not somewhere else, we'll be here when you get back."

I had ventured a short distance into this working pit only once before on a Sunday when nobody was around, going far enough to see the daylight disappear behind my back. But then I lost my nerve and never made it to the coalface, which could be anything up to a mile underground.

EIGHTEEN

As we started down the unlit tunnel I looked at the crude timber pillars and crossbeams used to support the roof. There was no reason why the pillars should collapse this minute, and yet I had to put out of my mind the extreme pressure they must be under from the untold weight of slate and rock pressing down from above. My mother would have a conniption if she knew where I was headed. But there were plenty of lads like Gerry McPadden working underground who'd quit school when they were only a year or two older than me, so losing my courage now was not an option.

After walking a short distance into the pit we came to a picture of the Sacred Heart in a gold frame with a red bulb burning under it on a shelf full of little cards with prayers and holy medals. Eugene took off his helmet, paused in front of the picture, and made the sign of the cross.

"Hard men came here to work in the pit," Eugene said, "and when they saw what they were facing they never got past this picture."

"Lead the way," Frank said, refusing to be overawed.

"Suit yourself," said Eugene, "though you should

140

always say a prayer at the picture since you could be meeting the man himself before the day is out."

Before we went any further, Eugene took each of our lamps in turn and primed the lower chamber with dusty white nuggets of carbide from the supply he kept in an Andrew's liver salts tin in his jacket pocket. Next he saw to it there was water in the top compartment and he thumbed the lever to allow water to trickle down onto the carbide to dissolve and release gas. With an expert swipe of his hand he flicked the spark-wheel and a jet of flame appeared.

Each time after he lit a lamp and adjusted the flame he asked for a helmet and fitted it to the holder on the front and passed it back. He did Frank first. Then he stood in front of me and settled the helmet with the burning lamp on my head.

He made a final adjustment to the flame to see it wasn't smoky and smudging the reflector, allowing it to cast the brightest possible beam of light. But the light it gave looked poor to me in comparison to the daylight we were about to abandon. Also, the helmet felt loose and wobbled if I moved my head too quickly, and it took time to get used to the bobbing light as I struggled to see where I was putting my feet.

We were in pitch blackness now, and the twin set of steel tracks underfoot meant it was best to walk in single file close to the sides of the pit. Every so often there was what Eugene called a sump, a hole under the tracks filled with burnt engine oil to lubricate the hutch wheels as they passed through. We had to be careful not to step into these sumps and twist an ankle.

Rough-ends of broken rock jutted from the side walls and we had to watch out also for low hanging rocks sticking out from the roof that Eugene called 'bullets'. Even though we had helmets on, Eugene said we would end up seeing stars if we smacked our heads by accident into one of these stone bullets.

The air began to feel dank and chilly and our breaths began to fog. Even though there was constant water coming in through the roof and splashing onto the uneven floor around us there appeared to be a haze of dust in the air and caught in the beams of our carbide lamps.

We turned off the main tunnel and started up what Eugene called a branch 'road'. It felt like the walls were closing in tightly around us, and the roof dipped lower. The pillars and props here looked a lot newer, and the fresh timber bore the traces of the blows where wedges had been hammered between the upright props and the roof to keep the supports in place. I didn't want to think what would happen if one of those pulpy pine-wood supports gave way.

A single line of track lay at our feet. It was used by the pitmen to push their hutches loaded with coal, by hand, out as far as the main 'road' before they could clip them to the steel haulage rope. We passed the opening to another branch and pausing a moment I could hear water splashing and running down the length of the tunnel as it stretched on into absolute darkness.

There were other noises, too, in the pit. Like in a hospital ward for old people at night, it was full of low whispers, though some of these sounds at least came from the chemical hissing going on inside the lamps on our helmets. Yet in spite of this steady hiss of gas the feeble light shed by my lamp left me completely disorientated. The shafts all looked the same and the floors felt level so we could be making our way towards the surface or going deeper underground and I couldn't tell the two directions apart. We would have to depend on Eugene to get us back safely above ground. And the same thought must have crossed Frank's mind.

"What happens when the carbide is used up and your lamp goes out?" he asked.

"Then all you can do is light the road with curses," said Eugene.

"I can imagine," said Frank.

"The men often hide stashes of carbide for themselves in case they run short," Eugene said. "I remember one time when Gerry's carbide got stolen and he wound up stuck in the dark waiting for help, you wouldn't fit the blade of a small knife between the curses coming out of him."

We kept up a good marching pace behind Eugene, but there was still no sign we were nearing the coalface. And even though there must be a couple of hundred men at work somewhere in this pit it was easy to believe we were the only people underground. Then a deep booming sound reverberated down the tunnel.

"What's that?" Frank asked. He was a short distance ahead of me and I couldn't see his face, but he sounded nervous.

Eugene didn't answer and, with Frank slowing his pace, a gap opened up between us and Eugene who kept moving briskly ahead.

"We need to keep moving," I said to Frank.

More unnerving noises brought him to a halt. This time the noises came in short but rapid bursts. They were followed by several hard thuds. Seeing the beam of his lamp swing about I realised Frank had flattened up against the side wall, as if anticipating a wagon train of hutches to come rolling along the single track towards us in the dark.

At this stage Eugene was out of sight, unaware we'd stopped. As I peered up ahead hoping to catch sight of his lamp a bright flash illuminated the tunnel.

Frank jerked back and his helmet came off and fell into

a pool of water on the floor. His lamp went out.

I moved closer to him to shine my lamp into his face to find out what was wrong. There was another eerily intense blue-white burst of light and I heard a crackling and fizzling sound.

"Get down," Frank shouted.

I ducked instinctively but then straightened up. A further rapid burst of echoing noise came down the tunnel. My first thought was that the roof was, in fact, caving in and the falling stones were making sparks as they fell. The other noises must be pillars splintering like matchwood as a whole section of the roof collapsed. That or the pitmen were using gelignite and we had strayed into a blasting operation underground and we were about to be blown to smithereens.

Even if we weren't directly in the line of the blast we could expect to be engulfed at any minute by a cloud of dust and choking fumes created by the explosion.

The beam of my lamp found Frank's face. It was drenched in sweat and his eyes looked wild. More rapid bursts of noise and flashing light filled the shaft where we stood. Frank winced but fought to keep his fear under control. Finding him scared and confused forced me to keep calm because having the two of us in a panic would surely get us into even deeper trouble. Holding my head steady to keep my light on him I laid a hand on his chest and found it falling and rising so fast he could be having an asthma attack or a fit of the panic that comes from thinking you're about to suffocate.

"Take deep breaths," I said, "and wait for it to pass."

"I thought for a minute I was back in the Congo," he said, his voice shaking.

"In the Niemba Ambush?"

"Operation Sarsfield," he said.

"Operation Sarsfield," Eugene said behind my back. "What about it?"

I hadn't noticed him coming back to find out what was keeping us. But he was right behind me now with the beam of his light shining directly into Frank's eyes, deliberately using his confusion to get information.

If Frank could just put one foot in front of the other it might bring the power of movement back to him, and I reached out to help him get back on his feet before he blurted out something important.

Only Eugene held out his hand to block me, and kept his light in Frank's eyes determined to take advantage of the situation.

"You don't have to tell him anything," I said, convinced that in the state of panic he was in Frank was about to blow his cover.

Aware of my concern, Frank let go of the rock wall at his back to stand upright. Using his right hand, he rubbed away the sweat streaming down his forehead and running into his eyes. Another burst of light pierced the darkness. But this time Frank kept his nerve.

I broke away from Eugene and put my hand on Frank's shoulder. Frank stumbled to get his balance and I encouraged him to lean on me until he recovered.

"His lamp's gone out," I told Eugene.

"At ease soldier," Eugene mocked Frank as he bent down to retrieve the fallen helmet and the extinguished lamp, friendly with us again as if nothing happened. "We're at the gob."

Up ahead I saw the glimmer of lights approach. We heard the sound of iron grinding against iron, and Eugene stepped aside while two pitmen went past us with a hutch so heavily loaded with glittering slabs of newly cut coal they weren't remotely interested in us, only in keeping their heavy burden moving towards the main road.

The loaded hutch on the track accounted for some of the sounds we'd heard, but not the unearthly bright flashes of light or the rat-a-tat sounds as we moved on again. Frank was still shaky and the lamp on his helmet was still quenched, but as we rounded the next bend we saw a pool of light and heard voices and found a bunch of pitmen hunkered down where the shaft ended.

The roof dipped sharply at this point and there was not enough headroom for the men at the coalface to stand up. The opening where they were gathered was really only a shelf cut into the rock face where a pitman lay on his side operating a pneumatic pick in *rat-a-tat* bursts.

The pitman wore a yellow oilskin jacket and I could see water spilling in through the roof on top of him. The other pitmen around him were handling a hosepipe attached to a pump powered by a compressor, which more pitmen were working on. Mossy Beirne, one of the younger and wilder pitmen from Arigna, was using an oxy-acetylene welding torch to make repairs.

A fresh burst of sparks and crackles came from the welding gear as Mossy dabbed a rod on the spot under repair and we had our explanation for the flashing lights, sparks and the eerie fizzling sounds.

Knowing the source of the noises meant they no longer unnerved me and Frank too looked composed.

With a build-up of rubble to clear away, the man in the oilskins stopped the pneumatic pick and got to work with a short-handled shovel. The men around him set to work swiftly installing timber props and hammering wedges between the props and the cross beams before the crumbly clay, slate and stone roof could collapse.

It all looked fairly chaotic but at the same time these pitmen were working closely as a team with a clear sense of what they were doing.

Another great burst of sparks went into the air around us from the welding torch and I spotted two very wet looking pitmen sitting with their heads between their legs.

"What's the hold up?" Eugene asked the pitman working on the compressor.

"They got stuck on the other side of the flood," said the pitman as he passed Mossy another welding rod. The two soaking wet coal miners nodded their bowed heads.

Eugene said, "But ye're all right now?"

The men looked completely done in, but they nodded their heads again, lacking either the will or the energy to complain.

"We're going no further with this seam," said another pitman holding the hose for the pump that still hadn't got to work on the water running round our feet and flowing away in a stream along the pit floor in the direction in which we came, making me wonder if the water might not be building up behind us, and if we didn't soon pull back we'd be trapped at this teeming wet dead end.

One of the pitmen passed another prop to the man lying on his side on the ledge and he hammered it into place. Even so, a fresh lump of stone and clay fell out of the roof.

None of the other pitmen seemed too concerned, as if these torrents of water and falling rock were everyday incidents.

"What do you think?" Eugene asked me. "Would you like to be a pitman?"

"Maybe," I lied, wanting to sound braver than I felt. I definitely did not want to stop my education for a job in this place no matter how much money a pitman could earn.

"The work is hard and the pay is small," said one of the nearly drowned pitmen. "And no matter how little you do, you earn it all."

"Good man Tommy," the pitman beside him said, also perking up.

"Yahoo," shouted another of the pitman for no reason that I could see.

Eugene looked at his watch. It was four o'clock and he told the two soaking wet pitmen their shift was finished. They got up on their feet for the trudge back to the daylight.

I stood over Frank where he had hunkered down to keep out of the way and reached out to him. He took my hand and used it to help himself onto his feet.

"Thanks," he said, but I could see he was in no mood to talk.

"Go on back with the lads," Eugene said, "I'll see to things here."

The welding gear sparked back to life and I was glad to be turning around and getting out of there.

In silence I trooped along with Frank and the other wet and bone-weary pitmen back the way we came, and when I finally saw daylight coming in through the eye of the pit as we neared the outside world, I realised we weren't nearly as far underground as I'd imagined. Lack of familiarity had made it feel like we'd penetrated much deeper into the mountain. All the same, when we came out through the eye of the pit into the daylight the industrial sheds and coal heaps never looked more beautiful, nor the fresh mountain air taste sweeter.

NINETEEN

Frank gave me his helmet and lamp to return along with my own gear to the rack in the big shed. When I got there I noticed straightaway my leather jacket was missing. One of the pitmen must have taken it. I was raging but also sick with disappointment at having survived the pit only for this theft to happen.

Bunches of black-faced pitmen were boarding the waiting coal lorry, getting into their own cars and mounting their motorbikes and bicycles while more took off walking their paths home across the mountain. Any one of them could have the jacket stuffed in his bag. Powerless, I went looking for Bernice to ask her if she'd seen anything.

I spotted her waiting patiently in the Land Rover, and when I opened the passenger door discovered she had my jacket draped over her shoulders.

"It got cool," she said, "I hope you don't mind."

It pleased me more than I could say to find her using my jacket to keep warm. It was the next best thing to having her in my two arms.

She cast her eyes over my appearance and said, "Look at the state of you."

My hands were filthy but I had no idea my face was so black until I checked my reflection in the side door mirror. Frank looked the same, and the state we were in made me smile. He didn't see the funny side and sat holding the steering wheel waiting for me to get into the Land Rover. Impatient to get going, he took off without a word as soon as I was aboard.

"Did something happen?" Bernice asked.

Frank didn't answer.

"How did you get on with Gerry?" I asked.

"He asked me out."

"What did you say?"

"I told him 'no'. And he said if I went out with him he'd take me anywhere I wanted. He's getting a car."

"Has he suddenly come into money?" I asked.

Frank shot a hard look at me. It was his first real reaction since he got the collywobbles down the pit. But he quickly turned back to his driving.

"He will soon, or so he says," Bernice said.

We drove down the mountainside, taking the shortest way back to the valley by the Top Road. Frank stopped at the pub, climbed out quickly, opened the back door of the Land Rover and rolled out the wheel for Daddy's travelling shop.

"I'll take that," I said, and balanced the upright wheel between my two hands so I could roll it as far as the van waiting up on blocks.

"See you later," I said.

Frank nodded and got back into the Land Rover. Even when Bernice waved him off he stayed looking straight ahead. Anyone would be upset if they lost their nerve down the pit. But he didn't have to be so mad at himself. He hadn't let anything important slip.

The Land Rover crossed the bridge and we watched it

go until it was out of sight.

"What's eating him?" Bernice asked.

"He got a fright."

"Why, what happened?"

"The banging and the flashing down the pit made him think he was back in the Congo under fire."

Bernice looked concerned. "Is he all right now?

"I'd say so," I said with worries of my own over how to get past my mother with my hands and face as black as a pitman.

"Can you smuggle me into the house?" I asked.

But even before Bernice could respond my mother came out of the pub and found us.

"Well?" she said.

Deliberately taking one hand off the wheel for the van, I wiped my face to make it even blacker than it already was and said, "They're expecting Daddy in for new tyres on Monday."

"Leave that for your father and get up them stairs and get washed."

She turned around and went indoors.

When I had the wheel left safely by the van Bernice handed me my leather jacket. "You're as lucky as a black cat," she said and laughed.

After a quick scrub I dried myself off and then, back in my room, stood in front of the dressing table mirror in new clean underpants only. The leather jacket rested on my bed and I reached out to try it on. Turning up the collar I struck a pose, admiring again its zips and spare pockets. I'd never had much interest in how I looked, but even minus my shirt and trousers I liked how I felt wearing the jacket. Then turning at the sound of a gentle tap on my door I found Bernice entering the room.

"Sorry," she said and backed out quickly.

She waited on the landing while I pulled on jeans and a T-shirt.

"You can come in now," I said.

Re-entering the bedroom she said, "I'm worried about Frank. I'd like to see him. But I won't go to the river field on my own. Will you come with me?"

"I'll bring the flash-lamp for getting back," I said.

We left the house by the back door, trusting the bolt would still be off when we got back. We ducked between the crates full of bottles in rickety stacks in the yard and crossed the back garden to go through the hole in the hedge. Dressed in the leather jacket and jeans I felt ready for anything. Though it was a bit disappointing to find she'd brought along a handbag.

The riverbank was thickly screened by rank smelling elder bushes and clumps of nettles, and luckily Bernice wore high boots so her legs were safe as I led the way through the undergrowth. The light was going, but through the arches of the stone bridge the water gleamed and clouds of insects danced over the calm surface as swallows skimmed the air over our heads feeding. The honeysuckle too was just starting to release its powerful night perfume, and this was exactly the kind of escapade I had been longing to share with Bernice. Reaching out my hand I helped her to scramble up the embankment and we came out onto the public road safely out of sight of the pub. We crossed the bridge and walked past Doctor Ballintine's house, and kept going without meeting a single car until we reached the gate into Red Paddy Reynolds's field. Crossing the field I could see Frank had a campfire lit in front of the tent where it stood in the shelter of the whitethorn hedge.

Frank sat cross-legged by the fire wearing a blindfold. He had his wristwatch on the ground alongside the dismantled parts of the Carcano rifle. He quickly reassembled the rifle, tested the action and whipped off the blindfold to look at his watch.

"What are you doing?" Bernice asked.

"Stripping the rifle and reassembling it, and timing how long it takes."

"With a blindfold on?" she said.

"In case it jammed in pitch dark conditions."

"Like you'd find down the pit," I said.

He didn't answer. And conscious of the unhappy silence Bernice demonstrated the handbag and said, "I brought you some supper."

"What have you got," Frank asked, brightening.

"Let's see," Bernice said, opening up a selection of brown paper parcels. "I have ham, boiled eggs, bread, lettuce and tomatoes and sweetcake."

"I'll put the kettle on," Frank said.

He had a primus stove with a brass plunger he pumped to get the paraffin into the jets and then he lit the ring with a safety match, returning the spent match to the box before handing the box to me to return to the tent.

The inside of the tent was stuffy but very neat, with a cot bed, hurricane lamp and a folding chair and table. On a small table rested for steadiness against the centre pole was an enamel basin, and beside it a silver safety razor, a bar of Palmolive soap, a shaving brush with clean bristles, a jar of Brylcream for his hair and a bottle of Old Spice aftershave. The set-up appealed to my sense of order and I wondered if I might not enjoy army life

We shared a tasty supper on tin plates and ate sitting around the campfire in the deepening twilight. There were "emmhhhs" and "ahhhs" in appreciation of the food and Bernice waited until Frank was almost finished before she asked, "What happened today in the pit?"

"Was Leo talking to you about that?"

"I knew something happened the minute I laid eyes on you."

"I lost my nerve," he said.

We waited for him to say more but the silence continued.

"You can tell us," Bernice said.

"Not if it goes any further."

"We won't tell another soul, honestly," Bernice said.

"Cross my heart and hope to die," I said, and immediately regretted sounding so childish, though it seemed the right thing to say.

Frank took up a long stick and poked the fire. Sparks flew into the air.

"When the banging and the flashing started in the pit today," he said, "I thought I was back in the jungle in the thick of battle. 'Bomb-happy' they call it, when a soldier's nerve goes like that."

He didn't look up to see how we took this admission and we stayed quiet while he mulled over the fire.

"I went to the Congo thinking I'd volunteered for a peace keeping mission," he said. "I was interested in seeing what the place was like, not in fighting or getting killed, but that changed. The whole of the Congo is one giant battlefield over who gets control over the country's uranium. The Superpowers all have operations and counter-operations going on. Unfortunately, it was the Irish forces serving with the UN that got mustered to retake a town called Elizabethville from the breakaway Katanganese. Even before our Dakota plane landed ahead of what the top brass called Operation Sarsfield, our fuselage got riddled with shrapnel from anti-aircraft fire from the ground. Swedish troops were meant to back us up, but I can tell you now it was the Irish lads who had to take the tunnel on their own."

"A real tunnel," I said "like the pit today only full of uranium."

"Quiet Leo," Bernice cut in on me.

"We called it the tunnel," Frank said. "In fact it was a railway bridge crossing the main road into Elizabethville."

I knew better than to interrupt again. And Frank said, "With a pre-dawn attack we thought we might have the element of surprise. But straight away we came up against a well-armed opposition. They were organised and led by hardened mercenaries – Belgians and Germans and ex-French Foreign Legion. And Irish lads too, like 'Mad Mike Connolly'. There was mortar fire and rifle fire, along with sniper fire. We were being cut to bits. And we had monsoon rains that were like standing under a waterfall. Our gunners never saw anything like it. They might have been handy lads firing on the range in the Glen of Immal, but they had no experience of the conditions we found ourselves in, firing live rounds over the heads of their own soldiers. They had a fire-plan they were meant to follow, but the mortars misfired in the wet and burned the hands off the gunners and their compasses were antiques going back to 1915. The base-plates went skew-ways in the mud, so you had rounds going astray and our soldiers even ended up in the target zone though thankfully our own mortar fire didn't. Worse still, the Katanganese and their leader Tshombe's mercenaries had the high ground. They were firing at us from railway carriages up on the bridge and they seemed to have plenty of ammunition.

"And then out of nowhere this lad called Charlie Raleigh stepped out into the middle of the road carrying the recoilless anti-tank gun. I'll never forget him. He stood there and took aim straight at the enemy position. It was madness. He was bound to get shot. I already had one of their snipers in my sights. He was a young lad. Too young.

But that didn't mean to say he wasn't a killer. "

Frank broke off for a minute to pick up his rifle and run a cloth along the barrel to wipe off a dribble of 3-in-1 penetrating oil. Then he went on.

"It was a tricky shot," he said, "because of the rain. And he was using a tree to hide in. But I had special training. I knew what I was there to do. I knew what was expected of me. So, I got him in my sights and squeezed off a shot. I had to, I had no choice. I had to cover Raleigh."

In the flickering campfire light I saw Bernice put a comforting arm around Frank's shoulder and the two of them moved closer.

"The anti-tank gun round Raleigh fired took out the whole position," he said. "It went through the bridge and blasted right into the carriage. Later we found five bodies. And it was on account of that single round our No. 2 Platoon was able to advance on Elizabethville."

"What about the other sniper?" Bernice asked.

"I had him in my sights a long time," Frank said with a catch in his voice. "I could have pulled the trigger earlier, but I didn't because he was so young."

"Did you kill him?" I asked, not knowing what else to say.

"I saw his rifle fall out of the tree. And then he came tumbling after it."

"Leave it, Frank," Bernice said. "You did what you had to."

"My superiors have no idea I haven't been able to hit a barn door since," he said laying down the rifle. "I'm a crackshot who can't shoot straight."

"Should you be the one out hunting this wildcat?" Bernice asked.

I watched him carefully, wondering if he would tell

Bernice the whole truth. He forced a smile and said, "I didn't want to end up in a locked ward on sweet tea and injections, so I volunteered for this assignment thinking the fresh air, and keeping off the drink, would help."

The special training he'd mentioned suggested to me his skills as a sharpshooter were what separated him from an ordinary rank and file soldier and got him recruited to Army Intelligence as a field operative. And Bernice deserved to know about the dossier instructing him to gather intelligence on Eugene and Gerry McPadden's involvement with the IRA. Only sitting beside Frank in the campfire light she had that tender, devoted expression on her face I'd noticed before when she lit candles in church. It was the kind of dedicated look Mammy had for me whenever I got a serious asthma attack. Only Bernice was not in church and she was not Frank's mother.

The pockets of ground mist in the hollows were thickening into a fog, especially in the damp bottomlands by the river where the corncrakes had started their 'crake-crake' mating calls that would go on the whole night long. It never got fully dark at this time of year of course and the sky behind the mountain was still streaked with red and orange light. But it was getting late, and when Frank stood up I knew it was time to go.

"I'll close the tent and drop you back," he said.

We could have made it home on foot. But Bernice was happy to accept the lift. And riding through the pockets of ground-mist in the Land Rover, and seeing only the tops of the ragwort and thistles caught in the sweeping headlights we could have been crossing the Serengeti on safari. In spite of my suspicions it was easy to slip back into believing Frank Welcome's only purpose was to track down and shoot the wildcat.

We turned towards the village, a red sky overhead

where the sun had gone down behind the mountain.

"Red sky at night, shepherd's delight," Bernice said.

"Red sky in the morning, nuclear warning," I said to Frank, and he chuckled.

After he dropped us off outside the pub, Bernice and I managed to sneak straight into the house by the back door. She was 'bursting for a pee' and got first use of the bathroom. When she came out of the bathroom she went to her own room. I waited a while thinking she might reappear but she must have gone straight to sleep.

Though I didn't feel a bit tired I went to the bathroom, washed my hands and face, brushed my teeth and got ready for bed without bothering to take my tablets. My breathing was good, even though I'd been out in the damp night air and my hair smelled of campfire wood smoke. Hanging my jacket in the wardrobe I found I'd been so busy looking around the tent I forgot to return the box of matches. It wasn't a good enough excuse, however, to make a return visit, even if all I wanted was to spend the rest of the night in the field by the river with Captain Frank Welcome, building up the campfire to see us through the night as the summer ground mists thickened into a blanketing fog; the corncrakes making a racket like the jungle, the Carcano rifle loaded and primed, and both of us keenly looking out into the darkness sharing the ancient and uncomplicated silence of hunters with our secrets unspoken and our destinies unforeseeable.

TWENTY

In the morning Mammy said nothing to me about going to town yesterday without her permission, coming back home black as a coal miner, and then sneaking out of the house again with Bernice for a late-night supper around the crackshot's campfire. Instead she went to the kitchen press and took down the bottle of cod-liver oil and, in a deliberate slow display of her authority, began to unscrew the cap off the horrible tasting tonic for me to get a clear picture of what lay in store.

Daddy sat at the lower end of the table with the ledger from the travelling shop open in front of him. He kept separate ledgers for the shop next door and for the travelling shop to keep track of the porter and whiskey he took from the pub. Supplying drink to those who preferred to keep out of the pub was Mammy's idea, and it made Daddy nervous because he'd already had a warning from Sergeant Glacken telling him he wasn't supposed to sell beers and spirits outside of the premises.

Daddy had his glasses on and he was going over the figures in three columns marked L, S, and D, adding up the pounds, shillings and pence. He dipped the gold nib of his fountain pen into a bottle of Quink ready-made ink and used the lever on the side to suck up the deep blue liquid, then he put nib to paper again. When he had entered the total at the bottom of the page, he laid a sheet of blotting paper over his work and waited for the ink to dry.

"Down again, I'll bet," Mammy said.

He lifted his eyes from the figures to meet hers.

"And they'll all be looking for credit for another week or longer you can bet."

"It's not their fault the bank got robbed."

"Open wide," Mammy said turning to me with a brimming desert spoon full of cod-liver oil levelled in her hand.

Normally I only had to take the cod-liver oil before my porridge on school mornings in the winter to stop me from getting colds and flu. And I knew well that forcing me to take the cod-liver oil this morning was her way of teaching me a lesson and that had I no choice other than to swallow my medicine.

"Euch – God that tastes awful!" I said, gagging on the fishy liquid as it washed past my tonsils.

"Mind your language," Mammy said. "Or I'll wash that mouth out with soap."

"Does he have to take the stuff?" Daddy asked.

"Have some yourself," she said. "It might put a bit of jizz in you."

Daddy bowed his head and went back to the accounts.

Alongside the bottle of cod-liver oil on the kitchen table Mammy had a big brown glass jar full of malt extract. I had to follow up the cod-liver oil with a spoonful of the gooey malt extract, which tasted sweet at least and a whole lot better than the fish oil.

"This late in our lives we should be running our own business," Mammy said.

"Don't start that again," Daddy said without looking up.

"We can't keep putting it off."

"We're doing all right as it is."

"Only for as long as it suits the owners. And when they don't need us any longer they'll run us like a dog at dinner time – same as the Kinsella's did in Wexford."

"Not in front of Leo, Monica," Daddy cautioned.

"We should be making plans to buy our own place," she insisted.

"Are you getting ready for Mass," Daddy said to me, squirming at having me witness this row.

But I'd heard this argument before.

Daddy was cautious in everything, and he didn't want to take on the responsibility of owning his own shop. Mammy did. Routine suited him while she wanted a challenge, or that's how I saw it anyway. True, Daddy was good with people, but she had a harder head for business. And to be fair to Mammy, if he would just let her have her way they probably should go it alone instead of relying on unpredictable shop owners who could ask us to move on any time they liked, in a repeat of the way Daddy had been let go in Wexford after years of loyal service. It is possible too that Daddy hadn't got over the shock of finding himself out of a job, and in taking up this manager's post he needed to prove his capabilities in the one line of business he knew best. Maybe knowing this Mammy didn't push him quite as hard as she might have wanted. But you could feel her frustration looking at Daddy with his inky fingers, pioneer pin, and sober Sunday suit, while she sported a tight-fitting jacket and skirt in the latest fashion and puckered her lips to redo her racy pink lipstick. He seemed colourless in comparison, and she was over-dressed for mass, but couldn't resist trying on the new outfit meant to catch the eye of the American President if only she'd made it to Dublin.

An hour later, with no breakfast but the cod-liver oil taste thick in my mouth, I stood on the altar with our Parish Priest, Father Canice Boland. He had a big square head, square shoulders and huge square feet in scuffed shoes. He was inclined to be impatient. And I was glad to have another altar boy with me since I wasn't exactly sure of the prayers. I was good at Latin in school but inclined to forget the words of the prayers as I never thought of the church as the house of God. To me, it was more like a War-Room with stained glass windows – the place where the pit owners, the school teachers, and the doctor sat nearest the altar in buttoned up coats like Generals. And my father and mother knew their place, a set behind the top brass.

A good foot soldier like Nora Greene, however, kept me on track, for she was always a step ahead of Father Boland saying the prayers out loud the whole way through mass.

At Nora's back the congregation divided in two, the women seated on the left hand side, and the men on the right. There were cross-houses also, on either side of the altar, where the women sat in one cross-house and the men sat in the other cross house looking at each other. The women covered their hair with hats and headscarves, the men prayed bareheaded. The church was not quite full, and there would have been room for more at the very back. But certain men like Red Paddy chose to stay outside in the porch, and more chose to climb the stairs and sit up in the gallery where they kept out of sight. I knew from my mother the gallery was not a respectable place to sit.

Pope John had died, and Fr Boland asked us to pray

162

for the Cardinals and grant them wisdom and God's grace in helping them to choose a new Pope.

When it was time to take up the collection, Eugene McPadden and Gerry left their seat and walked along the aisle, Eugene on the men's side, Gerry on the women's side, carrying long handled wooden paddles with a velvet-lined box fixed to the end of each paddle for gathering money. Fr Boland went to the golden door of the tabernacle in the fancy marble altar against the gable wall, and began the Communion Rite with his back turned to the congregation. I rang the bell when he raised the host. Then I walked alongside him with a golden salver in my hand I kept level under each chin as the pitmen and their families lined up along the altar rails to kneel with their tongues out to receive the Eucharist.

Eugene McPadden and Gerry also knelt at the altar rail, and it was odd to look down on the bowed heads of the two suspected IRA men as they received the sacrament the same as everyone else.

When mass ended, Fr. Boland had to see the women who hadn't been at communion. Since they had babies, and were thought to be unclean, they couldn't receive the sacraments again until they'd been 'churched'. Fr Boland didn't agree with the ritual, and I once heard him mutter under his breath, 'bloody nonsense'. He was hoping a new Pope might put a stop to the practice.

There were two women this morning he would have to 'church'. Luckily it wasn't my turn to wait behind and stand holding the candle.

Apart from the spoonful of cod-liver oil I'd been fasting since midnight like everyone else in the chapel was required to do, and I'd already seen one woman faint and have to be carried out to be revived. I felt weak with hunger myself. And while Fr Boland stood wiping the chalice clean after communion, and the congregation reflected and coughed and shuffled, all I could think about was getting home and putting on a pan full of sausages.

Yet even though everybody was starving, the men waited on for a while after mass ended and stood in a line along the gable wall beside the porch to smoke and talk amongst themselves. I had no choice but hold on while Daddy joined the pitmen for a short chat, and Mammy talked to Miss Costigan.

"It's a shame neither of us got to see the President in person," Mammy said.

Miss Costigan said that at least the State Visit was a resounding success. And President Kennedy had promised to come back. She had the President's parting words off by heart: "'This is not the land of my birth but it is the land for which I hold the greatest affection and I certainly will come back in the springtime'," she said proudly. "So we'll get our chance."

Amongst the line of men at the church gable I was familiar with Eugene and Gerry, Mossy Beirne and Peter Tim the Firesman from Rover Pit, Mattie Scanlon and Timmy and Tommy, the twins, who didn't look a bit alike. The other men I had no names for. Though I thought I recognised a couple of the pitmen from the coalface yesterday, but clean-faced and dressed now in their best suits I couldn't be certain. One thing about the pitmen of Arigna, if they spent the working week going around filthy, on Sundays they scrubbed up and dressed well. And even Red Paddy Reynolds wore a long Sunday coat and a good hat with a feather in the brim.

When Fr Boland came out of the chapel the pitmen stopped talking. The priest came down the steps to have a word with Red Paddy.

"I heard about your misfortune, Patrick," he said. "You

lost your Honda 50 in the fire. But have faith, Patrick, and the Lord will provide you with another."

"The Lord could have left me with the one I had," Red Paddy said straight out.

Seeing that he was wasting his breath, Fr Boland nodded to the two women who stood off to the side of the church yard. They followed him into the church, their heads covered and eyes cast down as they passed the line of pitmen.

"How many babies has the young Kelly one now?" Mossy asked.

"Five, counting the twins," said Eugene.

Gerry pursed his lips. The men laughed.

"Come on you," my mother called to me, casting a severe look at Eugene.

We could easily have walked to mass, but it was important to my mother we arrive and leave in the washed and polished Mark 1 Ford Cortina without a speck of dirt on the chrome bumper and trim.

Our first stop on the way home was the butchers where the car came in useful because Daddy had a box of meat to collect that he delivered in the travelling shop on Tuesdays.

I followed him into the clammy concrete stall with the big window. Condensation ran down the inside of the glass. The place smelled damp since it wasn't used all week. And I didn't like Ambrose Luck the butcher or his meat. He had a face like a fried egg. His meat tasted 'carney' like it had picked up the dampness in the shop. My mother thought so too and bought the meat for our meals from another butcher.

But the people from Arigna were loyal to Ambrose Luck, who allowed them credit during strikes when their pay dried up and now, too, on account of the wages theft. His main business was in town in Drumshanbo, but on

Sundays he opened up this smaller outlet for an hour after mass. On a bare plank table at his back, orders were laid out already wrapped in brown paper with his clients' names written on the outside ready for collection. All he had to do was hand out parcels of meat. He kept a few trays of cutlets on display just in case anyone wanted extra.

Daddy's order was ready and waiting in a flat brown cardboard box. When I picked it up the box buckled as the parcels moved around, each joint of meat a surprisingly dead weight.

After running his eyes over the docket Daddy opened a big velvet wallet with separate pockets for the different notes. He would not be getting paid by his customers until the stolen wages were replaced, but he did not keep Ambrose Luck waiting for his money. To be friendly, as he settled up the bill he said, "A fair exchange is no robbery."

"I'm not trying to make it all the one day," Ambrose said.

"He got you there," said Red Paddy.

We left to the sound of laughter at my father's expense, and I couldn't wait to get home. But we had one more stop. For with Daddy's shop closed on Sundays, people got their Sunday papers from a tin hut down the road from the booth belonging to Ambrose Luck. So I had to climb out of the Cortina again to collect our papers, - the *Sunday Press* for Daddy, the *News of the World* for Mammy – for which my reward would be a packet of Silvermints and the spare change to keep as pocket money.

Bernice helped the newspaper seller, Grace Nail, to cope with the rush after mass. Nearly everybody bought the *Sunday Press*, but Grace had everyone's name written on their own paper, so depending on what order her customers came into the little hut after mass, Bernice had to keep searching the pile until she found the paper with the right name on it.

The crowd in the paper sellers hut was often three deep at the counter straight after mass, but it was quieter now with only two or three people waiting their turn. Frank Welcome stood amongst them. Not having a paper on order he was obliged to wait and see what might be left over once everyone else had been served.

He was smartly dressed in the tailored dark suit, white shirt and a narrow tie. A hanky peeked from his top pocket and his Chelsea boots were highly polished. Out of uniform he looked even thinner and younger. But he seemed a lot happier than he did last night confessing to a loss of confidence in his marksmanship after what happened in the Congo.

Bernice gave me the papers and the usual pack of mints and then came around the counter. She handed Frank a *Sunday Independent* and said, "It's the last one." Then she lowered her voice and asked, "How are you feeling?"

"More sociable," he said.

Watching the two of them closely I couldn't get over the change in Bernice whenever she was around Frank. Somehow she became more timid and more forceful, more courageous and yet needier.

"Can I treat you to Sunday lunch in Flanagan's Hotel in Drumshanbo," he asked.

"Mrs Rossiter will have the dinner ready for me," Bernice said. "But we could go for a spin beforehand."

"I'd like that," said Frank.

With the last of her customers served, Grace Nail put the cash-box with the takings and the boxes of sweets back up on the counter to take home again until the following week.

"Here, have this," she said, pressing money into Bernice's hand.

Another change in Bernice was the way she didn't make a fuss accepting payment.

To allow Grace to lock up the hut we stepped out onto the road. The Parish Hall stood on the opposite side, and the players for Saint Ronan's football team were starting to file out carrying sandwiches in their hands, grabbing a quick bite to eat before the warm-up. Already, in the football field across from the pub, several of the younger players were kitted out and running and passing the ball, shouting for possession, while others trotted around the sideline.

What the stocky young lads of Arigna lacked in footballing skills they made up for in physical strength from working in the pit. And if a high ball gave them trouble because they were stocky, they were nearly impossible to knock off their feet. They didn't always win, but the other team generally had a higher rate of casualties.

Gerry came out of the hall wearing his jersey and togs and studded boots, and chewing on a ham sandwich.

Seeing Bernice along with Frank Welcome he moved to intercept her. But he found the studs in his football boots tricky on the tarred road, and when he reached Bernice he grabbed hold of her arm.

"Are you shouting for me today?"

"Let go, Gerry," she said.

His hand stayed on her arm. "There's a match on."

"Just let her pass, Gerry," Frank said.

"Who's talking to you?" Gerry said. He pushed with the flat of his hand against the lapel of Frank's suit. Frank raised his hand and pushed back against Gerry's football jersey.

"Try that again —" Gerry said, but he never got to finish the threat. Instead, Bernice took Frank by the hand and brushed past Gerry to break up the shoving match.

Watching what was going on from the Cortina,

Mammy leaned across Daddy and beeped the horn impatiently as a signal for me to hurry up.

Bernice turned to me and said "Tell your mother I'm sorry I'm going to miss dinner. I'll be back in time to do the switchboard."

She got into the Land Rover along with Frank and they drove off.

Gerry tracked their departure with an unfriendly eye and spat the end of the sandwich in his mouth onto the road.

"What's she doing with him anyway?" he asked me.

In an unnerving way I understood how Gerry felt. He had his sights set on Bernice, and so had I, which presented both of us with an unexpected rival in Frank Welcome. And even while knowing I was too young for Bernice to look on me as a boyfriend; it upset me to see her take off with this handsome newcomer for the day, leaving me high and dry. Sharing Gerry's jealousy, though, didn't make me like him any better.

"Will ya come on will ya?" a team mate called across the road. Gerry grunted and tottered off towards the playing field on his notably white legs that rarely got the sun.

"Poor Gerry," Mammy said when I got back into the car. "The girl that marries that man will wipe her eyes more times than she'll ever wipe her mouth."

TWENTY ONE

After the Sunday dinner, Daddy fell asleep in the armchair in the kitchen by the Stanley Range with the paper open in his lap, and Mammy went upstairs for a nap. The card game on Sunday nights in the pub often went on late and it could be three in the morning or later before she got to bed.

I felt heavy and full after the mid-day meal of roast beef with fresh garden peas and new potatoes that I'd washed down with a glass full of milk and then enjoyed a dish of jelly and ice-cream afterwards for dessert. Now with the household nice and quiet, and a long summer Sunday afternoon to kill, I had the perfect chance to collect the satchel with the length of cart rope from the back of the wardrobe and set out for the mountain.

I got out of my Sunday clothes, and put on an everyday shirt and jeans. Leaving the house I wondered if I needed the leather jacket but I wore it anyway.

The houses of the village stood with their doors and windows open. I could hear the same football match on the radio in every house with Michael O'Hehir doing the commentary. Leitrim were playing Galway in the Connacht

Final. I passed the church and on Chapel Hill saw a rabbit skip into the graveyard.

A mound of freshly dug clay in the graveyard where the rabbit went marked Francie Curran's grave. I hoped he'd understand why I didn't stop.

On the Top Road I slowed down for a quick look at the house where Gerry lived with his father and mother. Their cottage was a short distance in from the road along a grassy lane, and I got a whiff of cabbage boiling for the dinner held over on account of Gerry's team having a match on earlier.

Before the start of the Bog Lane I stopped to catch my breath and look towards the shores of the lake where the single slim chimney stack of the coal burning power station stood fuming like a rocket. That chimney always made me think of a nuclear missile ready for launching.

In the real missile crisis, President Kennedy's naval blockade had finally faced down the Russian ships loaded full of atomic warheads destined for Cuba, and the Russians would think twice before they set up nuclear missile bases again on America's doorstep. And yet I couldn't help thinking that some quiet Sunday there would be a surprise attack, and the inter-continental ballistic missiles with their atomic payload sulking in their silos would rise from their launch-pads at the press of a doomsday button and land on Arigna with everyone either asleep in an armchair after the Sunday dinner, or following a football match on the radio.

Aware that it was taking me much longer to get from the valley floor to the mountain top on foot than it did to cover the same ground in Frank Welcome's army Land Rover, I put on a burst of speed when I took off again. Where Frank and Bernice were right now I had no idea. But I pictured them together walking arm in arm by the sea along the promenade in Bundoran, or strolling the pathways of the Forest Park. And I had to control a moment's panic at the thought Bernice might never want to come back.

A tickle in my lungs made me speed up more to get rid of the sensation as I marched hard up the hill. Then, where the Bog Lane rose steeply near the gateway to Nora Greene's cottage, I put my hands on the calves of my legs to give myself a breather. I considered calling on Nora, then decided against it knowing I'd be working against the clock.

Branches would have to be gathered to cover up the pit meant to trap the panther; branches strong enough to support camouflaging heather but flimsy enough to give way under the weight of a panther. Next I'd have to scour the mountain for moss and mountain grass and wads of heather to make the trap blend in with its surrounds. And before I did any of that I had to climb down into the hole itself and use the loose stones at the bottom to make certain any animal that fell into the trap couldn't escape.

I was sweating and red in the face by the time I reached the rock-line, but I felt a sense of satisfaction at having overcome the earlier breathless feeling and made it onto the mountain. When I located the hole and peered down into it, however, it looked a lot deeper and more treacherous than I remembered from first scouting it out.

The rim of the hole had an apron of ferns and heather growing around it that served to conceal possible footholds or a handy way to reach the bottom. Taking the rope out of the satchel I searched for the trunk of a tree or a boulder to tie it to. This was easier said than done. The trees were saplings, while the closest boulder proved impossible to lasso.

Then an idea came to me. I carried a heavy stone up

close to a gap in the rock, threaded the rope through the gap, and set about looping the end of the rope around the stone the way my father tied up a parcel in the shop using brown twine. Going around to the other side of the gap, I pulled on the rope. The boulder slid along the ground until it lodged in the gap and wedged tight. I pulled on the rope as hard as I could several times more until I was satisfied the boulder was as sturdy and reliable as an army commando's grappling hook.

Unfurling the rope I carried it to the edge of the pit and allowed the free end to drop into the hole. It ended short of the bottom. But it would have to do. Using both hands I grabbed the rope and began to lower myself into the hole, my back facing out and my feet against the side wall the way a commando would rappel down a cliff face to an enemy gun emplacement.

The first part of the descent proved awkward and slippery. But it didn't take long to lower myself far enough into the hole for my shoulders and head to disappear. The lower I went, unfortunately, the more the sides of the hole angled away from my feet, and I found myself scrabbling for a toehold.

It was tough work keeping a grip on the rope. To move my hands I had to slide them one at a time down the rope bearing my weight, getting rope burn from the pressure. I should have knotted the rope at regular intervals to make handgrips. But it was too late, and before I knew it I found myself dangling in mid-air. My neck and shoulders ached, and I was totally dependent on the rope to keep me from falling. But under the pressure of my own weight I couldn't help feeding the rope faster and faster through my burning hands until I was forced to let go.

I hit the bottom, somehow managed to land on my feet, and righted and balanced myself. Craning my neck up

I gauged it must be at least three times my height to the top of the hole. I felt nervous and exhilarated.

The space where I stood was a lot darker than I'd hoped. And even with the rope to help me, getting back up to the surface would be a challenge since the sloping side walls widened out as they descended. And there were large fissures going back into the mountain which made footholds scarce and had caused my feet to find only fresh air while scrabbling downwards.

I'd have to deal with those complications when the time came. But right now I stopped and listened, partly fearful of being discovered and having to explain what I was doing in such an odd place.

In my eagerness to get to the mountain I forgot to bring the flash-lamp, but there was enough natural light, for the moment, to work by. Gathering up the stones under my feet I did my best to fix them into the gaps, first to stop the panther escaping, and second to make sure it couldn't hide in the crevices. I didn't want anyone to think that just because they couldn't see it, the panther wasn't down here if I was lucky enough to trap it.

The job kept me occupied and helped me put to the back of my mind the tricky position I was in. And though I had been sweating earlier I soon cooled off and had to keep my jacket on working in the dank dim conditions just like a coal pit.

It took a couple of attempts to build, with the rocks available to me, anything resembling secure dry-stone plugs for the gaps between the upright slabs. But I got the job done.

Sizing up the climb back towards the daylight I took hold of the end of the rope. It would have been better if the rope had been longer and I could tie it around me now in case I lost my grip. I should have thought of that, too.

As it was, I found when I pulled my weight upwards I hadn't enough strength in my upper body to lever myself up the rope the way every action hero I knew of could, able to scale the sides of buildings without the slightest bother.

I dropped back to the floor of the pit and tried again. The rope had a life of its own and seemed determined to wriggle out of my grasp. Little prickles of panic began to tell me I was in trouble: I'd lowered myself into a trap I hadn't the ability to escape.

Reconsidering what to do, I decided to climb up the side of the pit without using the rope. It was tricky but not impossible, and although I couldn't trust the soft, slimy foliage to use as handholds I made better progress climbing free-style than with the rope.

Using even the smallest ledge or pointed stone for support I employed my elbows and even my chin to keep my balance while pressing tightly up against the side wall, taking a breather and then wriggling cautiously higher with my muscles aching from the contortions needed to keep moving upwards.

It felt like I was wrestling with myself as my arms, my legs, my chest and even my head got in my own way. And I had to grit my teeth and try not to despair.

I was well on my way towards the top when I suddenly realised that further progress was not possible from my position. Taking another breather to consider, the rope, now, seemed to offer the best chance of getting unstuck. I reached out to grab hold of it.

Big mistake.

The rope swung away from me the instant I grabbed hold, I lost my balance and toppled into empty space.

My one thought was that at least I'd cleared the stones off the floor and I wouldn't be landing on a pile of rocks. But the impact jolted and winded me and my head jerked back and cracked off the side wall.

The pain was so far off the scale I felt it only as a blinding light: a detonation inside my head like a brilliant Atom bomb blast swelling upwards as the rings of energy around the base of the mushroom cloud engulfed me in a hurricane of hot agony.

Instead of being crisped to a cinder though, a sick feeling rose from the bottom of my stomach making me want to throw up. This would be what advanced radiation sickness felt like, only unlike my nightmare nuclear attack where I had the power to try and act to save myself; I was paralysed and couldn't stir a muscle.

The pain and shock from the sudden fall eclipsed the ringing in my ears for a time, but as the pounding pain began to blast my eardrums I knew that other sounds too were escaping from my lips. Moans and groans. My legs and arms arranged themselves awkwardly, like a broken puppet. Any attempt to stir caused my surroundings to crack and splinter into shifting streamers of light and coloured spots.

I must have lost consciousness and then somehow come round again. My eyes rolled towards the mouth of the pit. The brightness of the light made it hard to see but I sensed a presence above my head. A black shape looked down on me as it circled the rim of the pit.

Whatever it was moving up there, it looked weirdly flattened out, like a shadow; only this shadow had two blazing eyes. It opened its mouth full of glistening white incisors and cried out in terrible triumph at having cornered me in the very spot where I had foolishly thought to trap it.

I watched the dark outline of the panther pad around the rim of the pit, a hungry, sleek prowling jungle cat drawn by the smell of the blood that must be pumping from my head. I was its helpless quarry now. All the panther had to do was jump down on top of me where I lay and rip me asunder with its ferocious teeth and powerful claws and make a meal of my inner organs and then rest by the bloodied leftovers of my corpse purring with contentment. And it served me right.

Why had I ever believed I could use this damp useless hole in the ground to capture such a fantastically clever, beautiful and deadly creature?

TWENTY TWO

The dazzling brightness of the sky behind the panther began to fade. The big cat moved out of sight. Sensations of cramp and pressure returned to my limbs. There seemed to be gaps in the stages of coming round fully to my senses as I blacked out and revived again, with each return to consciousness bringing power back to my limbs.

A creeping cold seeped into my bones, and I felt numb more than grievously injured, although the pain level shot up each time I tried to stir. At last I managed to move one leg, and then an arm and my neck.

However serious my injuries I wasn't paralysed, and I comforted myself with the thought that I'd gotten a harder knock the day I'd been pitched over the handlebars of my bicycle while learning to cycle.

Now when I moved my head the streamers of Atom bomb bright light began to fade into ordinary grey daylight.

The only reason I could figure out why the panther hadn't jumped down into the hole and eaten me alive was that either it believed I was dead, and it only went for fresh kills; or more likely it decided if it jumped down into the pit after me it wouldn't be able to get back out. Especially if it wanted to drag away what was left of my carcass to dine on later.

I'd been spared from the panther but I was still faced with getting out of this treacherous deep hole in the ground that threatened to become my ready-made grave.

It made sense not to move any time soon with the panther waiting up above. And with time on my hands I began to plot a better alternative to my first effort. There was a series of footholds and handholds I could use that I hadn't taken full account of before. First, I had to find a way back onto my feet. And it was the need to keep the newly worked out plan of escape clear in my mind that finally drove me to shift position and attempt to stand up and see if I could straighten my spine.

The seriousness of my situation gave me greater focus and a new determination. And even though my head hurt, and my body ached, I not only got to my feet, I climbed steadily and methodically back out of the hole in one strenuous effort.

I stopped only when I neared the top to improve my footing and chance taking a peek above the rim. With one swipe of its waiting claws, or a lung at my windpipe, the panther could take my life. And it was with the greatest of care I inched my head out of the hole.

A cautious three-hundred and sixty degree sweep of the terrain revealed no trace of the panther. That didn't mean to say it wasn't hiding behind a boulder or crouched down in the heather. But seeing no trace of movement, and having clambered successfully near the opening of the hole, I had no choice but to climb clear the rest of the way and take my chances out in the open.

Gaining the upper world again I rested for a second on my hands and knees. I felt shaky and weak with relief. The danger remained that the panther was close by, hanging back until it had me in plain view. But if it suddenly reappeared and came bounding towards me I could probably grab hold of the rope and drop myself down into the pit again where hopefully the panther still wouldn't be prepared to follow.

In spite of the danger of encountering the panther I didn't feel like hanging around. And when I had enough strength in my legs I took off, hobbling at first but picking up speed as I put more distance between me and the hole. And it was only when I reached the Bog Lane and began running hard for home I realised I'd left my satchel and the rope behind.

By the time I reached the Top Road I felt out of danger. The panther must have gone off looking for an easier kill. And in place of fear for my life I began to feel foolish and conspicuous. My jacket was scuffed, but thankfully not torn. And there had to be blood in my hair and on my face.

I really did not want to attract attention to the state I was in since it was entirely my own fault. I could already hear my mother saying, 'Well, isn't this a nice how-do-you-do?'

Bernice and Frank Welcome might be back by now and he was bound to know a thing or two about first aid. He could patch me up. So instead of turning for the house I forked right after Chapel Hill and took a short cut through the siding.

As I crossed the weighbridge its massive cast iron bulk stirred under my feet like a steel barge on water. I crossed the coal yard into the shadows of the bunkers and the heaps of stockpiled coal. Most days there would be lines of Volkswagen cars with small trailers hitched to the back and tractors with transport boxes and plenty of asses and carts too, all queuing to load up with coal. Today, being Sunday, there were none of the usual figures bent over the coal heaps removing slates and stones by hand to pick out the best slabs and lumps of good coal before returning to the weighbridge and taking their hand-picked loads of fuel home.

Technically I was trespassing, but I didn't think anyone would mind me visiting the siding as long as it was clear I was passing through and not playing games around the dangerous bunkers and heavy machinery or trying to steal coal.

At the far end of the siding I stood on top of the derelict reservoir wall to look into the bottomlands by the river. I could see Frank Welcome's tent but there was no sign of the green army Land Rover parked in the field.

Disappointed, I left the wall and slithered down the embankment through thick undergrowth, getting stung by nettles. I felt too dazed to care about the stings or to search for a dock leaf to rub on them to ease the pain. Allowing my feet to carry me I followed the riverbank and reached the bridge without meeting anyone. Crossing the road quickly I dropped out of sight again to make my way under the alder trees overhanging the river which ran clear and peaceful in the shade.

Entering the back garden through the hole in the hedge, I followed the path between the ridges where Daddy's potatoes and onions grew. More than likely the bolt would be off the back door since Mammy had her washing hung out to dry on the line. And spotting her laundry basket with one lot of dry clothes fresh off the line resting on the ground beside the outhouse I was on the alert as I dodged behind a stack of wooden crates full of empty mineral and porter bottles.

I did not want my mother seeing me until I could inspect for myself the extent of my injuries. Using the stack of crates for cover I edged along the space between them and the back wall of the house.

"Oh Monica!" a man said.

He was breathing hard and he sounded like he was running up a hill.

"Stop," I heard my mother say, but not like she meant it.

"Don't worry," the man said, his voice dropping to a husky whisper.

The voices fell silent and I edged closer to the doorway of the outhouse used to store porter kegs and the crates with the full bottles, which were kept under bolt and padlock. The lock was off now and the door stood open an inch or two. I flattened myself against the wall and edged forward.

To avoid being spotted I kept my head level with the ground. It was the only way to avoid blocking the light, since any change in brightness might alert them to my presence. Hunkering down, with my head bent sideways and my ear almost brushing the ground I chanced a careful peek. Straight away I caught sight of my mother standing with her back to the door. Eugene McPadden stood directly behind her.

He had one arm around her chest and his hand was moving inside the top of her dress where the buttons must be undone. He had his other hand down lower, moving out of sight under her hiked-up skirt. He kept pressing himself up tightly against my mother who tilted her head back allowing him to kiss her bare neck. She was breathing hard through her mouth and her hair fell into his face.

It made me feel sick with shame and anger. But I felt an ugly fascination, too, and could never until this moment have imagined my mother allowing anyone to maul her that way, not even my father. Disgusted and fascinated, I got so carried away watching what they were up to that when Eugene shifted to bring my mother around to face him, wanting to kiss her full on the mouth, I was too transfixed to move.

The eyes of a cobra ready to strike could not have rooted its victim more completely to the spot as I froze where I lay, knowing I was about to be caught red-handed. My mother was bound to see me the instant she turned around and our lives would be changed forever in a flash. And it would be my fault because I was too stunned to move.

Only my mother didn't want to turn around to face Eugene. Instead she gripped his hand harder and began to show him how she wanted it to move under her skirt, moaning and breathing hard and telling him, "Don't stop."

Eugene grimaced at being handled so firmly. But he did what she wanted him to do, and she began to wriggle more energetically, squirming and pressing her hips back tighter against him. And although I wanted with all my heart to put a stop to what they were doing, I understood that making it known I'd caught them in the act would do far greater harm than any Atom bomb going off.

I drew back and got to my feet. In place of the disgust and horror I felt an uncontrollable fury. I had to do something to release my pent up rage over what I'd witnessed, so I deliberately put my shoulder to the stack of crates next to me, bringing it down and causing crates and bottles to spill and smash loudly across the yard.

With the racket of the toppled crates ringing in my ears, I ran for cover through the hole in the hedge to reach the river before my mother or Eugene could muster themselves and find out how the yard ended up littered with fallen crates and broken glass.

The sound of shattering glass was replaced by silence as

I backtracked along the river bank as far as the bridge, crossed the road like a convict newly broken out of jail, and darted for cover again feeling alone and hunted. Adopting a running crouch I came to the fording place where I crossed the river and headed directly for Frank Welcome's tent. I was raging with my mother and Eugene, but I was glad I'd found a way to give them a hop and break them up.

When I reached the tent under the hawthorn hedge I pulled the pegs out of the ground holding down the front flap and opened up the ties keeping the door closed and went inside.

It was as muggy as a greenhouse under the canvas but I felt comfort hiding there. I considered lighting the lamp; only I had such a headache I decided against it. Feeling as though I was about to pass out, I went straight over to the cot and lay down. My head throbbed and my ribs and knees were sore, my feet and lower legs were soaking and I'd gotten more nettle stings and briar scratches, but all I wanted to do was close my eyes in the only safe retreat I had left.

TWENTY THREE

I woke to find Frank standing over me and Bernice along with him looking anxiously down into my face. Feeling groggy, I tried to smile but my mouth was dry and my face felt numb. Bernice bent down beside me and put her soft cool hand on my forehead.

"What happened to you?"

"I saw the panther," I said.

"Where?" Frank asked.

It was time to come clean and I told him about my trap on the mountain and about losing my grip on the rope and banging my head when I fell. Frank looked at Bernice and nodded towards the tent door. I understood he wanted her to step outside to discuss what to do about me.

On the opposite side of the canvas they kept their voices down, but by closing my eyes and concentrating I could make out Frank saying, "He needs to go home."

"He's upset," Bernice said, "And for some reason he's relying on you."

"What do you want me to do?"

"Let him hang on here for a while."

Frank didn't speak.

"Please," she said.

From the intimate noises Bernice and Frank made next I guessed they were kissing. And I screwed my eyes shut tighter to avoid thinking about what my mother and Eugene McPadden had been getting up to.

Bernice and Frank fell quiet. Soon all I could hear was the gentle flapping of the tent fabric in the light summer breeze. It made me feel sleepy again and I was strongly tempted to nod off. When I opened my eyes Frank was pouring warm water from the kettle into the basin he used for shaving. He found a clean hanky to dab away the mud around my head wound. Next he got a bottle of liquid iodine and dabbed it around the cuts and scratches on my hands, leaving them as stained and yellow as a smoker's fingers.

"It's a bump more than a gash on the back of your head," he said. "So you'll have bruising but you won't need stitches."

"I'm feeling better already," I said. "And please don't tell anyone what happened."

Again I noticed Frank and Bernice trading private glances.

"If you feel a headache coming on, or if you get drowsy again," he said "you're going to have to see a doctor. You might have concussion."

I wanted allies badly and I promised I'd warn them if I started to feel poorly.

The short rest calmed and steadied me and the pain from the bang on my head was almost gone. I'd been more shocked than injured by the fall. Back on my feet I was excused from duty as I watched Bernice make tea that Frank insisted I drink with extra sugar and he also gave me several fig-roll biscuits.

By the time we closed up the tent and left the field in

Frank's Land Rover I felt almost back to myself. Now it was nervous pressure I felt. I did not want to meet my mother. I felt myself growing queasy and light-headed at the memory of what she and Eugene had been up to, and the shaky feeling increased wondering how long this had been going on behind everyone's back until I found them out.

"Leo," Bernice said, "You're as white as a sheet."

"Is the pain in your head back?" Frank asked, concerned.

"I'm all right," I said half-heartedly opening the passenger door and climbing out of the Land Rover to face the music.

Bernice went into the pub first, then Frank and then me.

It was my father and not my mother behind the bar.

"There you are," Daddy said when he spotted me. But he had nothing further to add and turned back to the shelves to fill a whiskey from the optic for Red Paddy Reynolds. It dawned on me my whereabouts hadn't crossed his mind the whole day.

"Where's Mrs Rossiter?" Bernice asked.

"She went to bed with a headache. She'll be down later."

A twitch started in my right eyelid. Bernice noticed it and said, "Are you sure you're not having one of your attacks?"

I shook my head. "I'm going to have a bath," I said.

While I moved to enter the house, Bernice took a seat across from the television to wait while Frank ordered two lemonades, their day together not finished yet.

A quick peek out the kitchen window into the back yard revealed how no effort had been made to tidy up the fallen crates, and I felt guilty seeing the empty bottles and broken glass scattered about the place, knowing the disarray was my doing.

With the stopper firmly fitted into the plughole in the bath I left both taps on full while I got out of my clothes. Feeling a stickiness that seemed to penetrate deep under my skin I opened a jar of bath salts and poured a good half into the water instead of relying on the bar of soap. The hotter the water, too, the better, and when the bath was full enough it took me a good minute to immerse myself fully in the scalding, frothy water.

Sinking slowly downwards, I let the hot water cover my shoulders to the point where the suds lapped around my chin. Then I raised my hand and cautiously touched my fingers to the wound on the back of my head, which felt raw and tender but hadn't drawn the attention I'd feared. I stayed in the bath until the iodine stains were gone and the water cooled down. Then I drew a deep breath, shut my eyes tight and went fully under. When my head came up again the water streamed out of my hair and I shampooed and rinsed it clean.

By the time I had dried myself off, an edgy and restless feeling kept bringing to mind my mother's wriggling and moaning and wanting Eugene's hands on her body. It disturbed and repelled me to think of it, but I understood how this craving could blind a person to everything but the hunger for satisfaction, since all I wanted was to get back to Bernice. I buttoned down the collar of my best shirt, straightened my tie and put on my good shoes from Tylers. My thoughts were in a whirl, but looking smart at least gave me a sense of control.

The public bar downstairs had filled with younger pitmen. They too were spruced up in their best clothes, getting ready to go to the Silver Slipper Ballroom in Drumshanbo. When I joined Bernice and Frank I found him trying to convince her to take advantage of her night off and join the crowd headed for the ballroom.

"It's a mad place," she said.

"When were you there?" he asked.

"I hear the stories."

"Well let's go and see if they're true."

"Could I come?" I asked.

"You're too young," Bernice said. "They wouldn't let you inside the door."

After the effort I'd made to look as grown up as possible it stung me to hear her call me too young, though she was right of course.

"So you're thinking about it at least," Frank said.

"Only if we can go soon and get back early."

"Deal," said Frank.

Despite my longing to stay close to Bernice it was clear I ought to leave her and Frank alone. And the jumble in the back yard troubled me. It had been a stupid, vindictive and bad-tempered thing to knock down those crates. So, I quit the bar and went out to the back yard and got hold of a brush and the navvy shovel.

Having lifted aside the fallen crates, I tackled the broken glass. There were scattered shards everywhere, and I had to pick up the ladder used to erect the television aerial on the chimney and rest it against the edge of the flat roof to get it out of the way. The sorting, the sweeping, and the tidying were hard work, but it satisfied me putting order on the mess. After about an hour, with the crates built into neater stacks than before, Bernice came outside to find me.

"Try this," she said handing me a motorbike crash helmet.

"Where did you get it?" I asked, catching an unwholesome whiff off the greasy, padded lining.

"It belongs to Red Paddy. He left it behind when his

bike caught fire."

"I'm not wearing it."

"It's only to get you past the doorman into the Silver Slipper."

"Really?"

"I know what goes on behind the ballroom," she said. "But if you're with me Frank can't try on too much hanky-panky."

I hardly heard her reasons for wanting me along, knowing only that when we were together we gave each other courage.

A short time later, if Frank Welcome was annoyed to find me playing gooseberry, he didn't mention it as we drove into town. In fact he wanted me to tell him about the panther sighting, and whether I was still certain I'd come face to face with the creature.

"If Leo says he saw the panther, I believe him," Bernice said.

While I was grateful for her faith in me, I confessed I couldn't be absolutely certain what happened. As much as I wanted to believe what I'd seen, I'd been out cold after the fall, and the panther appeared only briefly as I came around. Maybe I wasn't fully conscious and, come to think of it, there were aspects of the animal's appearance that matched how things looked in my dreams about nuclear attacks. So maybe I had only dreamt it.

"You took a hard knock," Frank said. "But it's possible you stumbled on this wildcat's hunting grounds."

"We could leave some meat out and see if it comes back," I said, wanting the panther to be real.

"A pot roast from Ambrose Luck," Frank said.

"I'd say his meat would be too tough even for the panther," Bernice joked.

She was in high spirits and giddy, probably thinking

about where we were headed. And I felt a gathering excitement too, stronger even than the thrill of having enlisted Frank Welcome's help to lure the panther into my trap on the mountain to catch it alive and not have to shoot it.

By the time we arrived at the Ballroom the regular Sunday night dance goers' cars were parked in orderly lines out front. Where the cars ended the rows of Honda motorbikes began, the tail end of the line made up of bicycles. A Volkswagen mini-bus stopped near the front door to offload a gang of girls from Carrigallen. Most Sunday nights the management ended up having to turn away people it got so crowded, Bernice said, but we should be fine as the busses were only starting to arrive. I fitted the reeking crash helmet, mindful of the bruise on my forehead.

"Try these," said Frank, passing me his sunglasses.

He led the way, I followed, and Bernice took up the rear. The man at the ticket hatch hardly looked at us. Frank got the tickets and passed one to me and Bernice. Next we met a man called McGuinness, the head bouncer; beefy and pink and squashed into a black tuxedo with a thin dickey-bow knotted tight under a triple row of chins. He was too busy chatting up the Carrigallen girls to take any notice of me. A second burly bouncer, also wearing a black suit and dickey-bow, stood alongside a lanky man in a dress-suit collecting tickets. With the helmet and the sunglasses to hide my age I kept my head down, and had just got past the ticket collector when I felt a tap on my shoulder. I stood stock still, my hopes dashed, ready to be ejected.

"Check the helmet into the cloakroom," the ticket collector said.

"I'll see to it," Bernice said and put her arm around me so we entered the ballroom together like girlfriend and boyfriend.

TWENTY FOUR

The dance floor was almost empty with most of the men lined up three deep against the left-hand wall, while the girls stood against the opposite wall across the divide where a few couples stood at a loss out on the floor waiting for the band to play.

I took off the helmet.

"It might be safer to leave it on," Gerry McPadden said.

He'd been standing near the door watching us come in.

"Why's that?" Frank asked.

Bernice said, "The lads from Arigna only take a break between fights for a dance."

"And there's a gang in tonight from Dowra," Gerry said. "So a man could get a chance to redden his knuckles yet."

Watching Gerry's eyes dart around the ballroom it struck me how his bragging and posturing was a way of covering up exactly the kind of nervousness I felt, especially in front of the daunting ranks of partner-less girls watching our every move from the other side of the room.

I could smell beer on Gerry's breath as he started to

tell Bernice about Mossy Beirne.

"Mossy had a rake of pints downtown," Gerry said. "And he wasn't in the door five minutes when he knew he was going to be sick. He made a run for the toilets and only got his head inside a cubicle when he threw up – but wasn't there a Dowra man there already sitting on the toilet."

Gerry had to wipe a tear from his eyes he was laughing so hard at his own story.

"So Mossy sees this man with his trousers down around his ankles covered in sick but getting to his feet fast. And he draws out and hits him a box."

"Ah no!" said Bernice.

"He knew if the other fellah got the chance to come after him he'd kill him," Gerry said, "so Mossy floored him first."

Even as Gerry said this I spotted a Dowra lad bump his shoulder off an Arigna pitman standing near the men's toilet door. Without a doubt there was trouble brewing between the two factions.

We began to move off.

"Give us a dance later, Bernice," Gerry said.

She said, "Gerry, I'm with Frank."

I wished she'd said she was here with me and Frank, but I took the hint.

Leaving the two of them in peace I moved off towards the stage where the band had started to take their places. They were a bunch of older men dressed in identical blue suits: a drummer and a saxophone player and two men with guitars and a lead singer. They started to play. The short-winded saxophone player's swollen face soon turned a spectacular range of colours as he belted out a big-band medley. Then the singer grabbed the microphone and launched into a passable imitation of Bill Haley's 'Rock around the Clock'.

The empty floor filled up with energetic dancers while I stayed close to the stage amongst the fans shouting encouragement at the singer. I could smell talcum powder and sweat and eau de Cologne. The walls turned clammy with condensation. After a couple of numbers, and to look less conspicuous, I headed for the back of the ballroom, climbed the stairs up to the balcony, and crossed to the mineral bar. Waiting my turn to get served helped to pass the time, and I was in no hurry to catch the attention of the big-chested woman behind the counter. Eventually I exchanged a fistful of coins for a bottle with a paper drinking straw stuck in the glass neck. I took the drink away in my hand.

The best view of the dancing was from the front of the balcony. Leaning my elbows on the guardrail I sipped from the bottle of Cidona and watched the action below. The floor was full now of jiving couples and the glittering mirror balls in the ceiling sent sparkles swirling around the sweltering hot room.

Without wanting to be obvious I inspected the wallflowers left standing on both the men's and the women's sides of the dance floor. It was mainly men because the women who hadn't been asked to dance were willing to get out and jive with their women friends whereas the men resolutely held their lonely ground. I spotted Bernice happily dancing with Frank. He didn't seem to have a whole lot to do to keep her pleased, mostly he held out his arm and encouraged her energetic whirl and twirl around him.

The man standing beside me at the rail moved off and I found myself next to Gerry. He'd been standing there the whole time watching Frank and Bernice. Now he moved closer to me and said, "Tell Welcome to watch his step. The Dowra lads think he's with us."

"You'd better tell him yourself."

Even though no alcohol was being served Gerry must have his own supply because he wasn't as sober as he'd been earlier.

I waited where I stood another minute or so, and when it was clear Gerry didn't intend to move on I went back downstairs. At the foot of the stairs I met Bernice and Frank holding hands. They'd just come off the dance floor.

"Give us a swig," Bernice said, "I'm boiling."

I handed her the mineral bottle and she put the straw to her lips. One of the Dowra lads coming down the stairs shouldered Frank. The impact caused him to bump into Bernice and splash the mineral.

"Watch it," he said.

"You watch it," the Dowra lad said back.

"Mind who you're talking to," Gerry McPadden cut in. "That man is just back after fighting in the Congo."

"Is that right," the Dowra lad said. "Tell him if he gets in my way again tonight he'll hear three bangs. He'll hit into me. I'll hit him back. And he'll hit the floor."

Gerry scoffed and said, "I seen bigger men on top of a wedding cake."

The Dowra lad jerked his head and said, "Outside."

Bernice handed back the mineral and tried to lead Frank away, "Let's go," she said.

Nothing further might have happened only Gerry shouted to Frank loud enough for the Dowra lad to catch the insult, "Pass no heed, he was never more than a mile from a cow-dung in his life."

Straightaway the Dowra lad threw a punch at Gerry. Gerry deflected the blow with his shoulder and struck back with a left hook that caught his opponent squarely on the chin and sent him back reeling.

A second Dowra lad lunged at Frank who swivelled

sideways and grabbed the outstretched arm. Yanking the arm swiftly downwards he used his opponent's momentum to flip him right over so he cart-wheeled like a circus acrobat doing the wildcat and landed flat on his back at Frank's feet.

"The bacon is no match for the slicer," Gerry shouted impressed, just as McGuinness arrived, grabbed the first Dowra lad by the scruff of the neck and pulled him backwards so hard his feet left the ground.

The scuffle at the foot of the stairs alerted the other lads from Dowra who began to move in a line through the dancers towards the action only to find their path blocked by an opposing line of Arigna pitmen, made up mostly of the parish football team and headed up by Mossy Beirne who drunkenly shouted, "The rebel hand was raised, and the heather blazed."

Bouncers in their black suits and dickey-bows arrived from every corner of the ballroom. Frank put his arm around Bernice and guided her swiftly around by the side of the stairs to leave by the front door. I took a step back but collided with the bottom step of the stairs and fell backwards into a sitting position just as a bottle thrown from the balcony whizzed past, narrowly missing my head and hopped off the wall without breaking.

The fight moved to the middle of the floor as the music stopped, the stage emptied and the band withdrew to the supper room.

I caught sight of Mossy Beirne being taken in hand by McGuinness. "I have me man," McGuinness shouted and skull-dragged Mossy towards the exit.

Before the same thing happened to me, and anxious not to lose track of Bernice and Frank, I abandoned the helmet in the cloakroom and followed Mossy and McGuinness out the main door.

A sizeable crowd milled about the car park waiting until the fight ended before they'd pay to go inside. But I came on another fight outside. For several minutes I stood and watched two grown men grunt and roll around on the ground, their shirts bunched, their midriffs exposed. Then a split appeared in the backside of one man's trousers as the whole seam burst. The onlookers, gathered in a loose ring around the fierce fighters, cheered and shouted encouragement and held back third parties to allow the two men to sort out their differences between themselves.

When I'd seen enough I went looking for the Land Rover which was easy to pick out in the line of regular cars. Bernice and Frank were in the front, necking. In fact, their faces were glued together and Frank had his arms around Bernice, embracing her shoulders as their kissing continued.

I might as well have been kicked in the stomach by one of the Dowra lads the sight of their passionate kisses hit me so hard. I didn't want to break them up, however, I wanted to trade places with Frank. That I hadn't found a way before tonight to kiss Bernice the way he was kissing her right now proved I was too young and immature to know how to turn wishful thinking into action. So while I wished with all my heart Bernice had never set eyes on Frank Welcome in the first place, most of all I wanted to be him.

TWENTY FIVE

When we got back to Arigna, my mother was up and dressed and back in charge of the bar. Why she supposed she could curb me anymore when she couldn't control herself, I couldn't say, although I expected her to leather into me straight away for going to the Silver Slipper without her consent, and for wangling admission into the ballroom while underage.

She noted my arrival, and fixed her eyes on me tightly; her restraint more disconcerting than an immediate telling off.

"Do you know who knocked over the stack of bottles in the yard?" she asked.

"No," I said, and felt the heat rise in my face.

The lobes of her ears, too, coloured red.

When you do not want to acknowledge what you have solemn grounds for believing to be true, the easiest option is to act like nothing is going on. And as full disclosure would have untold repercussions for both of us, we stood there blankly staring at each other until a customer hailed her to order a drink and the stand-off ended with nothing said.

Frank and Bernice took seats in the upper corner of the American Lounge within sight of the table where the regular Sunday night game of poker was about to start. It was a relief to have other things going on besides having to get used to Frank and Bernice as a couple, and the contest of wills between me and my straying mother while Eugene darted glances in her direction. So I was happy to shift my attention onto the card game.

The usual players were already in their usual places. Eugene McPadden sat at the top of the table. He had an empty chair on his left where his son Gerry would join the game later after he got back from town. Doctor Ballintine sat on Eugene's right. Tommy 'the Twin' Leonard sat on the left. Tommy was a pitman, but a quiet sort with a high voice who bet carefully and only ever drank tea while his twin brother Timmy Leonard, on a high stool at the counter, drank enough for both of them. The fourth player was Johnny 'Click', so called because of his badly fitting dentures.

It was early in the night yet so my father had a place at the table. He would play for an hour or so and then quit whether or not he was losing or winning. Nobody minded since any winnings he took away early one night would be matched another night by his losses. And it would be hours after my father left the table before the betting got high, and play could stretch on until one or two or even three o'clock in the morning, with the seriously high stakes games finishing at first light.

Returning with a mineral each for me and Bernice, but a whiskey for himself, Frank said, "I'm feeling lucky tonight."

"The cheek of you," said Bernice.

I got the joke, but kept my mouth shut, keeping tabs on my mother and Eugene.

"I'm going to ask if I can join the game," Frank said nodding towards the poker players.

"Don't," Bernice said. "Eugene McPadden cheats. And he doesn't like seeing you with me when he thinks I should be going out with Gerry. So you're never going to win."

"If I can figure out how he cheats then he might be stopped."

Bernice said, "Even if you catch him at it, Frank, he'll get you back another way."

Eugene went to the bar to order a drink where my mother pretended not to notice him. Did she regret losing the run of herself with him earlier? Had the threat of being so nearly caught in the act brought her to her senses? She had definitely cooled off, for even though Eugene tried to get her attention she let Bernice serve him.

"How do you cheat?" I asked.

Frank's eyes were on the poker players and he said, "Sorry – what did you say?"

"How is Eugene able to cheat at poker?"

"Well, he could have something like a cigarette case on the table to catch a reflection of the cards as he's dealing," Frank said. "That's known as a shiner. Or it could be a pub mirror somewhere behind the other players or a reflection in picture glass giving away what cards they're holding."

"I can watch out for that kind of stuff," I said, realising how keenly I wanted Frank to take on Eugene at his own game and give him his comeuppance.

"Or he could be using marked cards," Frank said. "That's not too hard to spot either if there's a pinch or a nick with a fingernail at the edge of a high card or the pattern on the back is faded from rubbing in a certain spot."

"But if it's so easy to spot, why has no one ever caught Eugene out before?" Bernice asked.

"In a regular Sunday night game," Frank said, "someone like Eugene could have gotten the other players used to seeing him hold his cards below the table from time to time. Then it's a simple matter to slip an ace or a king between his legs and the seat of his chair. Or maybe he folds but only throws four cards back into the pile instead of five. That's another way to build up a spare supply of high cards. You need to insist that everyone keeps their hands above the table at all times. But the real problem is that you have to be completely certain you know what's going on before you call another player a cheat straight to his face. If there's collusion between two or more players then it's even harder to expose one of them. They could be using secret signals like the angle of one another's heads or a finger tapped to an earlobe to trade information. And even if nobody is cheating, where you have a regular school of poker with everybody knowing one another, an outsider like me is always at a disadvantage."

"So stay out of it," said Bernice.

Frank looked at her directly, like a man who wanted to tell her about the dossier he was holding on Eugene and Gerry, but he couldn't bring himself to say it – perhaps because I was there along with them. He had no way of knowing I already knew, and this was not a good time or place for either of us to show our hands.

"I don't want you worrying or getting upset by anything I do tonight," Frank said to Bernice, speaking slowly and picking his words carefully. "The stakes could go high, and I might even have to lose to flush out the kind of banknotes Eugene might be carrying. Is that clear?"

Bernice said, "Have you a gambling problem – is that it?"

"It's nothing like that," he said. "But it might look that way."

He stood up and went straight over to the poker players. My father smiled and offered the newcomer a place at the table.

"I might as well help your mother behind the bar," Bernice said lifting her unfinished mineral. I could read the upset in her face though she didn't want to show it.

Even though Bernice had left, I decided to sit tight and see how Frank got on.

The seat my father gave him meant Frank had his back turned to me. And the first thing I did was check for mirrors or pictures that could potentially reveal to Eugene what cards he might be holding. The surroundings looked innocent and the likelihood was that Eugene had some other craftier method of cheating.

Pretending not to be interested, I strained to hear Eugene tell Frank, "Draw Poker, jacks or higher to open."

The men around the table opened their wallets and left money on the table. Mainly coins.

"Is everyone in?" Daddy asked.

Eugene took the pack in his hand and dealt everyone five cards smartly and swiftly face down on the table with no trace I could detect of a shiner to catch a glimpse of the cards as they left the deck. There was no monkey business either slipping cards off the bottom. And the cards looked clean and new.

I got up and began to gather empty glasses from the surrounding tables. The change of angle allowed me to observe Frank's face as he picked up his cards. To my way of thinking, at least, his expression gave nothing away. He didn't move his cards around in his hand either, arranging them in value and suits, the way I'd done in games of poker played for matchsticks against my father at Christmas, which he told me after we finished playing was a dead giveaway I was aiming either for pairs or a run.

Nobody had a jack to start, and it went to a third deal before Frank finally opened the bidding by throwing in a shilling. Doctor Ballintine was a cautious but decisive player while Tommy the Twin was annoyingly slow to make up his mind. Johnny Click licked his dentures and said, "I'm in". Play was good natured, and at the finish Frank Welcome won with a pair of jacks and a pair of twos.

Daddy and Johnny Click folded early again in the next game, with Daddy showing the low cards in his hand and Johnny Click demonstrating his hand was no better. Eugene stayed in, but Frank soon folded. Doctor Ballintine laid out three of a kind.

"Can't top that," said Eugene.

"You didn't get what you were looking for?" Frank remarked.

"Curiosity killed the cat," said Eugene, putting his cards back into the pile unseen.

Daddy puckered his lips and the others did not comment, but the game was developing an edge from the tension between Frank and Eugene.

But it was Doctor Ballintine who did best with a lucky streak. And raking in his winnings he said, "O happy field wherein this fodder grew."

Tommy the Twin dealt next and play went on with the pile of discards growing and the deck shrinking. Apart from Eugene making it clear he would do the newcomer Frank no favours, the game went on without incident and I found my eyes wandering to Bernice.

She caught my eye and came over and stood at my side to watch how Frank was getting on. Doctor Ballintine was still coming out on top. My father added a three-penny bit to the pile of coins. Ballintine raised with a sixpence and said, "I want to see hounds chasing these hares."

Daddy dealt next and this time everybody appeared to

have confidence in the cards they were holding and the betting grew to a sizeable pot. By this stage Frank had already drank two pints of stout and a double whiskey. And when Bernice moved to the table to take an order from the players he asked for another double.

Bernice gave him a cautionary look but he ignored her. At the finish Eugene beat Doctor Ballintine with a pair of kings and a pair of aces.

My father was out of pocket when he stood up and said he was calling it a night. Johnny Click too was having a bad night and so also was Tommy the Twin. But Doctor Ballintine was doing well and Eugene and Frank were about even. All told, the players were equally matched and Frank had settled so comfortably into the game he could have been playing every Sunday night. Yet it was Frank, more than anyone else, who was doing the most drinking and also pushing for a bigger opening ante at every chance.

Engrossed in the poker, and worried that Frank's drinking was making him reckless, I didn't notice my mother standing over me until she said, "Time for bed."

"I don't have school," I said.

"You have bags under your eyes with tiredness," she said. "Now go to bed."

It would be useless to get into an argument with her, and even though I did not want to leave I could find no excuse for staying up longer. On tactical grounds I said goodnight.

Upstairs in my bedroom after I brushed my teeth I draped my clothes carefully over the back of the chair, wound the alarm clock and turned the hand for the alarm to set so I would have roughly an hour's sleep. It was possible my mother would call time before I woke, but if I got up and found the poker game in progress then more than likely that's when the cheating would happen.

TWENTY SIX

The alarm almost rang itself out before I woke and raised my head from the pillow. Momentarily forgetting why I needed to be awake in the small hours, I reached out to silence the alarm bell. My body felt stiff after the fall and the dull pain from the bang to my head had travelled like a crick down into my neck. But I turned back the sheet and got out of bed, rubbed the sleep out of my eyes and dragged on my clothes.

I needn't have worried the bar might have emptied. Although the Sunday evening drinking crowd had thinned, and it was quieter now with the blinds drawn and the lights lowered, the serious drinkers had settled in for the night with double rounds in front of them on the tables. And the poker game was in full swing.

"What are you doing up?" my mother asked when she saw me coming through the door.

I lied and said, "I can't sleep."

She had a load of dirty glasses piled up around the sink behind the counter and I moved to help her, plunging glasses into the water and working them up and down on the cleaning brush fitted into the sink directly under the running tap.

Bernice had shown me on the quiet how to pull pints. But my work for the bar had mostly been limited to sorting bottles in the back yard, and occasionally clearing tables in the pub itself. Working behind the bar was a new experience. Mostly, my mother had a policy of keeping me out from behind the counter; as a result of an incident when we first took over the business. As often happened, though I didn't know it at the time, Timmy Leonard had too much drink taken. I had never seen a grown man drunk before and, aged ten at the time, I found myself ready to cry and protest at the sight of an adult with his wits so hopelessly fuddled.

Of course I knew more nowadays about the lively range of behaviours brought on by the alcohol we served, although I never fully got used to pretending I found nothing odd or threatening about the behaviour of slightly less drunken men than Timmy Leonard that first evening, or drunken women either, trying to act like they were completely sober. Not to mention the preference amongst certain pitmen for ignoring the indoor toilets and going outside to piss up against the gable wall, or for lurching out the door to go home and falling drunkenly out of their standing the minute they hit the fresh air.

The job of dousing the smelly spots at the pub gable with Jeyes fluid and hot water from the mop bucket was routine to me now, as was seeing the swift staggers and falls off barstools, and the nonsense roaring and shouting in the street by customers well known for that kind of thing.

As soon as I had a good stock of clean glasses back on the shelf to prove my usefulness, I took up a tray to collect more empties and a cloth to wipe the newly cleared tables. My true purpose of course was to get a look at what was happening at the poker table.

My presence on the edge of the game went unremarked while Frank Welcome won a hand, then lost the next hand and then quickly folded in the game after that. At this stage in the night it was no longer coins but large bank-notes on the table. I wondered how much Frank was responsible for the high stakes. The general run of play appeared to have shifted from Doctor Ballintine to Eugene's favour. And Frank still hadn't found out how Eugene might be cheating because every time there was serious money at stake Eugene hit a winning streak.

The only thing that looked anyways suspicious was the way Eugene had a habit of flicking the cards he intended to get rid of over and back against the gold signet ring on his little finger. The flicking action against the ring could potentially mark certain cards before he returned them to the pile. But I doubted if Frank was even aware of this tell-tale action. He had loosened his tie carelessly and kept brushing away a bothersome strand of stray hair out of his eyes as he bent his head down low and passed the cards out clumsily when it came his turn to deal.

I didn't want to see him making a fool of himself, and I wondered if there was some way I could get a message to him that he needed to quit before he lost all of his money. But before I could think what to do, Gerry McPadden arrived back from the dance.

He entered the bar smiling and nodding like a duck in a downpour making a welcome for himself. When he reached for the edge of the counter he misread the distance and stumbled forward.

Seeing Gerry stumble in, Timmy Leonard said to Red Paddy, "Two o'clock and all is not well."

Ignoring the remark Gerry said, "Give us a pint there, Bernice."

My mother stepped in and said, "I'd say you've had a few already."

"I asked for a pint not an opinion," Gerry said.

My mother held her ground.

"I'm not going to stand here listening to town porter," she said. "Go and calve where you were bulled."

Eugene put his cards down flat on the table and moved towards the counter to rescue his son. Resting his hand on Gerry's shoulder he said, "Give the lad a drink, Monica."

My mother and Eugene locked eyes, a contest of wills going on.

That my mother's authority in this bar could be challenged in even the slightest way made it clear she had lost the power to stop Eugene doing anything he wanted by allowing herself to get involved with him in the way I'd witnessed. The most she could manage was to make her reluctance known as she nodded to Bernice to let Gerry have a drink.

"The problem with these men," Bernice said to me as she set the pint of stout under the tap and began to pour, "is they can drink more than they can hold."

Hearing what she said Gerry asked, "Why are you always so hard on me, Bernice?"

She moved off to serve another customer without answering. I took after her and said, "I'm worried about Frank."

"He's as drunk as a skunk," Bernice said. "And he has everyone around the table betting wads of money."

Frank had warned us he might do something of the sort, but I reckoned Bernice was right and that he'd slipped from pretence into genuine loss of control. To confirm my fears I offered to bring the next tray-full of drinks over to the players.

When I arrived at the table I felt the friction like heat

coming off an open fire. A lot of money was at stake, and I did nothing that might interrupt a crucial moment in the play.

Johnny Click stared at his cards for a full minute before he put down three and Eugene dealt him three new cards. Doctor Ballintine was more decisive and wanted only one card. Tommy the Twin folded, and Frank discarded a single card.

I inched up to Eugene and cautiously put a drink down at his elbow. Under the guise of being extra careful I sneaked a look at what he was holding.

Eugene had the three, four, five and six of diamonds and an eight of spades. With his free hand he drew the eight of spades out of the spread, flicked it over and back across his signet ring and added it to the pile of discards. Clearly he wanted a seven of diamonds to complete a Run, and with four diamonds already he could possibly find himself with a Blue through another diamond.

I moved around to Frank Welcome next, and set down his double whiskey while wishing he wouldn't touch it. When I tried to get a look at the cards in his hand, he was holding them too close to his chest for me to see if he could beat Eugene.

Catching sight of the worried expression on my face Frank lifted his whiskey, knocked a large swallow back and said, "It's all going to plan."

"What plan is that?" Eugene asked.

Frank tapped his finger against the side of his nose.

I felt like screaming at him that with the turn of a card Eugene could find himself with an unbeatable hand.

Any lingering hopes I had that Frank was in command of his senses and preparing to trounce Eugene by winning the biggest pot of the night outright, gave way to a sickening realisation that like many a poor hill-farmer and pitman before him, Frank Welcome had ended up stupidly drunk and totally at Eugene's mercy.

As I waited for the sorry outcome, Gerry left the bar to do a kind of sideways crab-walk across the room and take a seat behind me. Frank shielded his cards and turned and looked at where Gerry had positioned himself.

"I don't like having you at my shoulder," Frank said his voice thick with alcohol.

"A good soldier never looks behind him," Gerry said.

Out of the corner of my eye I spotted Eugene reach quickly under his seat while everyone's eyes were on Gerry.

"Are you still in or folding," Doctor Ballintine asked Frank.

Other drinkers, aware of the rising tension at the poker table, looked from Gerry to Eugene and then back at Doctor Ballintine and Frank.

My mother came out from behind the bar. She approached with the pint in her hand for Gerry but kept her eyes fixed on the card players. Bernice arrived and stood at her shoulder.

Instead of putting the drink down in front of Gerry, my mother stood over him, intending to lure Gerry away to another seat where he couldn't interfere with the poker game. But Gerry had no intention of moving or producing money to pay for his drink.

"I was thinking about joining the army and fighting in the Congo," he said.

My mother said, "Do Gerry – it would spare a good man from having to go."

Doctor Ballintine laughed.

Eugene kept a tight eye on the game and said to Frank, "Are you in or out?"

Frank made a conscious effort to refocus on his cards.

At the same time Gerry got to his feet and reached into

his trousers pocket from which he withdrew a tightly rolled wad of banknotes.

"Count me in," he said.

"Put that away," Eugene told him sharply.

"Your bet," Doctor Ballintine reminded Frank.

"See you and raise you fifty," he said.

"What with?" Eugene asked.

"Steady on," Doctor Ballintine cautioned Eugene.

"You'll get your money," said Frank, "as soon as the bank opens in the morning."

"The rifle," Eugene said, "if you want to see me that is. Or fold right now if you like."

"Hey, Leo," Frank called, producing his keys. "Get the gun out of the back of the Land Rover, and bring it in to me."

"The Carcano?" I said.

"You heard me," Frank said, tossing the keys in my direction.

It was a bad throw and the keys went sailing past me and hit the linoleum tiles and skidded off down the public bar floor.

"Stay where you are," my mother said.

"He's shy a hundred," Eugene said.

"He's too drunk to go near a gun," my mother said. "Cancel the bet."

Neither man looked like he intended to obey.

"Come on lads," Doctor Ballintine said.

"My hundred for your rifle?" Eugene insisted. "And I'll see you."

Frank slowly lowered his cards. He was holding a pair of aces and a pair of eights.

"Ah now!" said Doctor Ballintine.

Johnny Click's dentures popped.

Deliberately lagging behind Frank, Eugene laid out on

the table an ace, two, three, four and five of diamonds.

He'd gotten his Blue.

Yet I knew for definite he'd cheated. He had to have been sitting on spare cards, because even if he'd picked up the ace when he asked for a card, or the two of diamonds, he couldn't have picked up both, and the six of diamonds was no longer in his hand.

Gerry sneered and said, "That's your man now for you, Bernice – all powder and no shot."

Frank sat unmoving at the table with his chin down on his chest like a man who'd been hit over the head. I wanted to console him but I was too annoyed because getting stupidly drunk and betting and losing the rifle was his own fault. He was shell-shocked from the Congo and being off the drink was doing him good – he'd said so himself. So why couldn't he have stuck to his own advice and stayed sober. Although I knew from the way the rope got away from me trying to climb out of that hole on the mountain how speedily even a well laid plan could come unstuck.

"Why did you say 'ah now' when you saw Frank's cards?" I asked Doctor Ballintine

"A pair of aces and a pair of eights, the dead man's hand," Doctor Ballintine said. "It's what Wild Bill Hickock was holding when he got shot."

Eugene shared a sneaky smile with Gerry, and I knew then for certain Frank had been made to look like a fool. The others too must know he'd been tricked but nobody had the courage to object.

Gerry stood with one hand shoved into the front pocket of his trousers to fish for loose coins to pay for the drink my mother kept back. If she had failed to stop the poker game before Frank got fleeced, she meant to reassert her authority by making Gerry pay. Impatiently watching him feel around in his pocket she said, "Is it your money or your mickey you're looking for, Gerry?"

A glint came into Gerry's eye and he said, "Which would you prefer."

The colour left my mother's face. Her head jerked around to look at Eugene, knowing full well he must have bragged.

Eugene understood Gerry had dropped him straight in it, but he didn't get the chance to speak.

"Out," my mother shouted at Gerry. "Do you hear me? You're barred. Don't ever darken the door of this pub again."

"Now hold your horses, Monica," Eugene said.

My mother looked like she was going to round on Eugene next, but the hurt flooded into her eyes and her whole face began to quiver. She quickly passed the drink in her hand to me, turned on her heels and rushed shamefaced into the house through the door marked 'Private'.

"Time now, please," Bernice called. Then turning to Frank Welcome she said, "I expected more from you."

Tommy the Twin, Johnny Click, and Doctor Ballintine looked relieved to be under orders to go home. Others in the bar were also finishing up their drinks and putting on their jackets and coats getting ready to leave.

But Gerry McPadden had slumped down into the seat under the window. I wondered if I should insist on him leaving straight away, since my mother had made it clear he was no longer welcome in the pub. But when I looked at him again his eyes were shut.

"Is he passed out?" Johnny Click asked.

"He's putting on an act," said Doctor Ballintine.

"Well, if he's acting," said Tommy the Twin, "he's not very entertaining."

"Give me a hand." said Eugene, "and I'll link him out

to the car."

The door behind the bar opened, and while I was expecting my mother to reappear, her composure restored, it was my father in his slippers, plaid pyjamas and dressing gown who burst into the room.

My mother must have gone straight to the bedroom and either told him to go downstairs, or else he had come down on his own initiative to find out why she was so upset.

It was the nearest I'd ever seen my father to a raging temper. Quickly taking in the situation he said, "Bernice, help Eugene get Gerry out to the car. Leo, give her a hand. I'm bolting the pub doors so come in around the back when you're done. And Captain Welcome, if you'd be so good as to wait in the kitchen until I have the premises cleared I'll make you a cup of tea."

TWENTY SEVEN

My father opened the pub door and looked up and down the road to see that the coast was clear. The street light at the gable had a halo of mist swirling around it, and the ends of the street were hidden in fog. Apart from the travelling shop and Daddy's Cortina, only Frank Welcome's Land Rover and Eugene McPadden's Volkswagen Beetle stood outside the pub, their outlines blurred. Eugene took hold of Gerry and along with Bernice linked him towards the car. Gerry belched and said, "I have a heartburn you could boil a kettle on."

"Bad porter," Eugene said.

My father had seen enough. He retreated into the pub, closed the door at our backs and fastened the bolts. Straightaway Gerry perked up, not nearly as drunk as he'd been pretending.

"It's a wonder your mammy let you out from under her apron," he said to me.

"That's enough," Bernice told him.

"The stuck up bitch, she can't bar me," he said. "All fur coat and no knickers, is all she is."

"Less of that, Gerry," said Eugene.

Gerry straightened up and the two men moved apart. "You go on," Gerry told his father. "I'll make my own way home."

"Do what you like," Eugene said and turned up the collar of his sheepskin coat. "I'll leave the outside light on."

Chilled at the prospect of Bernice getting stuck with Gerry for the night, I watched helplessly as Eugene got into his car, drove away, and the retreating red tail-lights were swallowed in the gloom.

I looked to Bernice who made a face to say she wasn't happy but she'd manage.

"You go on to bed," she said.

I stood uncertainly for a minute and then, seeing I had no choice, moved off to use the back door to return to the house. Only I didn't go inside. As soon as I turned the corner I tucked myself tight up against the back wall close to where the ladder rested. For a minute the only sound was the electric hum of the fogbound streetlight. A match struck and I caught the smell of cigarette smoke, and felt a stab of envy at Gerry's absolute sense of ownership of the night. I cocked my head and listened hard; worried they might have moved out of earshot.

Then I heard Gerry ask Bernice, "Why won't you go out with me?"

"Because I'm seeing Frank."

"And you think you'll do better with him than me."

Bernice stayed silent.

"I have money too," Gerry said. "See, there's over a hundred in this bundle alone."

"Put your money away, Gerry."

"And I'm getting a car," he said. "I can take us anywhere we want."

"I told you before, Gerry. I haven't a notion of going out with you."

"You'd sooner be going out with a Squaddie who'll end up yet getting lead in his arse."

"He's fun and he's going places."

"And I'm just an ignorant pitman stuck down a coalmine."

"I didn't say that, Gerry."

"It's what you meant though, isn't it?" Gerry said, raising his voice. Then, in a harsh, fast whisper, "Well let me tell you something. I was the one who worked out how to hide the getaway van in Noonan's old pit. Bet you didn't know that, did you?"

"Gerry, I don't want to know," Bernice pleaded.

"Mossy Beirne had the acetylene torch trying to cut off the roof when I got there and said let the air out of the tyres to lower the height of the van, and that's how they were able to make it fit."

"The curse of the seven snotty orphans on you," Bernice cried. "Why did you have to open your mouth?"

"I wouldn't keep a thing like that from you, Bernice. I'm mad about you."

I heard the scuffle of feet and realised she'd broken away from Gerry. With nowhere to run I froze, so when Bernice rounded the corner at speed she ran straight into me.

"Bernice, wait," Gerry called after her out of the fog.

"Go home, Gerry," she shouted, widening her eyes imploringly for me to get out of sight.

An upstairs window rattled and I quickly darted behind a stack of crates as my father stuck his head out the top half of the window.

"Is everything all right, Bernice?"

"Go home, Gerry, like a good man," Bernice said.

My father watched from above until Gerry got the message to move on. As soon as Gerry was safely out of sight I gathered my courage and stepped out from behind the stack of crates. My father looked between Bernice and me more baffled than concerned and said, "Inside, the pair of you."

I followed Bernice into the house by the back door where she immediately spun around and said, "You're not to breathe a word about this to anyone."

I couldn't contain myself and blurted, "But the getaway van is in Noonan's old pit, Gerry said so."

Bernice grabbed the front of my shirt, brought her face up close against mine and said, "Swear to me you'll keep this a secret."

I was too surprised by the strength of her grip to be able to say a word.

"Say 'I swear'."

"I swear," I said helplessly.

"If it ever gets out about the van," she said, "Gerry will know it was me that squealed."

Until she put it that way I hadn't fully realised how forcing his secrets on her gave Gerry a way to entrap Bernice.

We were both breathing hard and I felt almost sick with giddiness at the position we were in. Then all of a sudden Bernice kissed me full on the mouth. Our lips stayed on each other for a kind of kiss I'd never known before in my life, and even when the kiss ended her full moist warm lips were slow to slide off mine. "You're man enough now," she said, "to keep a secret."

TWENTY EIGHT

My father had a light left on in the hallway and on the landing where we met him coming out of the guest bedroom.

"What happened to Frank?" Bernice asked.

"He's out for the count," Daddy said.

I leaned to one side and saw Frank Welcome stretched out on the bed in the guest room wearing his shirt and trousers but with his suit jacket and pointy boots off.

"He can sleep it off here tonight," Daddy said. "You two go to bed and I'll bolt the back door and knock off the lights."

Reluctantly I parted from Bernice. As soon as Daddy finished downstairs I wanted to go to her room. It was time to tell her the truth about Frank. I could also confirm Eugene cheated at the poker game, although it was hardly a revelation on the scale of finding out for definite that Gerry, and his father too more than likely, were accomplices to the robbery. If she wanted to keep the van hidden in the pit a secret she could not breathe a word to Frank; a troubling predicament for her but one that brought the two of us a whole lot closer having such a dangerous secret only we could share.

I switched off the lamp and sat on the edge of the bed in the dark tracking Daddy's movements by the sounds he made downstairs. He turned the key in the lock of the door leading from the house into the public bar, then he slid the top and bottom bolts on the back door in place, and finally he switched off the lights in the hall. At the tread of his slippers on the stairs I lay down and quickly pulled up the covers. My door was open a crack and Daddy came to the threshold, took hold of the handle and closed the door softly. The light went off on the landing.

Smothered by the heat under the bedclothes I felt a rush of tiredness that made me think I should just get undressed and go to sleep. Only I couldn't help fretting that Gerry would regret blabbing his secret to Bernice and move the van to another spot the first chance he got. The only certain way to know the van used by the armed robbers was hidden underground in Noonan's pit would be to find it tonight. And the more I thought about it, the more urgent it grew in my mind to know the truth. If it turned out Gerry had lied, Bernice wouldn't need to worry.

As soon as I was satisfied Daddy had gone to bed I changed into my everyday jeans and the leather jacket, got the flash-lamp out of my locker and took up my shoes in my hand. Easing the bedroom door open I tiptoed the length of the landing in my socks.

Frank Welcome snored loudly in the guest bedroom. Even if I'd wanted to alert him to my plan, he wasn't in a fit state to help. And I had no intention of breaking my promise to Bernice, although I felt a twinge of guilt taking advantage of how badly Frank had slipped up tonight. I paused again outside Bernice's door and considered enlisting her help. The light was off in her room and I could not find the courage to enter and wake her and tell

221

her what I had in mind, knowing she would do everything in her power to stop me.

Instead I moved towards the window at the end of the landing. With the front and back doors bolted and locked it was about the only way out of the house, even if I was bound to make noise opening it.

Luckily the catch wasn't fastened and the window was already open slightly at the bottom to let in air. Even so, a sweat broke out across my forehead and ran down the ridge of my spine, and I had to wipe the damp palms of my hands twice on my trouser legs, before I got the lower half of the window raised high enough to squeeze out through the gap.

With a final glance back down the landing I climbed out onto the flat roof, careful not to snag my trouser leg on the catch. I couldn't risk closing the window after me even if leaving it wide open was a dead giveaway.

Out on the roof I put on my shoes and checked my watch. It was shortly after three in the morning and with luck I would be home again before anyone woke and noticed the open window.

Stealthily moving across the flat roof of the American Lounge I found the ladder propped against the back wall from when I was cleaning up the broken bottles in the yard. I eased myself onto the first rung and it was a simple job to climb down to the ground. Then going around by the gable I felt conspicuous passing under the street light even though the fog was so thick the petrol pump outside the shop was barely visible.

Keeping tight up against the back of the Land Rover I got the set of keys out of my pocket Frank Welcome had tossed to me when he wanted me to fetch the rifle. I fitted the right key into the lock and, knowing there was a slight trick to getting the Land Rover open, jiggled the key until the lock clicked. My chest felt hard with tension. But with a firm hold on the handle I eased the door open, climbed inside and pulled the door almost shut behind me. Crouched down I lifted the army blanket spread over the gear in the back. The Carcano rifle rested in its case. I doubted he'd leave the pistol behind in his tent either, and the leather panniers were stored close to the wheel-well. When I opened the flap and looked inside there were no documents but I spotted the belt, holster and revolver.

Undoing the fastener on the holster I reached for the gun. Taking careful hold of the butt I eased the revolver free. The braided cord uncoiled and I was able to unclip it from where it was hooked to the holster.

The army issue revolver was bigger and heavier than I expected and it did not fit comfortably into my hand. As far as I could tell the chamber carried six live rounds and the safety catch was on. Although I took care not to put my finger inside the trigger guard. The gap between the handle and the curved trigger in any case was far greater than it looked in cowboy and war films. It seemed practically impossible to level such a heavy weapon without my arm aching with discomfort, and taking accurate aim would be a problem if I had to shoot.

With luck it wouldn't come to that. The gun was for protection, since I had no desire to end up the helpless prey of a predator big cat on the mountain in the foggy dark. And while I might not know how to shoot straight, I counted on being able to fire a warning shot to prevent an attack and ward it off.

I got out of the Land Rover, eased the back door closed and locked it. I was tempted to run, but the sound of running feet in the street might wake someone and attract unwanted attention. Instead, I took off at a brisk walking pace. My plan was to keep the revolver out of sight in my jacket pocket or tucked into the waistband of my jeans. But it was so heavy this wouldn't work, so I slung the braided safety cord over my shoulder and let the gun hang down by my side.

The gun thudded against my lower ribs and I had to keep my right hand over the revolver to hold it more securely as I kept up a fast nervous pace leaving the village behind and climbing Chapel Hill, the road ahead shrouded in fog. Apart from the dimly burning street lights I saw no other lights on in the houses of the valley and no cars on the move either. I wouldn't feel safe, however, until I reached the Bog Lane and my progress had the sweat rolling off me. I didn't care that I was sweating heavily or that I could feel the beginning of a stitch in my side. I just wanted to get clear of the village. As I gained height I expected the fog to thin out, but it clung about the headstones in the graveyard, and drifted in swirls over the mound under which Francie Curran lay buried. I could only hope his ghost would understand what I was doing passing the graveyard at such an ungodly hour with a stolen gun in my possession.

TWENTY NINE

Anyone who bumped into me was bound to stop and ask my business. So I scouted the ditches on either side of the Top Road for gaps and gateways if I needed to duck behind a hedge for cover. At the start of the Bog Lane I put on a fresh burst of speed and I didn't stop again to catch my breath until the lane levelled out and I knew I was on the mountain. My heart thumped wildly and I laid my hand on the revolver to confirm its ribbed deadly presence.

Strangely, the gun added to my nervousness not my feeling of safety. Rather than give me confidence it forced me to ask hard questions of myself. I could imagine using it to scare off or kill the panther if it came to it. But suppose I met one of the robbers? What would I do? Could I point the gun at another person and pull the trigger? Could I live with their blood on my hands? And having these thoughts I began to feel more forgiving towards Frank Welcome for his bout of the jitters in Rover pit and getting stupidly drunk tonight at the poker game from being forced to live with the consequences of shooting an enemy soldier I imagined my exact age.

In spite of the fog I could see more clearly now, either

because it was already starting to get bright, or my eyes had fully adjusted to the summer half-light. Setting off again I soon crested the next rise and found myself at the start of the track that would take me as far as Noonan's pit. The mountainside was criss-crossed by these paths the pitmen had used for generations as shortcuts to get to and from work. It was too early yet for any of the pitmen to be out and about, but they would have to be at work by eight o'clock and I quickened my progress in the pre-dawn summer morning greyness.

My progress was surefooted and swift along the path through the heather and over the stone outcrops, driven by the exhilaration of having made it this far without a snag. At the same time I kept a close eye out in places where there was extra cover for a panther to lie in wait.

Once or twice I spotted black shapes on the mountainside. Each time I put my hand on the revolver, but the panther-like silhouettes turned out to be a sheep, a rock, a clump of bracken, and after a while I found it best not to think about the big cat's whereabouts and just keep moving.

Noonan's pit finally came into view where it stood at the end of a roughly paved lane with jumbles of iron wheels removed from broken hutches, old planks and oil barrels scattered around a block-house with only a couple of sheets of rusty corrugated iron left on the roof. Past the industrial scrap and ruined shed a cutting in the embankment led towards the mouth of the pit. The entrance to the pit itself was hard to make out, but there was no mistaking the life-size Marian Year plasterwork statue of the Virgin Mary erected by the pitmen to stand watch over the opening.

Although the disused pit looked abandoned, I crouched down behind a boulder and studied the layout.

After the effort to get this far on foot inside three-quarters of an hour, I could feel my heart hammering and it was racing even faster now at the prospect of entering the pit to go in search for the bank raiders' van.

The entrance to the pit was solidly boarded up and it appeared Gerry McPadden had in fact lied to Bernice about the getaway van being hidden inside because there was absolutely no trace of any visitors to this deserted spot other than the wandering sheep whose droppings were scattered everywhere.

A few of the offending sheep stood close to the original bunker, and I watched closely for any sign of movement to unsettle them. Even then I couldn't completely rule out the possibility the robbers were taking it in turns to keep an eye on the place from a distance, just as I was doing before I made my next move. Or, what if the police had located the van and they were lying in wait right now for the robbers to return. If they found me going into the pit they were bound to conclude I was involved, especially if they nabbed me carrying the stolen gun.

But I had come this far and I couldn't lose my courage now. With the pistol dangling from the strap around my shoulder, I advanced towards my goal. Having to cross the open patch of ground before the entrance to the pit made me highly visible, but no voice called out of the surrounding fog to arrest me or threaten to gun me down.

The horizontal boards across the entrance to the pit made a secure barrier and I ran my hands along their rough surface to find out how firmly they were held in place. It hadn't occurred to me to bring a pinch-bar or a claw-hammer. I might even have decided to abandon my search only I noticed that while the planks blocking my way were old and weathered, the nails fastening them to the timber surround were shiny, their heads bright from recent hammer blows. Someone had taken the boards down lately and then replaced them as before using new nails.

THIRTY

One of the wider planks near the bottom looked like my best bet, and using short quick bursts of strength to jerk it back and forth the nails began to work lose. One end pried free and with more leverage available the opposite end came loose easily. I was careful not to remove the plank fully.

With just this single plank out of the way a tight but manageable gap in the partition gave me space to crawl through. I took hold of the pistol and reached through the gap and left it down on the other side to have it there waiting. I did the same with the flash-lamp. Then I put one leg through the opening and lay along the top of the lower plank, my chest and stomach sucked in to force myself through. It was a seriously tight squeeze, but I angled my head and took a last look at the daylight as I squeezed painfully through into the pit.

Once inside I expanded my chest and drew several deep breaths to get my wind back. I lit the flash-lamp and the beam of light played over rock and clay and dripping water.

It could have been my imagination, but the atmosphere

in this abandoned pit seemed even darker and wetter than the working pit at Rover. It felt a whole lot more dangerous too, if only because I knew that nobody worked here so there was no one to maintain the props holding up the roof.

Down the entire length of the pitch-dark tunnel falling water splashed as it hit the floor, which was mostly one big standing pool. I aimed the lamp down the shaft and the beam tailed off into darkness.

Slinging the pistol over my shoulder again I moved deeper into the tunnel. The floor slanted slightly downwards, the water at my feet running on into the tunnel, probably ending in a pool deep enough to block the shaft up ahead. But I was hoping not to have to go too far into the abandoned pit. Using the beam of the flash-lamp to inspect the roof it barely seemed possible a van could squeeze past the jutting rock or make much headway underground.

Behind me, what little light came through the opening I'd made in the planks across the entrance began to fade as I went deeper into the pit. I had no idea of the distance I walked, but if I didn't soon come across the van I would turn back. Off to my right-hand side a second passage opened up. I shone the flash-lamp into the opening and reckoned it was too tight for a van. Straight ahead was best, though my feet were soaking wet as the level of the water rose above my shins. I hadn't bargained on having to cope with flooding.

Out of the corner of my eye I glimpsed a sudden movement as a huge pit-rat jumped into my path, stopped and stood defiantly in my way. I froze but finally the rat turned around and splashed on ahead. Trying to see where the rat went I got the strongest feeling that just up ahead an entire army of rats stood ready to attack. I gripped the revolver and raised it to be prepared. Then armed and ready I got the nerve to push ahead.

The shaft began to curve towards the right, and where the angle of the turn increased the beam of light from the flash-lamp glinted back at me from a pane of glass. Every instinct told me I was alone, yet I froze, never taking my eyes off the stationary van. The strangeness of the presence of the van underground was enough to set my heart hammering far harder than at any point during the race to get here. But if I was trembling and giddy with fright I was delighted, too, at the prospect of what this triumphant discovery meant. My stratagem had been worth it, and edging forward, I could see scorch marks from an acetylene cutting-flame on the roof of the van, confirming what Gerry said about Mossy Beirne having failed to remove it. All four tyres were flat, and I wondered if Gerry himself had driven the van into the pit in this state, or had there been a bunch of men along with him to push the van by their own strength.

I brought my face up cagily to the back window to shine a light inside, but the glass reflected the light of the flash-lamp back at me. Worryingly, the light had a dull orange tint from the battery wearing down.

I shook the flash-lamp and the light brightened up again, at least for the time being. But I needed to get a move on before the battery went completely flat. I reached for the handle to open up the back, and only realised at the last second I must not leave behind any fingerprints.

It was stupid of me not to have brought gloves or even a handkerchief. But I scrunched my hand up into my sleeve and used the fabric of the cuff around my bunched fingers to take hold of the latch.

My hopes of finding the back of the van full of sacks of money were immediately dashed. There was absolutely nothing inside. It made sense the robbers had taken the money with them but I felt bitterly disappointed. Foolishly I'd believed that by finding the van I'd also recover the money. I shook the lamp again to brighten up the beam and moved to investigate the front of the van.

It was a tight squeeze to get past the side of the van and the wall of the pit, but I made my way forward to the driver's door. Here it was painfully awkward to get the driver's door open wide enough to fit myself into the gap between it and the frame, and I had to push hard with the edge of my shoulder to force myself into the space.

A musty chill tinged with petrol fumes escaped from the interior of the van. If I hadn't known in advance this was the getaway vehicle there was nothing whatsoever to point to it having been used in an armed bank raid. No balaclavas, no guns, no spare banknotes scattered on the floor from the robbers having to make off in haste with overly full sacks of money.

Manoeuvring myself to look all around while keeping the van door open I found I was sweating heavily. I eased my shoulder away from the van door and it swung shut. It closed harder than I intended and the bang resounded along the tunnel.

I froze. My imagination ran wild. Would this be the signal for the robbers or the police to pounce?

Nothing happened. I was completely alone. And my relief was mixed with frustration that there wasn't the slightest trace of the proceeds from the robbery.

The flash-lamp battery was now practically useless. I needed to get back to the outside quickly before total darkness closed in around me. I reversed free and straightened up my clothes and double-checked the revolver.

Now that I'd found what I'd come looking for I

wanted to get out of the place as quickly as possible. Speeding up my pace I found it hard to control the rising fear I was about to get tripped up on the brink of my daring success. But I kept my mind on seeing at any second the thin bar of light coming in between the slatted boards offering my passage to freedom.

Though I was in a rush, and didn't mind how wet my feet and trousers ended up, I took care not to trip or to strike my head off a low rock as the eye of the pit appeared up ahead. On reaching the timber partition I crouched down to clamber out head first. It looked a lot brighter outside than when I first went down the pit, and I was anxious to keep moving and avoid bumping into early rising pitmen crossing the mountain on their way to work. I passed the gun and flash-lamp out first before squeezing out after them. Then partway through the opening I heard a car coming.

THIRTY ONE

With sickening certainty I recognised the sound of a Volkswagen engine. Lots of people owned Volkswagen Beetles, but I had to expect this one belonged to Eugene McPadden. Gerry had probably told his father he'd revealed the whereabouts of the van and they'd decided to move it. Urgently reversing, I grabbed back the gun and the flash-lamp. I wanted to race back into the pit to put as much distance as possible between me and the approaching car. But if either Eugene or Gerry spotted the missing board they'd know someone was having a snoop.

With only seconds to spare I got my head, shoulders and arms back out through the gap, grabbed hold of the plank I'd disturbed, and raised it again to fix it in place. The nails were slightly out of line with the holes but mercifully the points bit into the surrounding timber. I pulled the plank hard towards me and when I released my hold it stayed in place. How long it would stay there I couldn't tell. Trusting it to hold, I shrank back far enough from the entrance to conceal myself and yet have a view through a slit between the uneven planks.

It was Eugene's Volkswagen that pulled up beside the

abandoned shed, but he was alone in the car, with a small trailer hitched to the back full of sheep.

Eugene must have just taken a cup of tea when he got home, changed into his old clothes and gone out to load the sheep. In the same way his son Gerry planned to buy a car with his share of the proceeds from the robbery, Eugene seemed to have bought sheep to add to his flock. Or maybe moving the sheep was a cover for checking to see nobody had been near the abandoned pit. Either way, I was absolutely certain Eugene knew the van was hidden in this sealed-up pit and he had masterminded the operation. I hadn't found a shred of evidence to connect Eugene to the robbery, but I was convinced Gerry was too much under his father's influence to have taken part with just Mossy Beirne as an accomplice.

The car door opened and Eugene got out. Pressing myself back tightly against the rock wall I barely dared to draw a breath.

Reluctant as I was to use it, the moment was at hand to arm myself with the revolver. And feeling for its cold presence I took firm hold of the grip while keeping my finger safely on the guard and not the curve of the trigger. The weight of the handgun meant I would need both hands to steady, aim and fire. And for the moment I held it in my right hand only, my elbow bent to keep the barrel pointed upwards.

My mouth tasted dry and I swallowed and tensed and tried to focus the power of my thoughts on keeping that loose board in place. If it were to come lose now Eugene would definitely be driven to investigate and I would have to shoot.

Easing ever so slowly away from the entrance I caught a glimpse of Eugene going around to the back of the trailer to lower the tailboard. The sheep cowered away from him in a bunch and he had to reach in and grab the first of the animals by its fleecy back and neck to get it out of the trailer. With one sheep set loose the others took their chances and followed. Then as he raised the tailboard he looked towards the pit. It was the action of a man deliberately keeping an eye on the pit while maintaining an alibi he was engaged in ordinary farm work in case there was a swoop and the authorities demanded to know what he was up to.

He must have spotted something out of place because he kept on looking in my direction until I grew absolutely convinced he could see me. Yet I didn't dare blink an eyelid far less make a run for a better hiding place.

My arm began to ache under the weight of the army revolver. I had to think hard about whether I would use it or not if Eugene started towards me. If he entered the pit and found me holding a gun on him, and I warned him not to take another step closer or I'd shoot, then I had better be prepared to carry out my threat. Otherwise he would simply call my bluff and, finding me unable to shoot, he could easily disarm me. And then I would be at the mercy of a man Nora Greene said with the help of his father had dumped a helpless old woman down an airshaft never to be seen again.

I enjoyed reading *Commando* comics and watching action films, but now that I had a gun in my hand I realised I could never bring myself to use it. The consequences of one bullet fired would follow me for a lifetime, in the way Frank Welcome was haunted.

Inching further back into the covering darkness I lowered the gun and felt the circulation return to my arm. But the movement must have caught Eugene's eye. He started walking in the direction of the pit with a purposeful stride.

I took off running at a crouch back towards the van.

My feet splashed through the standing water but I kept going, relying on blind instinct to guide me until I collided with the van in the dark, leaving fingerprints no doubt, but squeezing past the van hurriedly to get to the other side. I had no way of telling if Eugene had second thoughts about entering the pit, or if he was hot on my heels. The safest course of action was to keep going deeper into the pit whether he was after me or not, to avoid getting caught at all cost.

Running blindly in the dark was impossible so I had to risk using the flash-lamp, keeping the beam pointed straight ahead and relying on the van between me and the entrance to hide its glimmer. The flash-lamp offered only a poor light anyway but it was enough to keep me moving, taking a side passage to the left and branching right again to put myself beyond pursuit. My plan seemed to be working because when I stopped and knocked off the light I could hear nothing, not a sound to confirm Eugene was after me.

The minutes passed but no matter how long I waited my eyes could adjust no more to the darkness. The blackness around me was so pure I could have been looking into a blinding white light.

For as long as humanly possible I tried not to move a muscle or make a sound. In all that time I saw and heard nothing only the constant patter of dripping water the whole dark length of the tunnel, and possibly the splash of a pit rat. I gave it as long as I could, until the freezing cold started to get the better of me. My teeth began to chatter and my whole body trembled, and I had to accept I could no longer endure another minute of this bone-penetrating cold. The danger remained that Eugene had decided to play me at my own game and stay silent until I made the first move, but I'd had enough of hiding in the dark

237

When I clicked the switch on the flash-lamp there was barely a meg left in the battery. I looked into the light and saw the flimsy wire filament in the round-headed bulb produce the tiniest glow for the shortest time and then it faded away entirely. With the flash-lamp dead the darkness engulfed me. Doing my best to stay calm I felt about inside my jacket pocket. Alongside the keys for the Land Rover was the box of matches I'd neglected to return to Frank's tent.

From the way the coarse powdery heads of the matches crumbled under the touch of my fingers I knew the majority if not all of them were spent, and I cursed the fact that Frank Welcome was in the habit of returning used matches to the box. So any plan I might have to strike matches one after the other to give me enough light to help me find my way safely back to the surface had to be abandoned

Before I used up whatever few matches I had left I needed to think through my plan of escape. Having turned full circle at least twice while listening for sounds around me I figured I must now be looking back the way I entered the pit. But a panicky doubt started in my mind and I couldn't be absolutely sure where I stood. My gut instinct told me the way out lay straight in front of me, but when I groped forward carefully I touched a stone wall that by my calculations shouldn't be there.

Marooned in total blackness I had no idea which way I was facing. And minus my sense of direction I had to tell myself that just like getting into a panic about suffocating from an asthma attack, this awful rising fear of being trapped underground in the pitch dark served no purpose and would be my undoing unless I got a grip on my fear.

Perhaps I could fire the pistol for a quick burst of light. But what about ricochets? And I might need the bullets later to make enough noise to try and alert someone to my presence in a last desperate hope of rescue. There were few if any good matches left in the box but perhaps there might be a loose match or two in my pockets. My fingertips were numb with the cold as I fumbled around inside my jacket pockets for anything at all that might be of use. Finding my pockets empty made me sick to realise how badly I'd prepared for this whole escapade.

I tried my jeans and felt what I thought must be a leftover Silvermint. If felt small and flat but softer than a mint.

It was the candle stub I'd pocketed when Bernice lit a fresh one in the church in Drumshanbo.

Keeping hold of the candle stub I rubbed my free fingers hard on the leg of my jeans to ease the numbness and ensure they were as dry as a cork. Then I touched the scant few matches in the box and concentrated hard to keep my hands from shaking. I struck a match off the box several times in the pitch black but either it was a dud or the head got damp. With frightening certainty I realised it was never going to ignite.

In the dripping pitch black dark I brought to mind again my imaginary submarine crew trapped on the bottom of the sea with their air supply running out. I had to use the same kind of will power to get out of this fix. At this point I knew I was talking out loud to encourage myself, but what mattered now was to control the panic, keep hold of the candle stub, and work my way through whatever good matches I had left until I got one to ignite.

The spent matches were soon transferred to my pocket and I was down to almost the last match in the box. I struck it and it flared, flickered, and burst into flame. I acted quickly to bring the flame to the wick but the tiny end of wick resisted the heat and the match died. I swallowed hard and went through the whole tricky business again with the very last match.

It lit, glowed and died away.

But the wick had the tiniest flame at its tip.

"Bless you, Bernice," I said.

It didn't matter that the candle stub was miniscule, or that I risked burning my fingers as the tiny flame cast its sacred brightness: a ridiculously weak light, but after so much time in total darkness it had a heart-gladdening power and it allowed me to get orientated.

I was indeed facing a wall of crudely cut rock. And considering how the shafts on either side of me looked identical in both directions I had to study which way the tiny flame fluttered. It seemed to be bending to the left so I went right, facing into the direction of the current of air entering the shaft. I could only hope I'd made the right choice because the candle was quickly burning out.

I plodded through the freezing water, desperate to keep the faint glow alive, knowing that even if I had got the direction right I risked running into Eugene. But meeting Eugene was preferable to being stuck in this chilling darkness with nobody having a clue where I was and ending up food for the pit rats.

Keeping the flame protected with my cupped hand limited the light it cast, but by watching closely where I put my feet I made good headway. Quicker than I expected I came to a fork in the tunnel, and finding a left and then a right turn in quick succession boosted my confidence I was on the right track. And then I spotted something white at my feet.

A canvas bag with metal eyelets for the cord used to tie the top lay sodden in a pool of inky water. In faint lettering I read the words 'Great Northern Bank'. It was crumpled and empty but definitely one of the bags used to hold the stolen money. I looked around for a hiding place where the money might have been wedged behind a pillar or prop the way the pitmen stashed private supplies of carbide for their lamps.

Only the light was so poor and the risk of the candle going out so great I couldn't delay, and I cursed again the poxy flash-lamp battery. I had to keep moving but now I had in my hands physical proof I'd found the van. I bunched up the sopping, empty cash bag and stuffed it as best I could into the other pocket of my jacket.

Soon the shaft led me as far as the van which was concealed just beyond the point where a slight amount of natural light from the entrance offered relief from the pitch dark at my back. Even as I reached the van the nub of candle suddenly turned to liquid wax in my hand, the flame guttered and went out and the last dreg of wax fell away.

The darkness didn't trouble me anymore as I squeezed around by the van, knowing the boarded up entry was straight ahead. Being so nearly safe, only the prospect of running straight into Eugene kept me from making a last dash to freedom. Even if he hadn't chased after me, I could not rule out the possibility he had simply decided to wait out whoever it was hiding underground and now lay in wait to nab me the moment I surfaced.

I tip-toed forward, then peeked through a chink in the boards. Eugene's car and trailer were gone, and the evidence pointed to me having imagined that Eugene ever came after me. Right or wrong, I had no choice but to remove the loose plank and clamber free. And while I wanted out of there fast, I took the time to replace the board and give it a few smart taps with a stone to wedge it in place and hide the traces of my visit.

The fog hadn't fully lifted but the grey vapour was beginning to glow in the dawn light, and where before it had been like hiking in a black and white world now the world had regained its colour.

I met nobody on the path back across the mountain and the Bog Lane too was empty. After the downward slope of the Top Road I reached the crest of Chapel Hill, where I met a coal lorry taking the pitmen to work. With the revolver safely out of sight under my jacket I figured it might look out of character but it wasn't unreasonable to find me outdoors on such a pleasant summer's morning.

The strangest part about reaching the village was being conscious of everything I'd been through and not knowing what to do about it or who to tell. I knew only that I had to return the revolver before Frank Welcome woke and found it missing. The morning was getting on and I was counting on a sore head keeping him in bed for another while. A bigger risk was my father spotting me opening up the Land Rover with Frank Welcome's keys in my possession. In our house Daddy was the early riser, but I had to take that chance as I had no intention of keeping the gun a minute longer.

THIRTY TWO

The blinds were down but my father had the shop door open. A pitman stepped out and put a box of ten Woodbine in his pocket to bring to work. A car and two motorbikes went past followed by a coal lorry. My timing was bad on account of getting stuck down the pit and the best I could do was brazen it out and simply open the back door of the Land Rover like I was on a genuine errand.

With the key in the lock I jiggled it around until the door opened, climbed into the back and closed the door behind me. Wetness from the money sack had gotten onto the gun and I wiped it dry on the blanket and then got hold of the panniers. Reattaching the braided cord to the holster I had the gun in my hands when the door behind me opened.

"What the hell do you think you're doing?" Frank Welcome said. "Put that gun down this instant."

I did as he said, too surprised to say a thing or do anything other than follow his orders exactly.

"That's twice now I've caught you going through my things. What were you trying to do? Sneak off with the gun? Is that it?"

I was too startled and heart-sick at being caught just

when I thought I was in the clear to answer him. And the fact that he'd paid for the leather jacket on my back doubled my helplessness to explain how my actions were not the betrayal of his trust that he supposed. I was returning the gun unused having borrowed it only for my protection, not stealing it for some underhand purpose.

"I thought you were more grown up than that," he said. "But this is what you get up to behind my back. If your father hadn't been so decent to me last night I'd haul you by the ear into him right now and tell him about the deceitful prig he has for a son."

His face was pink and his eyes bloodshot and he was so angry I understood this wasn't the moment to offer a defence. Gutted, I surrendered the keys. He snatched the keys out of my hand and I stood on the roadway and watched him secure the back door, climb into the Land Rover and drive away without a backward look in my direction.

Mrs Daly's husband pulled up in a Morris Minor to drop his wife off at the post office before going on to work at the siding. The post office van from Boyle would be arriving shortly with the day's letters and parcels to sort and deliver.

"You're up early," Mrs Daly said.

I was too upset to speak but I followed her through the open door into the shop.

"What are you doing out and about?" Daddy asked.

"Walking," I said.

"Out looking for this panther I suppose when you could be giving me a hand."

He had sprinkled water on the floorboards to damp down the dust and he took up his broom and began to sweep leaving me to do as I pleased. It was lucky for me the floorboards had been damped already for my feet were soaking and my shoes trailing water. I ducked under the counter and went on through into the house.

Exhausted and dispirited I climbed the stairs to my room, the window on the landing open wide. The only way to bring Gerry and Eugene's involvement in the robbery out into the open would be to tell someone in authority I'd found where they'd hidden the van in the disused pit, which meant breaking my sworn promise to Bernice. I couldn't do that, even though I badly wanted to get Gerry McPadden out of her hair, and break whatever hold Eugene might suppose he had over my mother. Instead of which I'd sacrificed my friendship with Captain Frank Welcome with no way back into his good books unless the truth came out. And that wasn't likely to happen any time soon.

The soggy canvas money bag stayed in my jacket pocket, and bending down wearily I loosened my sopping laces and got off my soaking wet shoes and socks. After I undressed I didn't even bother with pyjamas and climbed between the sheets in my underwear, feeling totally wrung out.

At some point my mother came into the bedroom, looked at me in my exhausted state and decided the best thing would be to let me sleep. I didn't wake again until three o'clock. But the light in the room looked wrong for that hour of the afternoon, and when I picked up the alarm clock I realised the hands were stopped. I got out of bed, went to the window and looked out. It was evening time, eight or nine o'clock or later maybe.

Daddy was below in the street in the summer evening cool, changing the wheel on the van, getting the travelling shop roadworthy for tomorrow. Other than that the place was quiet. No sign of Eugene's Volkswagen or Frank Welcome's Land Rover.

I went to the bathroom and brushed the sour coating out of my mouth and rubbed away the hard crusts of sleep gluing my eyelashes tight in the corners. The soreness had gone out of the injury to my head, but my legs felt heavy as lead, aching after the challenge of practically running up and down the side of the mountain in one night.

A smell of stale sweat clung to me and I squatted in the bathtub and used the nozzle and the rubber hose fixed to the taps to wash myself clean though hardly fresh as I was still woefully stiff and tired.

Back in my room I sat on the edge of the bed at a point of private decision that nobody could help me with. Nothing was clear beyond the certain knowledge that I could not endanger Bernice. I could only hope that having bet and lost his rifle in the poker game Frank Welcome would accept he was unfit for active duty, surrender the gun, or more likely pay Eugene the money he owed, and then pack up his tent and leave, having failed to crack the native code of silence.

A gentle knocking started on my bedroom door.

"Leo, are you dressed?" Bernice asked.

"Come in," I said.

The door opened and Bernice leaned into the room.

"You have a visitor," she said.

My first thought was that Eugene McPadden had come looking for me.

"Who is it?"

"It's Frank. He wants a word."

When Bernice noticed my reluctance to move she said, "He's in the post office, and I left the switchboard unattended to come and get you."

She had no idea of the dread I felt. But I understood the pressure she was under to get back to work and I said, "Tell him I'll be down in a minute."

Her footsteps retreated and a couple of minutes later, making my own way downstairs, I considered turning the opposite way to the post office and using the back door to slip away using the path by the river. I could hide in the big sycamore tree with its bird's eye view of the river field. And from there I could keep an eye on Welcome's encampment and know when he got back and if it was safe for me to return to the house.

Smothering the impulse to cut and run, I turned down the hallway and made my way between the cardboard boxes, sacks of onions and Indian meal.

Frank Welcome stood beside the switchboard where Bernice sat with the headset resting on the desk at her elbow. The roller blinds were lowered only part of the way, and I could see Daddy's comings and goings outside as he rearranged the goods stored in the travelling shop, making it ready for tomorrow.

Seeing me framed in the doorway into the shop Frank said somewhat awkwardly, "The man himself."

"You wanted to see me."

"I'm sorry I was so short tempered with you this morning," he said.

I didn't respond, accepting he'd been in his full rights to come down on me like a ton of bricks, having done a whole lot more than just messing with his belongings, though he wasn't to know that.

"I fell off the wagon last night, made a fool of myself at poker, and got up this morning like a bear with a sore head," he said. "I didn't intend for you to be on the receiving end of my disgrace."

It was decent of him to take the blame, but I hardly heard him because of the weightier problems on my mind.

"And you weren't really taking the gun, were you?" he said. "You were putting it back."

I looked to Bernice, but Frank cut in quickly and said, "I've told her I caught you stealing a look at my army revolver."

"What makes you think I was putting it back?"

"I checked the chamber and found water in it. What did you want the gun for?"

He had my full attention now because this was not an apology but an interrogation.

"You're not going to get into any trouble if you tell me," he said, "It wasn't loaded, so there's no harm done – is there?"

"I didn't realise," I said, although I was certain in my own mind there had been six bright brass bullets in the gun and he was just trying to make the incident sound less serious.

"Why did you take it, Leo?" Bernice asked. "Was it to hunt for this panther?"

If I'd known they were both going to gang up on me I'd have followed through on my first instinct to leave the house and hide until Frank Welcome went.

Maybe I was only imagining they were both against me. Could Bernice really have no idea that a more likely reason for arming myself was to go looking for the van after she told me where it could be found? Or was she deliberately trying to steer the conversation away from what she knew to be the truth and giving me hints to follow her direction. Either way I couldn't bring myself to co-operate.

"How much have you told him?" I asked her.

Now it was Frank's turn to look from me to Bernice to try to get at the truth.

"You should just go now, Leo," Bernice said.

For the second time in the space of a few minutes she had used my Christian name, making me realise that amongst the three of us standing here I was the outsider.

And with painful sharpness I understood how Gerry McPadden must feel; his helpless frustration and agony, knowing Bernice was totally smitten by this newcomer, a man I alone knew wasn't who he pretended to be.

It had been to my advantage to see Gerry rejected by Bernice when Frank came along, but only for as long as she continued to confide in me. That was no longer the case. And although I detested the resemblance, like Gerry I couldn't easily give her up without a struggle, without proving I knew things too.

From the pocket of my jacket I withdrew the canvas bag. Still balled-up I tossed it towards Frank Welcome who caught it in one hand.

"What's this?" he asked, shaking out the bag and starting to read the block print on the fabric that said 'Great Northern Bank'.

Realising what it was Bernice said, "You went looking for the van."

"I found it," I said, keeping a close eye on Frank Welcome's face.

"Where did you get this?" he asked.

"I know what you are," I said. "And I have the information you're after."

"Stop," said Bernice.

But I had no intention of stopping even if it meant breaking my sworn promise. My thinking had changed and I wanted to drive a wedge between them by outing him as working for the Military Intelligence Service without telling her, and at the same time revealing to him that Bernice had entrusted me with information she could not bring herself to share with him. If I had baulked at the prospect of using the borrowed gun when threatened, using this double-edged betrayal came frighteningly easy to me.

"Gerry told Bernice the getaway van is hidden in

Noonan's pit."

Frank Welcome appeared to rock back on his heels, though he recovered quickly.

"Put me through to Boyle, 512," he said to Bernice.

"I can't, Frank," she said, a look of wild panic in her eyes. "Gerry will know it was me."

Even though I should have anticipated what might happen next, to my horror, shame and dismay Bernice burst out crying.

"Do it," said Welcome, ignoring her tears.

Bernice's hands shook and she had trouble fitting the right jack-plug into the necessary socket. With the connection made she wiped the tears from her cheeks using the back of her hand. Then she re-settled the head-set over her ears. And as Bernice spoke with her colleague in the main exchange, asking to be put through to the number Frank wanted, a real gun might have been fired inside the post office from the way the air around the three of us thickened with a mood of bleak undoable harm.

THIRTY THREE

He did not have the authority, but Captain Welcome ordered me to stay in the post office, and sit alongside Bernice at the switchboard until the end of her shift. Outside the window by the petrol pump and telephone kiosk Daddy had stopped what he was doing to make conversation with late evening strollers. He hadn't the slightest idea what was going on behind his back.

Unlike the easy going chatter outside, Bernice didn't have a word to say to Frank. And he spent his time on the telephone talking to what seemed to be his real headquarters in Dublin, and making certain we told nobody what was happening until these calls were made.

I looked to the clock with the dockets on top on the mantelpiece behind the shop counter. Time moved desperately slow. Yet the atmosphere between us was as tense as I imagine it must have been in the War-Room in the Pentagon with the Russian fleet steaming towards President Kennedy's blockade of Cuba and the world holding its breath in case of all-out nuclear war.

On the dot of ten o'clock Bernice put down her headset and rose out of her chair at the switchboard. Frank

Welcome accompanied both of us into the house, and when Bernice went straight to her room he waited at the foot of the stairs until he heard her shut the bedroom door with more than usual force. Then he let himself out of the house by the back door.

As quietly as I could manage so Bernice wouldn't hear, I climbed the stairs and went to my bedroom window to see if he'd gone. His Land Rover was parked below in the street and he had in fact joined my father. I watched him kick the replacement tyre on the van to confirm it was solidly inflated. Then he lit a cigarette and sat down on the shop window sill where he looked like he was just killing time but he could also see into the post office. Acting like a man without a care in the world, he was making certain neither Bernice nor I could warn Eugene and Gerry that the authorities knew the whereabouts of the getaway van.

He didn't have to be so suspicious. Bernice was foremost in my thoughts. We had to prepare to meet the consequences now, not prevent the inevitable. And in the kitchen I made tea, ate a jam sandwich and kept an eye on the time. Eventually Daddy came in, but only to wash his hands at the sink and tell me not to stay up too late. Perhaps I should have unburdened to him, but there were so many things I would have to leave out it didn't seem worth it. Instead, I watched the clock until shortly before midnight when Eugene's shift ended and he always came into the pub for a drink. Would he be on his own, or would he have his son Gerry with him, though Gerry was barred? Or would both men find themselves under arrest after the phone calls Frank Welcome made.

Chancing my luck, I stepped into the public bar. My mother had a bunch of newspapers open on the counter and a scissors out of the kitchen drawer, and she was cutting out articles and photographs recording Kennedy's visit. The President had taken off without her ever getting a chance to see him in person, but she was putting together a scrap book in the innocent way I once preserved dried grasses and native wild flowers.

Red Paddy Reynolds sat watching her from his usual barstool.

I was tempted to help her go through the papers, but I sensed it was something she wanted to do for herself. And she had only just put the cuttings and her scissors aside when the pitmen off the backshift started to come in.

Timmy Leonard was the first man through the door and straight away he had news for my mother. There'd been a raid he said. Several unmarked cars full of Plain Clothes detectives, backed up by Free State soldiers, swooped on Noonan's pit. They found the getaway van from the bank robbery but no money. Sergeant Glacken, too, with several armed detectives, had Rover pit surrounded by a 'ring of steel' when the pitmen finished their shift.

"Why?" my mother asked.

"To lift Gerry McPadden," Timmy said.

But either Gerry had slipped past amongst the other pitmen because the Sergeant couldn't tell them apart, or he never came to the surface. Either way, said Timmy, he slipped through the ring of steel.

"What about Eugene?" my mother asked.

"No sign of him either," Timmy said. "He must have thought they'd lift him too."

My mother offered Timmy a drink.

"I'll have a brandy," he said. "The hands are worn off me drinking pints."

As she turned to the optic to get Timmy the drink I never before saw my mother's face look so care-worn and troubled. And her mood darkened as the other pitmen brought news how the getaway van was already on its way to Boyle barracks under tow behind an army breakdown recovery truck.

When Doctor Ballintine stopped in for a late drink and to hear the pitmen's news, my mother asked him why he thought Eugene and Gerry had gone on the run.

"Surely, to God," she said, "The Sergeant knows they had nothing to do with the robbery."

"True," said Doctor Ballintine, "But the robbers got help hiding the van."

Throughout the excited talk in the bar about the police raids on the pits and the manhunt for Gerry McPadden and the missing Eugene, I kept my head bowed over the sink washing dirty glasses. Even though I couldn't say it, I wanted to add that Eugene was slippery. If he'd dodged Sergeant Glacken at Rover pit he had a good reason for going on the run.

Having admitted to Bernice he was an accomplice to the robbery, Gerry was definitely in trouble with the law. But why wouldn't Eugene let Sergeant Glacken arrest him? Even if Eugene got held for questioning he knew how to keep his mouth shut, the way he did before in the pub. And after a spell in custody he'd be let out again with nothing proven against him. So if Eugene wanted to buy time before he let the Sergeant get hold of him he had a plan. The trouble was I couldn't figure out what he had in mind, though I was certain Eugene had some kind of dirty trick up his sleeve.

Later, in bed, I tossed and turned wondering where Eugene and Gerry might be hiding out. It was easier thinking about them than dwelling on the hurt I'd caused Bernice. I wasn't proud of what I'd done. I felt ashamed and wretched and couldn't explain my intentions nor come up with a single way to make amends.

One of the lads who worked at the siding arrived early the next morning to help lower the American flag and take down the bunting from the American Lounge. My mother on the ground shouted instructions, while next door Daddy treated this like any other Tuesday morning as he and Bernice loaded parcels of rashers and butcher's meat and other last minute goods into the travelling shop for his clients on the mountain. I wanted to help, but Bernice gave me an angry and wounded look and turned her back on me to climb into the van.

After the travelling shop pulled off I put on the leather jacket and got Daddy's binoculars from the top of the wardrobe. As I passed through the village, Grace Nail's hut was closed and so too was Ambrose Luck's flat-roofed booth, but the siding was busy with coal lorries coming and going and people loading solid fuel into donkey carts and car trailers and transport boxes on the back of tractors. Everything was getting back to normal even though we had a Garda checkpoint on the bridge.

Past the graveyard and Chapel Hill I turned onto the Top Road, and when I reached a good vantage point I climbed up on the ditch and lay there in the long grass to train the binoculars on Frank Welcome's encampment.

The Land Rover stood with its back door open as he stowed away his camping equipment. Seeing the empty spot where the tent had stood made me feel sad and friendless. But it confirmed what I suspected, that his job was done. The getaway van had been found and Sergeant Glacken had a summons out for the arrest of Gerry McPadden, his links with the IRA proven. Frank Welcome had no plans, apparently, to stay on in the area to shoot the panther and all of the so called sightings were, in the end, probably no more than hearsay and imagination and people believing in unfounded rumours that he'd used to his advantage.

My single sighting of the panther also happened after I got a knock on the head so the likelihood was I'd been dreaming or 'bomb-happy' as Frank Welcome called it, while thinking I was awake.

Then as I watched the campsite, Red Paddy Reynolds arrived and approached Frank Welcome. The two men stood talking, and it wouldn't surprise me if Red Paddy was looking for payment for the use of the field. With nothing further to see I decided to press on. And shortly before I reached the Bog Lane, Nora Greene swept past on her High Nelly. The sight of her freewheeling downhill towards the village increased my disappointment. She was probably the only friend I had left, and I had counted on calling in for a cup of tea and maybe even confiding in her.

Reaching the rock line I ignored the sweathouse and veered towards the deep hole behind the rock face that was to have been my panther trap. When I arrived at the spot the length of rope I intended to return to the shop was still there, with one end anchored to the boulder and the other end extending down into the pit. My satchel was on the ground beside it.

Looking at the set-up it was clear I'd never really stood much chance of catching a large predatory cat using such a conspicuous natural feature, but having cherished the hope of capturing the beast for so long I couldn't resist taking one last look down into the hole in the ground, just in case.

Approaching the edge I leaned out over the drop for a better view of the bottom.

A burst of movement made me fall back.

'Go-back-go-back-go-back...' went the squawky cry of a grouse as it flew past my face out of the hole.

I got such a hop I laughed to myself to recover, and then I picked up the rope, which was wet to the touch after

256

lying on the damp ground through two nights of heavy dew. It crossed my mind a short detour would take me to Noonan's pit. Having the binoculars meant I didn't have to get too close for a look at the place. Taking a pitman's path I walked along the top of a level ridge running parallel to the Top Road. Below me, a small plantation of pinewood trees grew on either side of a gully that fed water down off the mountain towards the river. A narrow hump-back bridge crossed the stream. The bump in the road at the bridge always caused the travelling shop to bounce at that spot and I raised the binoculars wondering how much of the run Daddy and Bernice had completed and if I could spot the big blue van trundling along.

A movement in the plantation caught my eye. Something black darted between the trees. Holding my breath to keep my hands steady I spotted it again. Yes, a dark shape in the plantation was headed for the gully.

THIRTY FOUR

The blur between the trees came into focus. It wasn't a large cat. It was a man dressed entirely in black. Was it Martin Foley in his torn coat and wool cap trying to keep out of sight? The figure vanished, and then reappeared. A man wearing a black sweater and a balaclava to hide his face was joined by two more men wearing balaclavas. One of them carried a sawn-off shotgun.

Even though I risked losing sight of the men in the plantation I swung the binoculars towards the road. Having chased down the bank robbers I expected to see the police or soldiers closing in. But it wasn't the law in hot pursuit; it was the travelling shop on the road headed for the bridge as it made its way back down into the valley from Whistle Hill.

I put the binoculars back in the case, shoved the case into my satchel along with the rope and slung the whole lot on my back and took off running. I had to be mindful where I placed my feet, skipping from rock to rock and not trusting the heather in between where there could be ankle-breaking dips. The secret was to picture where my feet should land and trust my brain to instinctively place my feet where I wanted them to go.

Running headlong I reached the edge of the rocks, where I had to clamber down a low cliff-face that dropped into a field full of head-high bracken which I pushed through blindly as though fighting my way through the jungle. Soon, I broke clear of the bracken and came into a soggy pasture field dotted with tussocks of green rushes. My feet slipped on the boggy ground as I picked up speed, and I felt a painful pressure under my ribs where my lungs were tightening up. My face was boiling hot and I could barely draw enough air into my lungs. It felt like a serious asthma attack coming on.

My body was telling me I could go no further, and yet to reach the road there was another rise I had to climb and then a major drain to cross that fed into the gully. It was on the downward slope of the hillock I lost my footing, flipped right over and rolled helpless into the drain.

I finished up on my hands and knees in the water.

Soaking wet, I took a moment's breather to collect my wits. I was drenched from head to foot, but the shock of the fall and the cold water had loosened the painful tightness in my chest and with the threat of the asthma attack gone I found my second wind.

Getting to my feet again I followed the embankment as it dropped towards the gully. The nearer I got to the bridge, the less certain my sense of direction. I had gone off track and I was still at the upper end of the conifer plantation. To reach the road I needed to find a way through the pine trees planted so close together and so thickly branched I was better off using the bottom of the gully and following the path cut by the water.

I pushed my way under a sheep-wire fence that straddled the drain and then made my way through an obstacle course of leathery bluebells and exposed roots and rocks and fallen branches that threatened to block my way as I splashed downstream.

At last I came within sight of the stone bridge and the road above where I spotted the van. It had stopped at the side of the road close to a fallen pine tree where it lay across the road.

I slowed my approach and edged forward, wary of coming face to face with the masked bank robbers. On the slope I could see a patch of fresh sawdust on the grass and the newly cut stump and smell pine resin where a conifer tree had been cut down to create the road block.

The tree was barely long enough to stretch across the road and Daddy must have thought he might be able to squeeze the van around it where the branches thinned out at the crown but then he had decided not to chance it.

Crouching low to keep out of sight I climbed the ditch to get a better view of the ambush. With my head level with the top of the roadside ditch I chanced taking a peek.

"Don't try anything stupid," I heard a man's voice shout.

I froze.

But it wasn't me he was shouting at. My legs felt watery and they were shaking badly after the hard run and the fright. But inching my head higher and looking down the road towards the van I saw all three of the robbers. The first man stood slightly apart and the furthest back from the van with his back turned to me. He was dressed completely in black and he had the sawn-off shotgun pointed at Daddy.

The second robber stood behind Bernice holding her by her two arms. He wore a green army-style jacket and also had his face hidden by a balaclava. The third man wore a polo-neck jumper as dark as his mask. He shoved Daddy up against the back door of the van.

When I saw Daddy being shoved around and Bernice being made to watch I wanted to jump up and shout at them to stop. But what good would that do? The first man would only swing around and shoot me, or else take me prisoner.

The man beside Daddy took a step back, turned his head and shouted at Bernice, "Down," he said. "Get down on the ground."

The other man holding Bernice put his two hands on her shoulders and shoved her onto her knees. It looked odd, but he carried a pillow which I thought might be for her to sit on. But he made her squat down on the tarred road.

"Just take the money and go," Daddy said.

"Shut up," the man beside Daddy shouted, and using some sort of baton or cudgel he jabbed it into Daddy's stomach. It winded Daddy, but he stayed on his feet.

"Easy," said the man beside Bernice.

The man with the shotgun had his back to me the whole time and he kept swinging the gun this way and that, pointing it at Daddy first, then at Bernice, and then back at Daddy. I'd say he was the most nervous of the three and he would probably shoot first and think later if he got a fright, such as seeing me behind him.

The man beside Daddy fumbled inside a bag like the ones the pitmen used to carry their lunches and spare carbide. He pulled a canister out of the bag and threw the bag at Daddy, whose reflexes surprised me when he caught the bag in mid-air. "Put the money in that – and cigarettes," the man who threw the bag shouted.

At first Daddy didn't budge.

"Move it," said the man prodding Daddy again with the cudgel to get him to co-operate. The nervous man with the gun aimed it right at Daddy.

"Leave him alone," Bernice shouted. She was sitting on the ground now with her hands on her head.

"Quiet, you," the man with the cudgel said. As Daddy climbed into the van to fetch the money, the second man moved closer to Bernice.

"Dirty little informer," he shouted into her face.

The cudgel now hung by a strap from his wrist and with the canister in one hand he reached around to his back trouser pocket with his free hand and took hold of a screwdriver.

"This is just a taste of what informers get," he threatened.

The man who'd forced Bernice onto the ground stood back and picked up the pillow. I got a sick feeling he meant to make Bernice put her face into the pillow as a blindfold so she wouldn't have to see the gunman shoot her in the head.

Desperate, but rooted to the spot, I didn't know if I should call out or make a run at the man nearest to me, and try to grab the gun.

The gunman didn't move any closer to Bernice so maybe he didn't mean to shoot her just yet.

Instead the man with the screwdriver used it to lever the lid from a can of UNO black paint.

"Squealer," he screamed in Bernice's face. "Tramp. Soldier's slut."

"Stop it, Gerry," she said. "I know it's you."

"Double-crossing bitch," he shouted. "Why did you do it?"

"Take the money and go," my father called, getting out of the van and moving surprisingly fast to put himself between Bernice and the man she'd identified as Gerry McPadden and not one of the bank raiders.

It was all making sense now. Gerry had gone on the

run rather than risk Bernice confirming what she knew to the police. If the first man was Gerry, then the second man with the pillow had to be, who? His father Eugene? You never saw one without the other. They had concocted a plan to dodge the law long enough to put the frighteners on Bernice, so any case against them would never come to court for lack of testimony.

And who was the third man with the sawn-off shotgun? His light build and jerky movements made me think it must be Mossy Beirne.

Eugene, who hadn't spoken, bent towards Bernice and said, "When the Sergeant comes asking questions you know nothing. Nothing. Is that clear?"

"Ah lads!" said Daddy.

Gerry swung the cudgel and gave Daddy a vicious thump into his stomach, shouting, "Shut your mouth."

Daddy doubled over, and as he sank to the ground Gerry hit him again across the broad of his back. Under the second blow Daddy collapsed onto the road and Gerry delivered a follow-up kick with his boot that laid my father out cold.

"Stop – will you for God's sake stop," Bernice screamed.

I was at my wit's end to know what to do when Mossy said, "That's enough, Gerry,"

"Shut up, will ya!" Gerry screamed back at Mossy for openly confirming Bernice had guessed right.

"I know it's you," Bernice sobbed. "I'll never forgive you."

"I'll put lead in you next – do you hear me?" Gerry shouted. The more he panicked the more violent he seemed to be getting.

Throwing the lid away, he tilted the can of paint and poured it over Bernice's head.

"This is what happens to traitors," he raged.

Black paint covered Bernice's hair, but at least she'd instinctively used her hands to protect her eyes. She began to gag and splutter to get the paint out of her nostrils and mouth. Then as the paint streamed down her face and onto her shoulders and chest like a cape, Eugene tore open the pillow and shook out white feathers that stuck like a covering of snow on the black paint.

Bernice's body stopped shaking and she seemed resigned to there being nothing more these men could do to make her feel more pain or fear. Defenceless and paint and feather covered, her silence and composure seemed to enrage Gerry.

"Don't you dare give me the silent treatment," he shouted in her face and having worked up his anger raised the cudgel to bring it down hard on top of her head.

I sprang up to my full height and sprinted towards Gerry shouting, "No – get off her."

Mossy swung around with the shotgun in his hands as I ran headlong towards him. He levelled both barrels at me and prepared to fire. I had time to think this is it, this is the moment my life ends, not with an asthma attack, or a swipe from a panther's claw at the bottom of a hole in the ground, but with a gun blast ripping through my chest.

Even with Mossy aiming the gun straight at me, my eyes went to Bernice as Gerry braced to strike her with blind brute force. The distance between us was too great, and with hopeless certainty I knew I would be dead long before I could reach her to stop him splitting her head open.

All of a sudden Gerry's leg jerked at the knee and a piece of fabric and gout of blood flew into the air, followed by the sharp crack of a rifle shot. The cudgel fell from Gerry's hand. He bent helplessly into a pain-contorted kneeling position as the shot boomed across the hillside.

With his back turned to the fallen Gerry, this was Mossy's moment to shoot me. Only he swung around again instinctively to respond to the rifle fire. Seeing Gerry on the ground gave him pause. On a distant elevation overlooking the road Frank Welcome stood braced against the Land Rover with the Carcano rifle raised and his eye tight up to the telescopic sight.

Gerry lay on the road, moaning and rocking back and forth in agony, and holding his leg as blood poured from the wound. Mossy realised that with the rifle and telescopic sight now trained on him he'd better freeze or take the next bullet.

Seeing he was in a tight spot Eugene turned one way and then the other, gauging what to do.

"Stay where you are," I shouted.

But Eugene grabbed up the bag with the money and cigarettes and using the travelling shop as a shield he vaulted the roadside ditch.

Seeing Eugene take his chances Mossy dropped the sawn-off shotgun and flung himself over the ditch after his compatriot. The forestry plantation sloped sharply downwards and both men zigzagged as they ran and were almost immediately lost from sight amongst the trees.

THIRTY FIVE

Frank must have judged it too risky to fire at moving targets at such long range with me and Bernice and my father in the line of fire. And I was more concerned anyhow with helping Bernice and Daddy who'd started to come around.

"Take it easy," I said, "Help is here."

Recovering his wits and catching sight of me Daddy said, "Get the turpentine out of the van and clean that mess off Bernice."

In the travelling shop I knocked aside besoms and bags of soda crystals to get hold of a bottle full of turpentine and then rushed to assist Bernice. Covered in household paint and feathers she sat perfectly still with her eyes shut and her hands now spread out flat on the road in a gooey pool. She was distressed and sobbing but otherwise uninjured.

Tossing away the satchel and removing my jacket, I pulled my shirt off over my head and balling up the shirt, doused it in turpentine and got down beside her.

"I'm going to wipe the paint off your face first," I said. "So keep your eyes closed."

"Where did you come from?"

"I was looking out for you," I said.

With the greatest of care I dabbed her face with the fabric of my turpentine soaked shirt to cut through the stickiness, tenderly wiping around her eyes and nose and mouth and ears and neck while Bernice moved her head from side to side to assist with the removal of the stupid paint and feathers.

"It's working," I said.

She tensed up with fear when an engine started somewhere in the conifer plantation below the road. It was a motorbike engine, and we listened to it rev and take off on a forestry track hidden by the trees. Next we heard Frank Welcome's Land Rover arrive and stop on the far side of the tree blocking the road.

My father was now bent over Gerry, tending to his wounded leg. He carefully wound gauze bandaging from the travelling shop around the gunshot wound with Gerry looking on submissively. Seeing my father behave so unselfishly towards his tormentor I did not know how I ever supposed he was a man who lacked bravery.

"I'm sorry," I said to Bernice. "This is my fault."

"They're animals," she said. "They had to be caught."

"I didn't mean to put you in danger."

"You had courage when it counted," she said.

Frank Welcome broke past the fallen tree carrying the big walkie-talkie he'd been using the first day I set eyes on him. He also wore the holster and pistol in plain sight.

"I've called for back up," he said.

Bernice began to shake violently, as if the shock of everything that happened only hit her fully when she heard Frank's voice. She immediately began to struggle to her feet.

Frank passed the walkie-talkie to me and wrapped his

arm around her waist to raise her up and support her effort to stand by herself.

"I'm going to link you to the Land Rover," he said. "And then I'm getting you safely out of here as soon as I've treated your attacker's gunshot wound."

Bernice nodded but did not speak. I stood aside helplessly as Frank led her away. I felt a crushing sense of having deservedly lost her, mixed with relief that the worst was over for her.

"Someone get the doctor," Gerry shouted.

In spite of my father's efforts to bandage the wound the blood kept pumping through the gauze, turning it soggy and red frighteningly fast. To stem the flow Daddy went to the travelling shop again to look for more bandaging.

Frank Welcome's uniform was smeared in black paint and dotted with feathers when he arrived back from the Land Rover. My father's first priority had been to treat Gerry's injury and he'd left the balaclava in place, but now Frank grabbed the balaclava roughly and tore it off.

Gerry's hair stood up on his head and his face was covered in sweat.

"I'm losing blood like a stuck pig," he said. "Get Ballintine."

I moved to hand the walkie-talkie back to Frank. It was switched on but making only static noise. Frank signalled to me to hold onto the walkie-talkie.

"In combat I've seen gunshot wounds like yours, Gerry," he said. "Unless the bleeding is stopped you'll die."

"You have to get help," Gerry pleaded.

"Where's the money Gerry?" Frank asked, standing over him with his arms folded.

"What?"

"The loot, Gerry – the proceeds from the robbery?"

"Leo, for God's sake," Gerry raised his voice to appeal

to me. "Help me. Get on that yoke and send for an ambulance."

Frank looked to me and I understood his intention. I turned the power knob on the walkie-talkie to the 'off' position.

"Gerry, you can come clean with us here, or you can bleed to death on the side of the road," Frank said. "You decide."

Frank waited for Gerry to grasp the seriousness of the fix he was in.

"I'm a political prisoner," Gerry said. "I have the right to medical attention. Besides, you've no proof."

Frank said, "In that case you're going to die an innocent man. And at the rate you're losing blood it won't be long. So if there's anything you want to get off your chest I'd do it now."

A low anguished groan came from Gerry.

"It wasn't my fault," he whimpered.

"What wasn't your fault?" Frank asked.

Gerry gulped a dry swallow and blinked up at me.

"What is it, Gerry?" I asked.

"That schoolmate of yours, Francie Curran."

"What about him?"

"It was me that tossed his helmet into the river."

"Start at the beginning," Frank said.

"After the hold up, we raced out of town," Gerry said. "I got out at the Iron Bridge while my father went on ahead to meet Mossy at the pit. The getaway van was due any minute. But Francie had this bloody plank across the bridge. He kept shouting, 'Halt – who goes there?' I only did it for his own safety to get him out of the way."

"Did you see him go into the water after the helmet?" I asked.

"It's where he ended up isn't it," Gerry said.

"So you invented a story about seeing the wildcat," Frank said, "and finding tracks at the river."

Gerry hung his head and watched the life-blood leave his body. "Tell my father I meant no harm."

He sounded sorrier for himself than for what he'd done.

Frank took the length of fresh bandage my father arrived back with from the van and wound the fabric into a cord which he looped around Gerry's upper leg and knotted. Then, with a pencil through the knot, he twisted so hard Gerry roared with the pain, but he continued to tighten the tourniquet.

"What are my chances?" Gerry said weakly.

"I'd say you can expect several years behind bars," Frank said. "And a limp for the rest of your sorry life."

Ignoring Gerry's confusion, Frank double checked the tourniquet, and when he'd done giving Gerry first aid he looked to my father and said, "Can you stay with him until the ambulance comes?"

"Ambulance?" Gerry said.

Frank glanced at me and said to Gerry in mock disbelief, "Didn't I mention, there's an ambulance on the way."

Gerry lay back on the road and closed his eyes.

Frank straightened up and walked back towards the Land Rover. I left my father with Gerry and fell into step alongside Frank.

"How did you know about the ambush?" I asked.

"Red Paddy came to the river field and told me he had masked visitors last night. They made him hand over his shotgun. And outside the post office I met Nora Greene. She'd come looking for me to report seeing men up to no good in the plantation. I took the high ground to scout out the situation, spotted what was going on, but was too far away to get to you in time."

"Nice shot," I said.

We went around to the far side of the fallen tree to where Bernice sat in the Land Rover, an army issue blanket around her shoulders. Her hair and clothes were soaked in paint and sodden feathers, but her face had a formal expression of immense dignity and composure. Our eyes locked on each other to memorise this moment and she released me from her gaze only when Frank got into the Land Rover, did a U-turn, and drove away.

Now it was just me and Daddy with the wounded Gerry McPadden who lay in the middle of the road in a dark red pool of his own blood, black paint and scattered feathers.

I wasn't much help to anyone since I was shivering uncontrollably, feeling the chill of going about without my shirt and in wet trousers and squelching sandals, along with the delayed shock of thinking about how close I'd come to getting shot; and how close Gerry had come to splitting open Bernice's head.

Daddy took off his jacket and gave it to me. I put my arms into its long sleeves and felt his manly warmth from the lining. We both smiled at the sight of me hugging myself for comfort in his outsized jacket.

It was amazingly quiet on the mountainside with only the sound of the water in the gully running under the bridge and an occasional crow call.

As the minutes passed it could have been an ordinary day with Gerry and my father hunkered down to talk like pitmen, my father offering Gerry a cigarette and lighting it for him. Except of course there was a fallen tree blocking the road after the failed ambush, and Gerry had turned out to be the monster whose heartless cruelty throwing the helmet into the river had cost Francie Curran his life.

"What?" said Gerry, catching me looking at him.

I didn't want Gerry to know my real thoughts so I said, "You do look like a prisoner of war."

Gerry snorted and said, "A hostage to fortune more like."

A coal lorry carrying Tommie and Timmy Leonard, the twin brothers, arrived and stopped short of the travelling shop. Wordlessly they inspected the obstacle in their path and finding the cross-cut used to fell the tree they took one end apiece and started to saw up the trunk.

Listening to the steady, rhythmic sawing sound made by the cross-cut in the expert hands of the twin brothers I barely heard the ambulance arrive. Sergeant Glacken followed behind the ambulance in his sturdy squad car.

The cut sections of the tree were moved aside, and Gerry got stretchered into the back of the ambulance. Sergeant Glacken retrieved the sawn-off shotgun and said he'd get a statement from my father later.

Daddy sat into the van, and when the ambulance and the squad car moved off we fell in behind, driving in convoy. After everything we'd been through I was happy to sit alongside my father riding shotgun as we rolled into the village in the travelling shop.

Only one loose end made me uneasy. Eugene and his sidekick had escaped and he would hardly take the arrest of his son Gerry lying down. And to judge by the way everyone looked at us when we pulled up outside the shop they knew we were the cause of Gerry getting shot.

The post office, the shop and the pub closed for the rest of the evening. With nothing else to do I waited until nightfall for Bernice to return. But she did not come back. At midnight I went to bed thinking Frank Welcome must have taken her to the hospital for medical treatment after getting the paint out of her hair and off her skin.

The next morning I went straight to Bernice's room. Her things were there exactly as she had left them; her shop coat and her sun shorts and top, the bottle of calamine lotion, her little transistor radio and her Beatles record, too, still on the record player turntable. Yet I knew in my heart she was never coming back.

Wednesday was a half-day. And on account of the hold-up on Daddy's van, and still no word from Bernice, I supposed the shop and the pub would not open. But we were in fact trading as normal. My mother especially wanted people to know that regardless of what happened we had no reason to keep out of the public eye.

At one o'clock Daddy came into the kitchen for his usual bread and honey. He sat at the lower end of the table while my mother stayed on her feet with a mug of tea in her hand. Daddy told her the attack must have put people off because the only customer he had the whole morning was Mattie Scanlon looking for cigarettes and matches.

Shortly before the four o'clock shift finished in Rover pit, my mother got a row of empty glasses and began to pour pints of stout at the tap. Then she lined up the drinks with more than usual care on the counter ready for the thirsty pitmen. The coal-lorry arrived full of pitmen but it went past our door and stopped on the far side of the bridge. Nobody came on motorbikes or on foot either. The only customer to come through the door was Red Paddy Reynolds. He took his place on the stool at the end of the counter and put his head back against the worn spot on the wallpaper.

He watched the freshly poured stout in the line-up of pints on the counter go flat and said nothing as my mother finally poured all but the pint she gave him free of charge down the sink. He said Sergeant Glacken had confirmed the sawn-off shotgun dropped by Gerry's accomplice was the one taken from his house the night before. The Sergeant told him he couldn't get it back as it would be needed in evidence, and it was useless anyhow, he said, because they'd butchered both barrels. He stayed until about nine o' clock. Red Paddy was the only customer the whole night.

The next day Daddy took in the bread delivery from the breadman but nobody came near the shop or the post office. Again that evening my mother filled the line of pints, and again she waited alone in the bar with no takers. Finally the door opened. It was Doctor Ballintine. He ordered a whiskey, drank it back, and left again with his protest made against the way we were being shunned.

"It's Eugene McPadden that's behind the boycott," my mother said. "He's the ring-leader."

"We don't know that," Daddy responded.

"He's doing it out of spite," my mother said.

I did not want to think about what she must be feeling, or going through privately.

If it had been a criminal gang who'd robbed the bank, the pitmen and their families might have reacted differently. But with IRA involvement they would not confront or condemn the perpetrators, and anyone who divulged information or co-operated with the law could expect to be treated like a strike-breaker, a scab-labourer, labelled a turn-coat and a traitor.

Even the retired miners left their old age pensions uncollected on Friday. Yet my mother – hopeful, hard-headed and desperate – wearing slacks, a turtle-neck sweater and her hair in a beehive, started the line of pints for the pitmen again that evening. As she got the drinks ready in the American Lounge, Daddy sat in the kitchen where he entered the amounts owed on the short term credit notes from the shop into the long-term ledger; the boycott a useful excuse for his customers to avoid settling their bills.

The lorry carrying the pitmen arrived and rumbled past without stopping. Daddy left the kitchen and stood behind my mother who had seven or eight freshly pulled pints lined up on the counter. The only sound came from the tap as my mother, a pint glass tilted under the nozzle in one hand, the other hand on the pump controlling the flow, filled a final pint. Daddy rested his hands on her shoulders and she eased back the leaver in mid-pour. Without a word exchanged between them she emptied whatever stout was in the glass down the sink and they left the bar together.

The next morning, my father in his good wool-mixture sports jacket and gabardine trousers and my mother, looking like Jackie Kennedy's double, went to see the colliery owners. The pub stayed shut; Mrs Daly and her daughter took charge of the post office and shop. That same evening we packed up: suitcases mainly, enough to fill up the Cortina. The rest we could load in the van and move another day. When we were ready to leave I went upstairs to Bernice's room and walked over to the record player. The Beatles *Please Please Me* LP with the Parlophone label rested on the platter. I put down the lid to stop the dust gathering on her record.

In Dallas, on the 22nd of November, at roughly half-past six in the evening our time – only months after his Irish visit – President John Fitzgerald Kennedy got assassinated. The sniper, Lee Harvey Oswald, used an Italian made Mannlicher-Carcano rifle. It even had an off-set telescopic sight like the one I'd used to hold President Kennedy's head in the crosshairs that Saturday morning on the newly arrived black and white television set in the American Lounge.

By the time of the Kennedy assassination we were living in Ballina in Co Mayo. My mother had a dressmaker friend living in the town, and with her friend's help and encouragement she'd gone into business for herself, setting up 'Monica's House of Fashion', doing a brisk line selling the locally manufactured Brendella skirts.

Daddy kept the travelling shop on the road serving Ballycastle and the Belmullet peninsula, but he switched to agricultural merchandise: shovels and spades and hedge-knives, pinch-bars and mallets, barbed wire and staples. It suited him calling from farm to farm and getting to know the people and the coastal countryside and leaving the running of the house of fashion to my mother.

There were advertisements for the business in the papers every week, and pictures too of my mother and father out enjoying themselves with their new friends at the Harriers' Ball. And I reckon it was through my parents' names appearing in the society pages in the local paper that Frank Welcome traced our whereabouts. He was an Army Intelligence agent after all.

About a fortnight before President Kennedy got shot I was sitting in our kitchen finishing a school essay when I heard the phone ring in the shop. Calls in the evening were a novelty even for my parents, and I certainly wasn't expecting my mother to run in from the shop where she and her friend were making alterations to tell me I had a phone call.

"Hello," I said when I put the receiver up to my ear.

"So you're in Ballina now?"

"Bernice – is that you?"

"How many girlfriends have you got ringing you?"

"None," I said.

"Too busy with the schoolwork I suppose."

"Where are you?"

"The Gresham Hotel."

"In Dublin?"

"I'm after coming from the Beatles concert."

"Seriously?"

"They were fabulous. And you should have heard the fans screaming. I thought the balcony was going to come down on top of our heads. And there was a riot afterwards. It was just like the Silver Slipper Ballroom."

"Is Frank with you?"

"He's ordering tea for two with all the trimmings. We're engaged to be married."

I should have expected the news but it left me dumbstruck.

"Leo, you want me to be happy, don't you."

"I do."

"And I am happy," she said. "The happiest I've ever been in my life."

It got noisy behind her.

"I have to go," she said. "Frank is going to hit George Harrison if he doesn't stop giving me the eye."

We left it at that.

A few days later in the post I got a photograph of Bernice and Frank taken in the street by Arthur Fields. They looked so happy linked arm in arm on Dublin's O'Connell Bridge. The following May they were married in Rome. On honeymoon, Bernice sent a postcard of a cloudless Amalfi Coast seen in golden end of day light.

ACKNOWLEDGEMENTS

Summer of '63 uses real places populated with fictional characters, streets and buildings. There are no actual people or incidents or towns and villages quite as they appear in the story, although I gratefully acknowledge the inspiration I've drawn from the coal mining industry in Arigna, along with the native outlook, humour, and turn of phrase. So thanks to Dermot and Terry, my brothers, who keep me in touch with the lingo. Thank you so much to Christine Breen. Through your comprehensive and expert editing of the original manuscript, and copious 'track changes' directions, this story grew into a novel. Thank you to Danielle Kerins for handling the editing, formatting and publication of the book. Thanks also to Niall Kerrigan who once again found the perfect cover. Thank you to Sean Golden, a man who knows his poker. Thanks to those who read the book in manuscript and said exactly what they thought: Susan Carton, Rosita Boland and Frank Golden. And as ever, a big, warm, loving thank you to Carmel – the very heart of everything.

ABOUT THE AUTHOR

Brian Leyden is an Irish novelist, short story writer, memoirist, playwright, screenwriter, librettist, and editor. His books include the bestselling memoir, *The Home Place* (New Island, 2002), the novel, *Death and Plenty* (Brandon Books, 1996), and the short story collection, *Departures* (Brandon Books, 1992). He has written extensively about his home area for RTÉ's *Sunday Miscellany*. His radio documentary work includes *No Meadows in Manhattan*, *Even the Walls Were Sweatin'*, *The Closing of the Gaiety Cinema in Carrick-on-Shannon* and *An Irish Station Mass*. He is also co-writer of the feature film, *Black Ice*, which premiered at the Jameson Dublin International Film Festival 2013 and received an IFTA Best Actress nomination. He has been a guest performer at The Frank O'Connor Weekend, The Green Ink Festival in London, the Ireland and its Diaspora Writers and Musicians tour of Germany and The Newport Festival in Rhode Island. He also toured with the Irish Writers Centre's *Peregrine Readings*—supported by The Arts Council / An Chomhairle Ealaíon (2010). Ireland's Age & Opportunity *Bealtaine* Festival National Writer in Residence (2016), he has won several awards, including the Francis McManus Short Story Award and The Arts Council / An Chomhairle Ealaíon Travel and Education Award. He is a recipient of a Norman Mailer Writers Colony Scholarship (USA), Broadcasting Authority of Ireland, (BAI) Sound and Vision Award (2014), and an Arts Council / An Chomhairle Ealaíon "Literary Bursary" 2014.

BRIAN LEYDEN

SWEET OLD WORLD

New & Selected Stories

"Life remembered with precision and love."

Bernard MacLaverty

In a story collection spanning three decades Brian Leyden is a master at evoking time and place and people with a voice that is consistently wise, observant and wonderfully entertaining. Every one of these New & Selected Stories feels like a homecoming.

BRIAN LEYDEN

The Home Place

A Memoir

"An absolutely beautiful piece of work"

Joseph O'Connor

The Home Place is a profoundly moving story of Irish life seen afresh where the intimate and the familiar are made unforgettable. This hugely evocative memoir will be a treasure for generations to come. In the words of the writer Carlo Gebler, "It tells so much, and what it tells is so rich".

Made in the USA
Charleston, SC
17 December 2016